The Amul

A supernatural romantic comedy

by

Effrosyni Moschoudi

For Andy, my very own guardian angel

Contents

Chapter 1

'Bring back the piiiiiiiiipes!!!!' shrieked Roula down the telephone line.

Katie looked up from her computer screen. *Damn . . . here she goes again…*

'Bring back the piiiiiiiipes!!!!'

Katie chewed her lip and ventured another look in her manager's direction. Beyond the large glass pane that separated her boss' office from her own, she could almost see Roula fuming through her ears. Her face was red and puffy, her chubby hands holding on to the edge of the desk as if holding on for dear life. She kept jumping up and down in her chair, the headset over her well-gelled coif making her look like a DJ about to break into a crazy jittery dance.

Katie let out a low gurgling sound of amusement. Roula had an affinity for clothes and hair accessories adorned with studs and glitter; this, along with the headset she used on the phone, meant everyone referred to her office as the D.M.R. (Disco Monster Room). Katie was responsible for that one. It wasn't she that had come up with the nickname 'D.M.N.' (Disco Monster Nut) for Roula herself, though – that was Vasso from Accounts. According to the office joke, if you spelled out the letters fast enough, it revealed Roula's real identity. Katie was still gutted Vasso had thought up that one first.

No one liked Roula. That was a fact. But that wasn't because she ran the show at the pipe-manufacturing company where she was top dog. No. Plenty of top dogs can be good bosses. But this one ran a tight ship where people walked the plank almost daily for writing with the wrong pen or not answering the phone fast enough. Every working day Roula followed the same nine-to-five abusive routine, throwing tantrums in the blink of an eye.

'I said, briiiiing back the pipes or eeeelse!' screamed Roula into the receiver, leaning back into her designer office chair and plopping her large backside down onto the seat so abruptly the poor thing squealed in protest.

Katie felt a tap on her shoulder and turned around to find her colleague Anna had come to slouch over her. She had an open notepad in her hands and offered it to Katie, raising her brows to give her a hint. Katie pretended to be reading something on it, even though it was a blank page, while Anna picked up a pen from Katie's desk and pretended to write something on the pad.

'What's the matter with her?' Anna whispered. 'You'd think she'll get a stroke any moment now.'

Anna was only new. She was still in the Innocent Newbie stage that lasted anywhere up to a week. She'd only started work three days earlier but had already seen enough to know there was something seriously wrong with the boss. Roula had spared her from her nasty moods, so far. Katie imagined it was all part of Roula's cunning plan. Perhaps the D.M.N. liked its new meat tenderized slowly.

Katie rolled her eyes. 'That? That's nothing. Last month she got so worked up with the guys down in Production she had three of them fired on the spot. That day we could hear her yelling all the way up here.'

'Really? Can she do that? Can she fire people in Production too? I thought she can only do that to us office girls.'

'Are you joking? The old man who owns the company has retired. He comes in once a week to have a chat with her over a cup of coffee and that's it. He trusts her blindly. She might as well own the whole factory now.'

'Bring back the piiiiiiiipes!'

Katie let out a laborious sigh. 'Here we go. She's off again.'

Anna gave a frown. 'What's going on? Do you know?'

'It's that new customer we sent pipes to this morning. They refuse to receive the invoice, saying the parts weren't up to scratch. Problem is, our guys have already offloaded the goods into their stores. Now, the customer won't allow them to take them back and won't commit to delivering them back themselves either.'

'So the customer has taken our pipes but won't pay?'

'In essence, yes. But they're open to discussion. I spoke to them earlier, and they said they want to negotiate a better price because the quality wasn't what they were hoping for. I put them through to Roula and . . .' Katie gave a cunning smirk. 'The rest is history, as they say.'

Right on cue, behind the glass, Roula shot up from her seat and banged her open hand on the table so loudly that Anna's shoulders jumped.

'*Now!* I want them back *now*, you hear?' shrieked Roula. 'You took them away from us and you have the nerve to want to negotiate a price? What you did is illegal, you hear? Bring them back or else!'

Katie sniggered. 'If I didn't know better, I'd think this is a hostage situation.'

Anna gave a low giggle. She opened her mouth to speak but her lips froze, alarm igniting on her face. Roula's all-seeing gaze had just turned to the girls in a scary, big-eye-in-the-sky-of-Mordor kind of way, her heavily made up eyes narrowing.

'Oops. Better return to your desk *pronto*,' whispered Katie as she pretended to key something into her computer, her head low so Roula couldn't see her lips moving behind her computer screen. 'Go! *Now*!' added Katie with a grunt.

Anna scuttled away to sit at her workstation in a remote corner, relieved to be out of Roula's direct line of vision again.

'Bring back the pipes *now*! I won't say it again! You have one hour, then I'm calling the police!' barked Roula and ended the call. Katie didn't have time to enjoy the amusing scene because Roula stormed out of her office and came up to her in a heartbeat.

Roula's eyes glinted, her breathing laboured. A strand of her dyed blond hair had managed to escape the thick layer of gel it had been plastered in and hung loosely over her greasy forehead. Roula huffed loudly, placing a closed fist on her waist. 'Why did you put them through to *me*?'

'Excuse me?' answered Katie. Although the D.M.N. was towering over her, she wasn't intimidated.

'I said, why subject me to this phone call? It wasted my precious time! You could have handled it yourself. Isn't this what this good company is paying you for?'

'Excuse me, Roula, but the customer asked for you personally. He said he wanted to negotiate a better price. I don't have the authority to do that.' Katie gave a sweet smile. 'Only *you* do, of course.'

Roula looked away and smoothed her hair, a chuckle escaping her ruby lips. 'Well, yes, of course. But this man had the nerve to call our products unacceptable. He said they weren't good enough.' She narrowed her eyes and bent over Katie, bringing her pudgy face closer, enough for Katie to feel claustrophobic. 'You should have tried to change his mind. Why didn't you tell him all about our quality controls, our certification? Isn't this what you're paid for? To actually *sell* our products?'

Katie leaned back in her seat to put distance between her face and Roula's. She took a deep breath as she studied her boss' frantic expression. The familiar nervous tic had made its appearance without fail, the way it always did whenever Roula lost her cool, which was a lot. Roula's lower lip twitched repeatedly, causing her right eye to blink in a frantic manner.

Katie counted. One, two, three blinks of the eye for every twitch of the lip. She knew it well by now. She'd been suffering her boss for three dreary years and knew exactly why she had come to her. All Roula wanted was to find the nearest victim and let off some steam. It wasn't the first time she'd picked Katie.

'I'm sorry, Roula. I thought I did the right thing by giving a customer what he asked for. And that was to speak to you. Is there anything you want me to do? Do you want me to call them and communicate something for you? Follow up?'

Roula pursed her lips, then stood straight again, squaring her shoulders under the tweed jacket of her designer skirt suit. 'No. That's fine. I'll let you know.' She turned on her studded stilettos and returned to her office, closing the door behind her. Katie turned to Anna who stared back aghast.

'What the—?' mouthed the new girl.

Katie gave a dismissive wave and returned to her work.

Chapter 2

'Oh, what a glorious day!' said Anna as she and Katie sat by the window in the staff room. It was lunchtime and they had exactly twenty-two minutes left. Roula often monitored these things so the girls made sure to keep checking their watches. Office staff had to use corporate software to register their activity throughout the day, including their lunch, bathroom and cigarette breaks.

Katie opened her plastic food container from home and started munching on her chicken and lettuce salad. Anna had just returned from reception where a young lad delivered a large *souvlaki* with *pitta* bread. 'You don't mind the onion smell, I hope?' asked Anna, showing her the delicious-looking *souvlaki* as if it were an article of incriminating evidence.

'Oh, that doesn't bother me. Eat away,' said Katie. 'Compared to what I stomach all day with Roula . . .' She shook her head. 'Trust me. I wouldn't mind if you were to eat a plate of bugs.'

Anna pulled a face of disgust, then slumped her shoulders, leaning forward and lowering her voice a notch even though they were alone in the small room. 'So, tell me, how much worse does it get in here?'

'I think you've seen the lot where it comes to Roula's appalling manners, but one thing you should remember about her is she can always surprise you. She can be sweet and friendly one moment, then sacking you the next.'

'Friendly? I'm yet to see her act that way.'

'It doesn't happen often. But she does have her moments. The right planets have to be aligned, of course.'

Anna sniggered. 'Does she have any friends in the company?'

'Are you kidding?'

'No, not us sales girls. I mean other managers maybe.'

'Who would want to be friends with her? She's arrogant, rude, and seriously unstable. As a matter of fact, if I had to choose between Hannibal Lecter and Roula for my next best friend, I'd invite Hannibal home for dinner and ask him to bring the Chianti.'

Anna let out a howl of laughter and took another bite of her *souvlaki*, her face alight with mirth as she munched. Katie watched her for a few moments and wondered how long it would take before Anna turned as miserable as everyone else in the building.

She took another forkful of salad and looked outside the window. Not a leaf stirred in the trees in the lush park across the busy highway. Katie let out a long sigh. 'Ah . . . it's the spring. And yet, here we are. Stuck in here, imprisoned for life.'

Anna shrugged. 'That's a bit heavy, don't you think? Everyone has to work.'

'I'm not against work, don't get me wrong. But I am against work that dampens my spirit and gnaws at my sense of self-worth.'

'You said you've been here for three years?'

Katie nodded, pressing her lips together.

'If you're not happy, why don't you look for another job?'

'In crisis-stricken Greece? No, thank you.'

'I guess you're right. Which is why I consider myself lucky for landing this job. I have a high rent. The job came at the right time to save me from bankruptcy.'

Katie gave a knowing smile. 'Still, I wish there was a way I could spend my days without being constantly on guard. This woman gives me the creeps. And the shouting . . . every single day. I hate working in an office as it is.'

'What did you do before this job?'

'I have a degree in Hotel Administration and have worked in various hotels in Athens. I got this job when I was last made redundant, but back then there was no Roula. The owner ran the company at the time and he did a wonderful job. When Roula came to take over the Sales Department, and especially after the old man retired, things started to get complicated. But, by then, I was trapped. The crisis got worse and . . . you can imagine the rest.'

'I see. Sorry to hear.'

Katie huffed. 'That damn crisis. It has lots to answer for.'

'That's true. If only we could give it a round with Roula, right?'

Katie gave a giggle as she picked the last forkful of her salad. 'That would be a bad day for the crisis, that's for sure.'

The girls laughed with abandon this time, and when Katie caught her breath, she leaned back in her chair, gazing at the deep blue sky, her eyes twinkling with longing. 'Aaah . . . If only I could be on the beach right now, on an island somewhere.'

'Wouldn't that be something?' said Anna, but made sure to check her watch again.

'No, I mean it. I'd love to board a ferry and get to an island in time for the summer. If I had the money, that's what I'd do. I need a change, an escape from it all. It would be wonderful to find work on an island . . . at a hotel. Anywhere.'

'Well, you never know . . .' said Anna and checked her watch again. 'Oh, time's up! Come, Katie. Let's head back before Roula exercises her vocal cords again.'

###

The girls emerged from the elevator, their expressions still amused from their earlier chat, but all that changed when they met their colleagues' anxious faces.

'What's wrong?' asked Katie and Anna in unison as they returned to their seats.

'Roula's in another bad mood,' said one of the girls, her eyes huge. 'Katie, she stormed out moments ago screaming your name!'

'Me? But why? Did you tell her I was at lunch?'

'We all did, but she didn't answer; just bolted out of here and went down the stairwell like a slinky on speed.'

'Do you think she went to the staff room looking for you?' asked Anna, panic alight on her face, but Katie seemed serene. Too serene for normality. It was like she was beyond caring. It made the girls look at her with incredulity.

Katie let out a long sigh and returned to her computer screen. At that point, the other girls dropped the subject and did the same. Not two minutes later, Roula returned.

'A-ha! There you are!' she shrieked, striding towards Katie to stand over her with her hands on her hips, her stumpy legs spread apart, skin straining to burst through her tights' delicate fishnet pattern.

Katie swivelled around in her chair and looked up at her slowly, as if in a dream. 'Can I help you, Roula?'

'I sure hope you can, for *your* sake! Tell me, have you posted the samples to Mr Sotiriou in Salonica like I asked you?'

'Of course. The package was shipped yesterday. I gave you the Airway Bill as soon as the courier left, if you recall.'

Roula's eyebrows shot up. 'No, I don't recall, but it's not my job to remember these things! I asked you a simple question. Don't evade it!'

Calm, Katie replied, 'I didn't evade it. As I said, the package went out yesterday. Just like you asked.'

'But we promised the customer a morning delivery! He just phoned and said the samples are not there yet.'

'Excuse me, Roula, but this is the first time I hear this. You asked me to give it to the courier yesterday afternoon. You said nothing about morning delivery, otherwise, I would have told you there and then there was no way the goods could be delivered in Salonica this morning. As you know, for next morning delivery, we need to hand a package by midday latest.'

'What?' shrieked Roula. 'How come you didn't tell me this before?'

'But, Roula, surely you know the courier needs a bit more time than this!'

'No, I don't. I don't have to know these things. That's what we pay you for! So I, the manager, don't need to worry about the little details!'

'Roula, you never told me you wanted morning delivery. Besides, I think it's evident there's no time for morning delivery in Salonica if the package is still in Athens at five p.m.'

Roula huffed, then shrugged her shoulders. 'There are night flights, aren't there?'

In lieu of an answer, Katie let out an exasperated sigh.

'What's that sigh for?' snapped Roula.

'I'm sorry. I've never worked for a courier company, I wouldn't know.'

'Are you being snarky with me?'

'No, no. I'm just saying, it makes sense.'

'Are you calling me irrational?'

'No, of course not!'

'Katie, do you know what your problem is? You have a big mouth; you talk too much. I've never heard of such insolence from a simple clerk! May I remind you I am your manager?'

Katie nodded and lowered her gaze. It was futile to argue with that lunatic, she knew it.

Roula gave a huff but now her eyes glinted with contentment. As soon as Katie met her eyes again, Roula shook her finger at her. 'Katie, really, things would be a lot easier for you if you started admitting your mistakes. You're forever giving me lip for this and that instead of simply saying "sorry". This long conversation that's wasted my precious time could have easily been avoided were you to simply accept your mistake at once.'

'What mistake? But you never said—'

'Really, Katie, you're unbelievable!' said Roula and turned on her heel. Katie's jaw dropped as Roula began to walk away, her high heels clicking on the polished wood, the sound drilling Katie's brain, her sanity hanging by a thread.

'Be more careful next time!' scolded Roula from the doorway and sauntered back to her desk.

Chapter 3

Katie stood at the bus stop and held the collar of her coat against the biting wind. Recently, the days had been lovely and sunny, but the temperature still dropped dramatically in the evenings. She couldn't wait another month for the summer to arrive. Already, she was looking forward to the possibility of relaxing on a beach during her weekends. She was lucky to live in the Eastern suburb of Glyfada, a short bus ride away from the beach. From the balcony of her one-bedroom rented apartment, she could see a tiny strip of the sea. It seemed to beckon to her every morning from the tiny open space between the two tall buildings that stood opposite hers.

Katie's parents still lived in the same seaside town in Epirus where she'd grown up. It was a beautiful place but also quiet and claustrophobic. Now that she'd become accustomed to living on her own in a big city, she could never go back.

Living in Athens on her own wasn't too bad, it was just her job she couldn't stomach and hoped a hotel job would turn up, somehow.

A tall, heavy-set gypsy woman in her sixties came to sit on the bench beside Katie and winked at her, breaking her reverie. Katie met her eyes and gave a tight-lipped smile, then looked quickly away. She still felt agitated from yet another difficult day at work and was in no mood for a chat with a stranger.

'Sure is cold tonight,' said the gypsy woman.

Katie threw her a furtive glance, then looked away again as not to encourage her further. 'Sure is.'

'Oh, how I long for the summer . . .' mumbled the gypsy woman.

Despite herself, Katie nodded her agreement.

'You agree then?'

Katie turned to look at the woman properly for the first time. The gypsy had her arms wrapped around herself and was shivering, which was no surprise as she only wore a skirt and a t-shirt. Her long hair was dyed raven black, long strands flowing in the sharp wind. Katie's heart went out to her. 'Yes, I do. Hey, you must be very cold.'

'Frankly, I am. You must be warm in that coat. I don't suppose you have an item of clothing to spare? Or maybe a bite to eat? I haven't eaten anything since morning. Being hungry doesn't help with the cold.' The gypsy gave a shiver.

'Of course. Let me look . . .' Katie didn't think twice. Her kind heart wouldn't have it otherwise. Having rummaged through her shoulder bag, Katie took out a half-eaten pack of biscuits. 'Here. Will this be okay? It's all I have.'

The gypsy's eyes lit up. 'Oh thank you!' She took the packet and started to munch hungrily while Katie watched, wondering how cold the gypsy must be in her flimsy attire. She wore no tights under her long skirt and only had a pair of sandals on. Katie removed her coat, took off the cardigan she wore underneath and offered the latter to the gypsy before putting her coat back on.

The gypsy put on the cardigan at once, a grateful smile playing on her lips. It hung loosely on Katie but for the gypsy, who was much larger, it was a close but comfortable fit. 'It's still warm from you – thank you so much!' Her eyes twinkled as she continued to munch the rest of the biscuits.

Katie felt an arrow of heat land on her heart, the warmth rising to bring a huge smile on her face, as she watched the gypsy devour the last crumbs from the packet. Katie saw her bus approach and stood.

The gypsy followed suit. 'May God bless you; you seem to have a good heart. Could you spare a ticket? I don't have any change on me.'

Katie threw her a sideways glance and raised a brow. *I gave her my cardigan, my biscuits, now she wants a ticket. What else will she ask for? A night on my spare couch?* Still, she had a few tickets to spare – she liked to buy them in advance so she never ran out. It cost next to nothing to her. She nodded her acceptance, took out two tickets from her purse and when the bus doors opened they both got on. Katie punched the tickets in the machine and handed one to the gypsy. They sat together, side by side.

'Where do you live?' asked the gypsy as soon as the bus began to move.

Here we go. 'Not too far. You?' said Katie.

'I live in the park,' replied the gypsy, pointing to the green mass on the other side of the highway from where Katie's work building stood.

'Oh that's nice,' said Katie, not knowing what else to say.

'Yes it is, although I miss the island . . .' She shook her head.

Katie whipped her head around. 'The island?'

'Yes. Sifnos. This is where I was raised.'

'I hear it's nice. Lovely beaches.'

The gypsy smiled, a dreamy look in her eyes. 'Ah, you couldn't imagine. And the beaches are unspoiled there. Not like the ones over here.' She scrunched up her face with disgust. 'I wouldn't swim here in Athens if you paid me.'

'Well, that's all I have so I do swim here in the summer.'

'If you swam in Sifnos even once, you'd never swim in Athens again.'

Katie chuckled. 'The beaches are that good, huh?'

'I don't mean you wouldn't *choose* to swim in Athens. I'm just saying you'd never swim here again simply because you wouldn't have the heart to leave the island again.' She gave a cunning grin.

'Oh, I see. I'm with you now.' Katie gave a tight smile. The woman sounded stranger by the minute. Thankfully Katie's stop was coming up so she stood to press the button. To her relief, she saw the gypsy didn't follow. Instead, she gave a broad grin and called out, 'Meet you at the bus stop tomorrow same time?'

Katie raised her brows. 'Excuse me?'

The gypsy gave a titter and pointed at the cardigan she was wearing with one sharp finger. 'To return you *this*!'

'Oh!' Katie slapped herself on the forehead and gave an awkward smile. 'Yes, of course, thank you.'

'No, thank *you*,' replied the gypsy, patting her heart with a sincere hand.

Katie pressed the stop button and stood in front of the closed door, waiting. When the bus halted, she turned her head one last time to say goodbye to the gypsy but, to her surprise, she wasn't there any more. A man was sitting in her place and was staring back at Katie, his face animated with intrigue.

Chapter 4

'Kaaaaaatieeee!'

Oh God!

'Kaaaaaaatieeeee!'

I'm on the loo, you mad cow!

'Kaaaaaaaaatieeeeeeeee!'

Katie dressed as quickly as she could, washed her hands and left the Ladies. As soon as she walked into the office, all her colleagues whipped their heads around, their expressions frantic.

'What's wrong?' Katie peered through the glass pane to find Roula wasn't in her office. 'Where's the D.M.N.?'

'She came out of the meeting room calling you,' said Anna. 'We told her you're in the Ladies. She said to tell you to go in the meeting room as soon as you return.'

Alarm flashed in Katie's eyes. 'Why? Who's in there with her?'

'Just the sales guys. They arrived earlier on. Didn't you see them?'

'No, I didn't. But why does she want me in the meeting room with Paul and Nick?'

All three of her colleagues shrugged, their faces full of sympathy. 'Better go in there soon. You don't want to vex her,' said one of the girls.

'Right, wish me luck,' mumbled Katie and paced to the meeting room down the hall. When she reached the closed door she took a deep breath to steel herself. As soon as she knocked, she heard Roula's voice prompting her to come in.

'Roula, did you call for me?' asked Katie as sweetly as her boss' sour expression allowed.

Roula gestured to her to approach. 'Come. Sit,' she said curtly pointing to a vacant seat beside her. On the other side of the table, Paul and Nick sat slumped in their crumpled grey suits, their ties loose, their hair tousled. Being typical Greeks, they both had a large Styrofoam cup of *Frappé* coffee in front of them. Being chain smokers, they'd already gone to work puffing away at their cigarettes, a small ashtray sitting on the table between them littered almost to the brim with ash and cigarette butts.

Despite her angst and mystification, Katie couldn't help thinking how similar these guys looked. Like a photocopy of each other. They were forever driving around Athens chasing new customers, and despite their formal attire, they always looked untidy like a pair of homeless tramps who had been handed out the wrong kind of clothes. It didn't help that they were never clean-shaven and Paul had a shock of thick curly hair. Katie wasn't friends with these guys. For a reason she couldn't fathom, she avoided them like the plague.

She wondered why Roula wanted her in her meeting with them but wasn't half as intrigued as she was afraid to know. When Roula cleared her throat, Katie averted her eyes from the trashy duo and turned her attention to her boss, trying all she could to conceal how she felt.

Roula flicked a blond tendril behind her shoulder with a perfectly manicured hand. 'Katie, I called you in here because of your seniority. I trust you more than anyone else in the office.'

Katie's eyes turned huge, her mouth gaping open. *What? Did she actually just say something nice to me?*

Roula looked pleased from her reaction. 'Therefore, I've decided you'll be the perfect girl for the task.' She met the men's eyes and they gave a low laugh that could also pass for a growl. Katie imagined because of their chain-smoking these guys' throats might as well be internally plastered with asbestos.

'What . . . what task would that be?' Katie leaned towards Roula despite herself.

Roula crossed her knees and gave a smug smile. 'Well, Paul and Nick here had a great idea. Our business is expanding and we should start from now to build a stronghold that will last against our competitors.'

Katie's brows shot up. 'Our competitors, you say? And how can I help?'

'Well, it has come to our attention that some of our ex-employees are now working for competitors around Athens. Several people from Production, a girl from Accounts, and a couple of sales staff too. This means that our company secrets could be compromised. We have to . . . Oh, how shall I put it?' Roula raised her eyes to the ceiling and made cartwheels with her hand in front of her face. 'Let's just say . . . that we need to supervise our staff more closely from now on.'

Paul and Nick nodded profusely, enthusiasm glinting in their eyes.

'Supervise?' Katie felt at a loss. 'You mean, *everybody*?'

Roula's eyes lit up. 'Yes! Everybody! And you are the perfect woman for the job!'

'But how?'

'Relax! We have it all worked out in every detail.' Roula gave a loud chortle, the unshaven hobos amplifying the annoying high-pitched sounds she made with their asbestos gurgles. Katie couldn't see them clearly by now; the cigarette smoke in the room had turned into a fog. It caused her eyes to water.

Katie blinked repeatedly a few times, her eyes misting up further. She was allergic to cigarette smoke and started to feel faint. It didn't help that she was taking in only shallow breaths, unwilling to breathe in deeply the toxic air.

Totally oblivious, Roula continued to blather on. 'We're buying top-grade camera software which Paul here will install on your computer. Paul and Nick will be installing the cameras in all areas. We'll do it on a weekend so the staff won't know a thing.' She winked, an evil gleam in her eye. 'Then, all you'll have to do is take the odd look on your computer during the day, make sure everyone is doing what they're supposed to be doing, that's all.'

Up till then, Katie had been staring aghast and now she found her voice, but because of the cigarette fog, it came out feeble, strained. 'What? You want me to spy on people for you?'

'Spy? What an ugly word! Of course not. This is for the good of the company, Katie.'

'But it's illegal to watch people through hidden cameras.'

'Oh come on, Katie! It's a private space – we have every right to protect ourselves. Besides, they say the end justifies the means, don't they?'

'But . . . Wait, I don't understand. How is this going to help you protect company secrets from the competition? What do you expect me to find out for you?'

'Oh – don't worry. The cameras are just to make sure they're not stealing stuff. It's the telephone reports that will tell us the rest.'

'Telephone reports?'

'Yes, Katie. Relax, already! Don't look so appalled. It's business, my dear, nothing personal.'

'Let me get this straight. You want me to spy on people with cameras all day *and* listen into their phone conversations?'

'Yes. I'll get some technicians from the telephone system company to set it up.' Roula flicked her wrist. 'Easy peasy.'

'But, Roula, how am I going to do my work if I am to listen to people's phone calls all day?'

'Don't be daft, Katie. Of course, you'll still be able to do your work!'

'When? Last time I checked I couldn't clone myself into two. Besides, there's no way I would do this even if I *could* clone myself!'

Roula huffed and leaned back in her chair. 'And why not?'

'Because you need a snitch and you're asking the wrong person. I am sorry, Roula. I'm just not built that way.'

'A snitch? That's harsh! All you'll have to do is listen into a few conversations around the office. And not just on the phone. You know, you could linger a bit in the stairwell, outside the elevator, in the staff room, wherever the employees tend to gather and talk. We need to know who talks behind our back, who is unworthy of our trust. This way we'd know who to send packing before they harm us; before they learn too much from our business.'

'What? You can't be serious!'

'Of course I am, Katie. I cannot believe you're so negative!'

'What else can I be? It's simple, Roula. You're asking me to be a snitch and I won't do it. I refuse.'

'Excuse me?' Roula's response came out as an ear-piercing shriek.

Katie's face had turned red, partly because she was fuming with exasperation, and partly because she was desperate for fresh air. She felt nauseous in every way. 'You heard!' she snapped back and jolted upright. 'Now, if you've finished with your proposal, I'd like to leave the room please. I'm not feeling very well.'

Roula jumped to her feet and stretched out her hand authoritatively, pointing at the table. 'No! Absolutely not! You sit back down! And how dare you talk to me like that? You forget your position!'

If Katie had a morsel of patience left it had just evaporated. 'No! I won't sit down! I won't sit here a moment longer! You're a lunatic, you hear? A lunatic *and* an idiot!'

'What?' Roula seemed so appalled it was comical. Katie had trouble stifling her amusement. Her boss huffed twice, her eyes bulging, mouth opening and closing inaudibly. She looked ridiculous, like a puppet. As expected, her nervous tic returned with a vengeance. But, this time, four blinks for every twitch of the lip. Katie found herself wishing she had a hidden camera. She'd make that tic viral on Youtube, no doubt about that.

'You can't talk to me in this manner!' yelled Roula.

'Sure I can! I'm only responding to your appalling suggestion! First of all, how dare you assume that I would willingly spy for you? For your information, if you want your company secrets to be safeguarded, the last thing you should do is spy on people! You should treasure them instead! That's how you win people's discretion and respect, and their good will!'

'You don't understand. We can't just trust these people blindly!'

'And why not? They're honest, hard-working people, Roula! They're not here to harm the company, they're earning a living! The only person harming the company is *you*! You are a menace, firing people whenever you have a bad day! That's no way to treat others, you hear?'

Roula put both hands on her waist, scowling. *'What?'*

Katie sneered. 'You heard! And now you want to spy on them too? Disgusting!' Katie leaned closer and shook a finger at Roula. '*You* are disgusting! Shame on you!'

'Get out! Get out *now*! You're fired, you hear? You're *fired*!' shrieked Roula, extending one rigid arm to show Katie the door.

In response, Katie gave a little bow and a wide grin. 'That's music to my ears, Roula! Thank you. Can't wait to leave this *hell* hole!'

Roula scurried towards the door behind Katie, who was now striding down the hall, her head held high. Roula teetered on her high heels, her legs shaking. She held on to the door jamb, her bottom lip twitching at an impossible speed. 'Make sure to go straight to Accounts. I'll call in a minute and instruct them to give you all payment due to you. I don't want to see you back here ever again after today, you hear?'

Katie stopped dead in her tracks, threw Roula a fiery look and curled her lip with disdain. Without saying a word, she resumed marching.

Roula's face contorted with rage. As Katie had guessed, her silence had vexed her boss further. 'I fired you; you didn't quit. Remember that!' shouted Roula. 'You'll never get another job in pipes, you hear? No pipe-manufacturer in the country will ever employ you while I'm still alive!'

Katie whirled around, her face animated with mock-despair, hands laced together. 'Oh please! Don't do this to me, Roula! How am I ever going to live without another shitty job selling pipes?' Katie gave an easy smile, the only real smile she'd ever given inside these walls. 'I'll sure miss you, Roula . . . no, wait a minute,' she brought a hand to her mouth, '*The hell* I will!' she yelled, then disappeared around the corner.

Chapter 5

Katie exited the building and marched to the bus stop, blurry-eyed. The glorious sunshine felt warm on her skin but did nothing to make her feel better inside. Even though it had felt amazing to give Roula a piece of her mind at last, a deep sense of sorrow had followed when a few of her colleagues gathered at Accounts to say a quick goodbye. Now, sitting on the bench at the bus stop, her feelings of loss and remorse were overwhelming. *Maybe I over-reacted. Oh God, what have I done? How am I going to keep the apartment? I can't go back to my parents' house!* Panic contorted her features at the thought of moving back home. She buried her face in her hands, and tears began to flow freely from her eyes. She didn't stop crying even when she felt the bench shudder for a moment or two. Someone had just sat beside her but she was beyond caring.

A hand rested softly on Katie's back, causing her to look up. She was teary-eyed but the blurry image was unmistakable. It was the gypsy woman of the previous evening.

'What's the matter?' she asked Katie, her eyes soft, a deep frown on her dark, weathered face.

'I . . . Oh, it's nothing.'

'Nothing? But you're crying, my darling, aren't you?'

'I . . . I just lost my job,' Katie confessed, shrugging her shoulders. She hung her head, avoiding the woman's eyes. She felt stupid for her angry outburst that had got her fired. *Why didn't I lump it the way I've done all these years?*

The gypsy gave a chuckle. 'These things happen. Look, it's a lovely day. The sun is shining. And you're young. That in itself should be enough to make you smile.'

'Young?' Katie turned to face the gypsy. 'What does this have to do with anything?'

'When you're young the opportunities are endless. Look at you! You're a beautiful girl, and I'm guessing you're single – you have no husband, no kids, or other responsibilities. The world's yours for the taking. Just reach out and grab it!'

Katie gave a bitter smile despite her sadness. 'I wish it were that simple.'

'I'm telling you it is.' She gave a lopsided smile and rubbed Katie's back.

Katie gazed into the gypsy's kind eyes and felt strangely comforted. 'I admire your optimism,' she mumbled with a wry smile.

'Optimism is a state of mind. And so is happiness.'

'I beg to differ. Happiness, in my book, comes with having enough money to pay the rent. Seems I just lost that privilege.'

'Are you saying there's only one job in the whole wide world and you just lost it?'

'No . . . I'm just saying I lost the one I had. But, trust me, getting another one is going to be tough.'

'And why is that?'

'Because we're in the middle of a crisis, that's why. And I'm no spring chicken. I'm twenty-seven. Employers like their staff young so they can pay them peanuts. I have work experience behind me. This is a disadvantage for me. I have the darn crisis to thank for that.'

The gypsy rolled her eyes. 'The darn crisis! Of course.' Something in her expression suggested she wasn't convinced, though.

Katie raised her brows. 'What?'

'Tell me something: if they told you on the nine o clock news aliens have invaded Earth, would you believe it?'

'No, I guess not; unless they had footage or witnesses to attest to that fact.'

The gypsy's eyes lit up. 'A-ha! Exactly!' Katie's expression was deadpan so the woman continued, 'You see, this is how they get you to believe anything they want.'

'They? Who do you mean?'

'Them!' The gypsy widened her eyes, her expression ablaze with mock-terror. 'You know, *them!* The powers that be. The ones who control the masses for their own gain.'

Katie wasn't a fan of conspiracy theories, but she decided to let that one go for the sake of conversation. 'So?'

'So, they fabricate a big bubble of nothingness, sprinkle it with doom and gloom and serve it to you every evening for dinner and you yum it all up. Then, before you know it, you blabber about it every time you see your family and friends, when you go to the dentist, when you buy your groceries, saying "the crisis this" and "the crisis that" until it becomes a big bad monster.'

'But the monster *does* exist.'

'Huh! As much as the Boogie Man does!'

'So, what are you saying?'

'I'm saying that you shouldn't believe what others tell you. I'm telling you, like I tell all the young people I meet, that your dreams belong to *you*,' she pointed a sharp finger at Katie, 'and so does your life. Neither is in danger of being lost to you unless you hand them over.'

Katie knitted her brows. 'Hand them over?'

'Yes. You hand them over every time you believe the lie, this crisis, this fabricated Boogie Man that numbs your thinking and makes you feel weak and helpless.'

'So what's the alternative?'

'Faith, of course. Determination. Optimism. Saying, "I'm young, I have dreams. I have drive. I'll be all right"!' She shook her fist in the air. 'Look at all those young entrepreneurs who have fresh ideas, and are operating successful new businesses in Greece right now. They are the exception to the rule, I know, but if they can do it, anyone else can. It's all a matter of focus and determination.'

Katie's jaw dropped as she watched the gypsy saying these things. She sounded like a public speaker, one of those inspirational gurus that leave you feeling empowered and super-charged with elation, as if you have wings on your back. That was exactly how Katie was feeling after that pep talk, even though consciously she wasn't at all convinced.

Out of the blue, the gypsy jumped to her feet and took Katie's hand to shake. 'My name is Esmeralda but my friends call me Esmera. Pleased to meet you, Katie.'

'Pleased to meet you—' Katie's eyes narrowed. 'Wait a minute! How do you know my name?'

A flicker of alarm ignited in Esmera's eyes, then she gave a little wave. 'You told me yesterday, of course.'

'No, I didn't! If I did, then how come you didn't offer yours?'

Esmera huffed. 'You girls talk too much. Now, come with me! I haven't got all day.'

Katie frowned. 'Where to?'

'To my humble dwelling, of course. I live in the park across the highway, remember?'

'Oh! Are you inviting me there? What for?'

'To return your cardigan?'

Katie's eyes lit up. 'Of course! I'd forgotten all about that, sorry.' She stood to follow Esmera but stopped short again when they reached the edge of the pavement. 'Wait a minute – is this why you came over? How did you know to find me here?'

Esmera shook her head and patted Katie's back. 'Lighten up, girl. Your distress is making you paranoid. It was coincidence, of course. I was taking a stroll and saw you. It's a good thing I did too, otherwise I'd never have been able to return your cardigan to you. I'm guessing you're not coming back here after today, are you?'

Katie gave a bitter smile. 'No, not if I can help it.'

Chapter 6

About a dozen people were milling about the gypsy camp that consisted of five tents, some larger than others. Kids, dressed in shabby clothes, chased each other around. Katie and Esmera emerged from a large tent and began to saunter towards the trees, leaving the camp behind. It was time for Katie to catch her bus home and Esmera had offered to escort her to the highway. Katie's frustration had eased by now. The gypsy women she'd been chatting with over a cup of Greek coffee had been very hospitable.

Katie and Esmera kept silent as they walked down a path through the trees heading for the edge of the park. In her hand, Katie held her cardigan. She could tell it had been washed; it smelled fresh, a fabulous scent of spring flowers emanating from the fabric.

When they reached a marble bench at the edge of a clearing that was strewn with delicate purple and yellow flowers, Esmera turned to Katie, her expression cryptic. 'I wonder, Katie, if I could keep you for a while longer? Would you sit with me on the bench for a minute?'

Katie was taken aback but she'd grown so fond of the woman by then she was happy to oblige her, whatever the reason.

As soon as they sat down, Esmera took something out of her skirt's deep pocket. 'It's nothing, just a goodbye gift.' She extended her hand, a delicate necklace inside her open palm.

Katie marvelled at it. Under the strong sunlight, it looked dazzling. She took it into her hands, mesmerized by the exquisite gems that covered one side of the silver round pendant. She imagined they were zirconia, even though they sparkled like diamonds. She turned the pendant over to find the figure of an angel, his wings open wide, inside a circle of gems similar to the others. 'Oh how beautiful!' she exclaimed.

'I'm glad you like it. It's an amulet. It'll bring you luck.'

Katie's eyes twinkled as she looked at the gift. She felt mesmerized. It took all her resolve to manage to take her eyes off it. 'Thank you, but I can't possibly accept this. It's too expensive a gift, too wonderful, and we've only just met.' She moved to return it, but Esmera put up a hand.

'Yes, Katie, it is quite precious, but not in terms of money. Don't worry about it. I'm happy to let you have it.' She leaned closer and winked, a glint in her eye. 'It's not your average amulet, you know. It has gypsy magic. It will change your life, and that's all I can say. Think of it as a reward for the kindness you've shown me.'

Katie smiled, amused, then tilted her head. 'Are you sure?'

'You're a good person, Katie. All good people deserve a little help every now and then. Consider this *your* turn. I'm happy to do it. Besides, you're going on a journey soon. You'll need a little something to bring you luck.'

Katie's brows shot up. 'A journey? What do you mean? Where to?'

'Well, I have a feeling you'll be going on a boat journey soon. Perhaps for a new job.'

'How do you know?'

Esmera gave a cunning smile. 'Well, you had coffee in the tent, didn't you?'

Katie gave a grin. 'You read the coffee grounds in my cup? I didn't realise.' She wasn't sure if Esmera was serious or joking but found it amusing all the same. She let out an easy laugh and Esmera joined her. Soon, they were both gasping for air in between excited squeals.

Once they calmed down a little, Katie patted Esmera's hand. 'Thank you so much, Esmera. I needed that. You can't imagine what a miserable life it's been, working in that awful place. Thanks to you, I now feel like a huge weight has been lifted off my shoulders. Had I gone home today without meeting you, I'd still be crying my eyes out now. I'm sure of it. And all because of that shitty job . . .' She pointed vaguely in the direction of the building.

It wasn't visible behind the tall trees that surrounded them, but Katie could still hear and see in her mind's eye all the things about Roula that had been making her sick to the teeth to the point of numbness. It had been a sneaky kind of numbness that had caused her to be patient for a long time; until today when her exasperation had finally reached boiling point.

Esmera leaned over and squeezed Katie's arm. 'It's over now. You don't have to think about it any more. Remember that: in this new beginning, you won't be alone. This amulet will bring you all you need to find happiness. I know!'

Katie gave a sweet smile. 'You're so kind to try to cheer me up. Thank you for your gift; I'm going to treasure it forever.'

Esmera pinched Katie's cheek lovingly, then helped her put the amulet around her neck.

They stood and Esmera announced she wouldn't escort her all the way to the highway, after all. She left a kiss on Katie's cheek, then began to walk away. After a few steps, she turned around and said, 'Enjoy Sifnos!'

Katie stared back at her mutely for a few moments. 'How do you know this is where I'm going?'

Esmera tilted her head and smiled.

Katie's eyes lit up. *The coffee grounds. That's how.* Whether Esmera had really read them or not, she was surely trying to amuse and comfort her and it was working. Katie let out a chortle, gave Esmera one last wave and resumed walking, the amulet around her neck catching the light. The angel depicted on it seemed to bounce as the golden sun rays touched it, a trick of the light that made his open wings look as if they were moving up and down.

Chapter 7

The next day, the new girl at the office, Anna, called Katie at home but it wasn't just a sympathy call to check on her. It was to bring her a piece of astounding news. Anna, who lived with her elderly father, had gone home the previous day to find him reading the paper. Upset as she was about Katie getting fired, Anna told him all about her. Then her father handed her the paper, saying it included a special section that day that listed hoteliers looking for staff.

Anna was amazed by the coincidence and skimmed through the ads, circling a few that seemed interesting enough. One of the hotels, Hotel Asimi, was on the island of Sifnos, and Anna was particularly excited about that one. Being a strong believer of fate, Anna thought it was uncanny since Katie had expressed the wish to work on an island. Now she had been fired out of the blue; the notion stuck in her head that perhaps this was a sign.

When she told Katie over the phone, it was Katie's turn to become amazed. She told Anna about Esmera and her reading of the coffee grounds in her cup, and they decided it was well worth calling the hotel. Everything that followed had worked out seamlessly, painlessly, strengthening Katie's notion that this job was meant to be.

Within three days, she had sent her CV to Hotel Asimi and done a successful telephone interview that had landed her the job.

And now, Katie had just boarded the ferry that would take her to Sifnos. She went straight to the top deck and found a seat to enjoy the view of the Pireas docks and the tall buildings that lined the seafront. It was a beautiful morning; the sea was calm and the cawing of birds delighted her ears as she watched the passengers arrive. Soon, they were all settling down, a bustling mass of humanity pulsating with excitement. Some chatted noisily and others just enjoyed the moment in silence or read quietly.

Katie turned her gaze towards the docks, a dreamy smile on her face. As she took in the view of the busy highways and the bustling docks, her fingertips caressed the amulet around her neck. It occurred to her then that it had been just over a week since Esmera gave it to her. Everything had happened so fast. Today, with one packed suitcase sitting beside her, she was off to Sifnos and already feeling like a different person. Gone were her tattered nerves she'd always had to hide; for the first time in years she felt restful inside, solid hope for better days causing her heart to swell.

Soon, the ferry left the dock and, as it began to sail, Katie stroked the amulet with her fingertips again and felt gratitude for Esmera, who had come to save her sanity. She had imparted a lot of wisdom the morning of her dismissal; she'd given her strength, made her laugh, and offered her this beautiful gift, telling her it was magical. She believed it in a way; Esmera had told her she was going to Sifnos and the job had turned up the next day. This amazing coincidence had made Katie see the world through new eyes. Now, she believed miracles could come true. She could see the truth in what Esmera had said: that faith, determination, and optimism can bring a better future.

One hour into the journey, Katie decided to have a stroll around the deck to stretch her legs and grab a bite to eat. An endearing elderly couple was sitting next to her on the bench. Katie asked them if they could mind her suitcase and her shoulder bag and they were happy to do it. Thanking them, she took her wallet from the bag and left.

She ambled around the deck for a bit, enjoying the view of the deep blue water and the distant shores from both sides of the ferry, then stopped at the cafeteria to get a fruit juice and a toasted sandwich.

Holding a tall Styrofoam cup of juice in one hand and her wallet and sandwich in the other, she strode along the deck, eager to get back to her seat a moment sooner. The fresh air had made her ravenous. Suddenly, a tiny toy car shot out from the row of benches to her left, and she stopped dead in her tracks, taken aback. She'd only missed it by an inch. Had she stepped on it, it would have been a disaster.

A little boy crouched in front of her and picked up the toy, then rushed to a sour-looking woman sitting on a bench. The woman offered Katie a tight smile and mouthed 'sorry', then took the toy from the child scolding him for nearly causing an accident. Katie resumed walking but could still hear the woman shouting at the boy for leaving his seat. She didn't seem to stop and that bothered Katie. She loved children and couldn't handle it when people talked to their offspring gruffly. She cast a backward glance over her shoulder to look at the boy one last time, but then her torso crashed against something soft. Startled, she whipped her head around and gave a groan, an excruciating pain shooting out from her forehead to her temples.

Chapter 8

'Argh!' exclaimed the young man Katie had just bumped into.

'Ouch!' came Katie's own reaction. Her brow had landed on the man's jaw since he was way taller than her. *Taller and rather gorgeous.* Through watery eyes, she could see him rubbing his jaw with urgency, his flawless features contorted with discomfort.

Once the pain subsided somewhat, Katie's eyes focused properly for the first time and she gasped. Her fruit juice had spilled, making a large ugly stain on the stranger's t-shirt. 'Oh, God! I'm so sorry!'

'It's all right, it's not your fault,' he said, offering a thin smile.

'Are you joking? Of course, it's *my* fault! I wasn't looking where I was going.' The man's gracious response had made her feel guiltier. She almost wished he'd shout a few expletives at her, just to make her feel better.

'Please don't mention it; these things happen,' the man insisted, waving his hand dismissively.

Katie's eyes darted around to the crowded benches. Many of the passengers were staring curiously, some smiling with amusement. Among them, that sour-looking woman seemed about to burst with laughter. *At least, she stopped scolding the boy. That's something.*

Katie pressed her lips together and turned her attention to the young man again. 'Let me make it up to you at least. I can't get you a new shirt on the ferry, obviously, but perhaps if I gave you the money to buy a new one?'

'That's very kind, thank you, but I have plenty of t-shirts in my luggage.'

Katie stared back at him, amazed. His kindness was out of this world, not to mention his beauty. He had to be, hands down, the most heart-stoppingly handsome man she'd ever laid eyes on, in an Edward Cullen kind of way, but without the rock-solid skin and the sparkle-in-the-sunlight effect, of course. For a few more moments her mind drifted as she stared into his big, twinkling blue eyes. He was freakishly tall, his shoulders broad and strong, and she felt tiny in comparison, not to mention dazzled.

Under the strong sunlight, he seemed almost angelic. Perhaps it was his impeccable white skin that made him look like someone who didn't belong to the earthly plane. She hoped, for his sake, that he had packed plenty of high factor sunscreen lest he'd burn like a roast lamb on Easter Day.

Katie realized in a panic that the man had been staring into her eyes all this time, waiting for her to say something. She cringed. Visibly. *How embarrassing! What's wrong with me?* 'I . . . well, sorry again. I'll let you go now, now I've messed up your holiday.' She gave an awkward smile.

'Don't worry. Really. I'll be fine. And who knows? We might meet again,' he said with a big smile and a wink, then wandered off while Katie watched him speechless. She wished that were true – that she'd see him again – she'd noticed how her heart thumped when their eyes first locked together. She'd been single all her life, never had a boyfriend, and at the age of twenty-seven she welcomed love to sweep her off her feet, but so far it hadn't happened. She hoped there and then that a man half as gorgeous as this one was somewhere in this world destined to love her.

The ferry was going to stop along the way to Kithnos, Serifos, and Sifnos, before reaching Folegandros, its final destination. Perhaps he'd get off at Sifnos too. One in four chances seemed good enough. Katie decided she'd take it. Since receiving Esmera's gift she felt empowered in a strange way, almost as if anything was possible now as long as she decided she had to have it.

As she watched the young man walk away, his head held up high, she wondered what it must be like to be as cool as he seemed to be. If she had to walk around with a big yellow stain on her front she'd be crouching more than the Hunchback of Notre Damme in an attempt to hide it from view.

Feeling even more ravenous now, Katie strode back to her seat to find the elderly couple in a frantic state. They were talking with three young women sitting behind them. As soon as Katie approached they told her a man had come to sit in her place while she was away. The elderly lady, who'd been keeping an eye on Katie's personal belongings, said the man had grabbed the shoulder bag, then began to run, before the woman could do anything to stop him. When the old couple began to shout in panic, a young man had come to the rescue throwing the thief to the ground, then pinning him down until two crewmen came to apprehend the thief and take him to the captain. One of them had just returned to say they'd found two wallets on the thief that weren't his. The crewmen had asked around and found the rightful owners.

Katie was speechless. Her mouth was gaping open as she listened.

'Have a look in your bag, young lady,' said the elderly man, 'see if anything's missing, just in case.'

Katie checked the contents. 'It's okay, everything's inside.'

'Oh thank goodness for that!' said the old lady with a long exhalation. 'You should have seen the young man who threw the thief to the ground. He was so handsome! Wasn't he, Jason?' she asked her husband, who nodded distractedly while picking up his newspaper.

'With his big blue eyes and sweet expression he seemed like a guardian angel when he came over to return your bag to us,' said the old lady. 'I don't mind saying he made my aged heart skip a beat or two. Especially as he was *really* tall!' She brought her voice down a few notches. 'I've always had a thing for tall men, you know!' She gave a wicked laugh and her husband issued her with a look of mock dismay.

'Oh! Come here, you,' teased the old lady and put an arm around her man. Katie watched, speechless, as the old lady gave her husband a peck on the lips to receive a big cuddle in return. It was such a sweet scene, but Katie's mind was miles away. *Really tall? Big blue eyes? Could it be? The man stops a thief to save my bag, and I give his t-shirt a bath to thank him? Great . . . Nice one, Katie!*

Chapter 9

Katie wasted no time when the ferry docked in the port of Kamares on Sifnos. With her luggage trailing behind her on its squeaky wheels, she marched to the taxi queue and was soon on her way to the seaside village of Asimi where her new job awaited. The middle-aged taxi driver chuckled, his eyes igniting with pride, to hear her exclamations of wonder as they drove past the golden beach of Kamares.

Asimi was a short drive away, a tiny village nestled, all white like a young dove, in a sloping space between two hills. On top of the higher peak, a single windmill graced the skyline. The hills themselves were barren, typically for a Cycladic island, but on lower ground, around the village, there were fruit orchards and vegetable fields – a green oasis amidst the golden brown landscape. The hedges glinted in the sunlight, all built with stones from a local quarry. It was silvery in colour and sparkled like fool's gold.

Katie smiled with delight at the dazzling sight. She thought perhaps the village was called Asimi (silver) because of that stone but decided not to ask the taxi driver who kept babbling as it was. At the time, he was busy complaining about the heavy taxation, speaking of the many locals he knew who suffered, some of them depending on a handout and the kindness of the church for their survival.

Katie pressed her lips together and nodded silently as she listened. She knew about all that from the news but had thought in rural areas things might be easier than they were in the big cities. To find out she was wrong made her sad. Still, this was a big day and she needed to stay upbeat to face this new challenge.

The taxi turned off the main road and continued along a dirt path towards the beach of Asimi. Thrilled to hear they were nearing the hotel, Katie whipped her head around to admire the village nestling in the foothills behind her. A wide, paved path ran from the village square to the main road she'd just left behind. She noticed a beautiful blue dome and a tall belfry at the edge of the square and rubbed her hands together with delight. Asimi seemed quaint and a joy to explore. *It's the perfect place for me and right on the beach!*

The taxi driver coughed fiercely and rolled up both the front windows that were, up till then, fully open. The path was covered with a mixture of fine soil and sand.

When they reached the end of the path, right on the beach, the taxi pulled to a stop and Katie jumped out to take a better look. The beach was strewn with beautiful sand dunes here and there. Clear, sparkling water and fine golden sand reached out, kissing each other softly, as far as the eye could see. On one side, a cluster of eucalyptus trees swayed gaily in the distance, the shoreline almost deserted and bordered by fields. A scattering of people lay on the sand.

On the other side, the beach was a lot busier. Several holidaymakers were swimming in the sea or lying under thatched umbrellas. At a close walking distance stood a tiny jetty, a small fishing boat tethered to it.

The taxi driver pointed to the jetty, shielding his eyes from the sun with the other hand. 'Hotel Asimi is right there. You'll have to walk along the beach to get to it.' He turned around and pointed at a fenced off field with a sealed iron gate. 'See that? That's their private property. Gate's closed right now. Happens sometimes.' He brought a hand to his ear and drew two circles in the air with his index finger. 'The owner's a little forgetful. Means I can't drive you to the back entrance of the hotel.'

Katie didn't mind walking. Excited, she gave the man his fee and set off, her luggage wheels not much use along the sand so she resorted to carrying it. As she went, she admired her destination, a happy grin plastered on her face, despite the heavy weight she carried. Unbeknownst to her, as she made her way, a faint golden glow emanated from the amulet around her neck. The wings of the angel it depicted sparkled in the morning light and seemed to move smoothly up and down with every step she made, in perfect synch with the excited beating of her heart.

Hotel Asimi was a medium-sized, three-floor building painted in pale yellow, its antiquated façade adorned with plaques made of the same shiny stone Katie had seen at the village earlier. She stood at the entrance to catch her breath for a few moments. Many of the sun loungers under the thatched umbrellas were vacant. It was the end of May, low season, so that was no big surprise. She faced the hotel again and walked along the cemented front path admiring the lush garden and the manicured lawn either side. A few steps from the doorway she turned to check on her luggage. The annoying earlier squeaking was gone and had now been replaced by a low, gritting sound. Her luggage wheels coughed up sand as she dragged it along and Katie smiled, finding it amusing.

She went through the arched doorway and looked around at the basic, yet quaint reception area. The big desk and the varnished panelling on the wall behind it were made of pine wood. It all looked neat and fresh, giving her the impression that particular corner was newly decorated. The rest of the open space looked shabby and old, including the few pieces of lounge furniture a stone's throw away from the desk.

To her left, a small lending library held dog-eared volumes waiting to please newcomers. To the right, a stone arch led to a staircase Katie could barely see. The tiny specks of silver on the stone caught the electric light overhead. There was no one at reception so Katie paced slowly towards the arch and, as she went through it, pricked her ears. A closed door near the bottom of the stairs bore the sign 'Private'. Katie stopped to catch her breath for a moment, then rapped lightly on it.

Shortly, the door squeaked open and a woman appeared behind it. She seemed to be in her late forties and was dressed in a shirt, woolly cardigan, and a below-knee pencil skirt, her salt-and-pepper hair pulled up in a tight bun. She wore bone-rimmed brown glasses that had slid down her delicate nose. The glasses looked ancient and suited her dull features perfectly. 'Yes? How can I help?' asked the woman with a tight smile, peering at Katie from over her glasses.

The woman's scrutinizing gaze made Katie feel apprehensive about her casual attire – a tank top and capri trousers. 'Um . . . sorry to disturb you. Are you Matina Mavros, the owner of this hotel, by any chance?'

The woman stepped outside and half-closed the door behind her. Katie darted her eyes inside, despite her best intentions not to. The moment the woman moved to close the door, it was like she was compelling her to. Katie caught a glimpse of the side of a computer screen and a bunch of magazines stacked neatly on the desk beside it. It was nothing worth hiding, so Katie was taken aback when the woman's features hardened, her hand reaching behind her to close the door further. She tilted her head and pushed her glasses back into place, then squinted her eyes. 'Yes, I am Matina Mavros. What can I do for you, young lady?'

Katie cleared her throat. 'Sorry to disturb you, Mrs Mavros. I am Katie Pavlides. I've just arrived. Pleased to meet you.' She offered her hand, half-expecting the woman to kick her back out.

To her surprise, she exhaled with delight in response. It was as if she'd been holding her breath until now. Her face lit up like a church on its festival day, and she welcomed Katie to the hotel shaking her hand with fervour. Katie was stunned to silence for a few moments. Before she could say anything, Matina strode to the bottom of the staircase and yelled, 'Spyros! Spyros! Come down! Miss Pavlides has just arrived!'

Within seconds, the sound of loud footfalls echoed from above, Spyros appearing bright-faced and eager. He was a tall man in his early fifties and rather large around the middle. His thinning hair fell straight and limp on his forehead over vibrant and large blue eyes. As soon as he came down the last step he offered Katie a firm handshake and a huge grin.

Spyros picked up Katie's luggage effortlessly and together with his wife escorted her to her private quarters. It was a tiny yet pleasant room in the back of the hotel on the ground floor. Katie was overjoyed. It didn't have a sea view as she'd hoped but, outside her tall French windows, she could see the distant hills and Asimi. The village lay at their feet like a shiny pebble she could pinch between her fingers and marvel at forever. She turned around to face her employers, her face ablaze with joy. 'Thank you so much! This looks wonderful.'

Matina moved to show Katie the en-suite bathroom. The girl was thrilled to see it was equipped with a glass-walled shower. On the sink, a soap dispenser was full to the brim with pink liquid. A tumbler held a packed toothbrush and, on the hanger, two towels hung neatly folded. It all smelled fresh and clean.

'I trust you're happy with everything. And you won't have to bother with cleaning the room. Our maid, Julia, does all the rooms in the hotel. She's an Albanian immigrant. Very reliable. We've had her for years,' said Matina, her chin raised.

Katie made sounds of appreciation as the lady spoke. She noticed her husband was nodding along leaving his wife to do all the talking.

As if on cue, Spyros piped up then, 'Well, we'd better let you get settled.' His eyes darted to his wife as if he needed to check with her before leaving.

Nodding her assent, Matina smiled. 'Miss Pavlides, I'm more than happy to let you have the morning off. But, I do hope you'll be ready to start work this afternoon.'

'Of course!' Katie nodded, her face eager, causing Matina to smile agreeably. Katie noted the woman had said 'I' instead of 'we' on both counts in her last sentence and wondered what that was all about.

'Miss Pavlides, the afternoon shift starts at five p.m. and ends at ten. After that, my husband and I handle any requests from the guests as they come. They know to knock on our door or phone our mobiles if need be,' continued Matina matter-of-factly. 'Your work day begins in the morning at eight a.m. sharp.' She paused to make sure Katie responded.

'Of course!' Katie assured her, but something pricked inside her. *Hope I haven't jumped out of the frying pan to land into the fire. Please, not another Roula!* Instinctively, she brought one hand up to her neck and caressed the amulet. *Hope Esmera's charm will do its magic.*

Unaware of Katie's apprehension, Matina kept talking, a satisfied smile playing on her lips. 'So, to sum up, it's eight a.m. till one p.m. – that's five hours – then five p.m. till ten p.m. That's a total of ten hours work daily, but you will be having days off as discussed.'

Katie nodded, tight-lipped.

'And you'll have the evenings free after ten p.m. on all your work days,' piped up Spyros with a wink as if trying to cheer her up. 'Although there isn't much to do around here for young people like you!'

'Really, Spyros!' admonished his wife with a huff. 'I'm sure Miss Pavlides isn't the party animal type, otherwise she'd have applied for a job on a more cosmopolitan island than our quiet little Sifnos. Mykonos or Santorini, perhaps.'

Katie darted her eyes to Spyros, who looked away, then bent his head. Feeling sorry for him, Katie turned to his wife and forced a faint smile. 'Yes. That's right. Not a party animal at all. I can't wait to explore Asimi and the island, though. Sifnos is so beautiful!'

'Yes, indeed it is, young lady,' said Spyros looking distracted. He darted his eyes to the door and rubbed at his forehead, shifting his weight from foot to foot.

'Please, call me Katie,' said the girl addressing them both, pretending not to notice the change in the man's demeanour.

'All right,' said Matina. 'I don't see why not. And you can call us Mrs Matina and Mr Spyros, if you wish.'

'Of course. I'll be happy to.'

'Oh! Before I forget, you can visit the kitchen downstairs after one p.m. to have lunch. I've told Eva, our cook, you'll be arriving today. You're welcome to have your meals there daily with her.'

Katie's eyes lit up. 'Thank you, I will. This is very kind.'

'The rest of the staff will be joining you at meal times occasionally.' Matina gave a little wave. 'It's a pleasure for us to offer this little perk to our employees.' Her eyes met Spyros' and his face lit up with elation. He took this little morsel of acknowledgment like a starved dog who's being thrown a treat.

Katie averted her eyes from the scene. It was too embarrassing to watch. Already she was wondering what she'd got herself into. She gave a sigh and smiled widely to hide her awkward inner thoughts. She forced a smile. 'How many staff do you employ, if I may ask?'

'Just four, including you,' said Matina. 'I've already mentioned Julia who does the rooms, and Eva, our cook. The only other member of staff is Julia's young son, Eddie. He's seventeen. A marvellous boy. He helps his mother with the rooms but also does various odd jobs and errands for us.'

'He's only seventeen and he works here?' asked Katie, before she could stop herself. 'What about school?'

Matina shook her head and gave a wry smile. 'I'm afraid his family is poor. He had to drop out of school a few months ago to start work and help with the expenses. It's not too uncommon these days, I'm sorry to say.'

'I see,' said Katie, now sorry she brought up the subject.

'Anyway,' piped up Matina and clapped her hands together. 'Eddie is an eager boy. Everyone working here is. I'll introduce you to them all in good time. So! That's all for now, I believe.' Matina gave a firm nod. 'Well, work awaits . . . and you need to rest. See you at five p.m. sharp!' she added and turned on her heels without waiting for an answer, Spyros jerking forward as if she'd dragged him along by a tether.

As soon as they were gone, the door closed behind them, Katie exhaled audibly, took another long look at the stunning view outside, and set about unpacking.

Chapter 10

Katie came down the stairs early for her appointment. It was ten to five when she stood in front of the reception desk to wait for Matina and possibly her subdued husband as well. The door to her employers' private office was shut. She could hear the whirring sound of a printer working away but decided not to disturb. *She can come out and see me when she's good and ready!*

Katie heard footsteps and turned to see Eva coming from the kitchen. She was carrying a small tray with a coffee mug and biscuits. Balancing it effortlessly in one hand, she knocked on the office door. Before going in, she gave Katie an easy smile and a wink. Katie beamed at her. She had lunch with her in the kitchen a couple of hours earlier. Eva was lovely to talk to. Even though she was from Albania, she spoke Greek like a native. She was a widower in her sixties, who'd been living in Greece for many years. Katie hadn't met Julia or Eddie yet, but thanks to Eva's chatty nature she felt like she knew them already. When it came to the staff, Katie felt lucky. It was her strange employers that made her feel unsure about which way this was going to go.

The sound of the creaky door opening made her jump out of her reverie. Matina spilled out of the office first, Spyros and Eva following suit behind her. Eva disappeared down the corridor past the staircase to return to the kitchen while her employers walked straight up to Katie.

After a quick greeting, Matina started to talk shop. While Spyros stayed put, his wife took Katie to the back of the desk, prompted her to sit down on the hard, wooden chair and began showing her where everything was. The first thing Katie noticed, to her dismay, was there was no computer at her disposal. In all her previous hotel jobs she'd always had one. Instead, this desk seemed rather basic.

Matina pointed to a thick, dog-eared volume that wouldn't have looked more discoloured and out of shape had it been dunked into the sea. 'This is where we register all our bookings. Make sure to use it carefully. I won't stand for mistakes leading to double bookings, Katie. Otherwise, any incurring expenses will have to come out of your salary.'

'Of course. I understand.' Katie nodded frantically.

'It has happened, you know,' said Matina, squinting her eyes. Behind her, Spyros stood tight-lipped, his expression apologetic. Katie took one look at him and wondered how patient he must be to be able to coexist with such a bossy wife. When Matina cleared her throat, Katie turned her attention reluctantly back to her.

'This is the phone, well, obviously.' Matina chuckled. 'I trust you know how to use the calculator?' She pointed to a dingy article of the solar variety, the kind you can get for a euro at the local thrift store.

'Yes, I know how to use this, of course . . .' Katie's heart sank. The realization she wasn't going to have a computer hit her hard. How was she going to pass the time during idle periods? Being denied the joys of social media, email or even Solitaire was bad enough, but being asked if she knew how to do calculations on a stupid piece of pastel-coloured plastic was a bit too much.

Katie's mind drifted for a few more moments. When she looked up from the desk, she realized her boss was still blathering on, oblivious. But in Spyros' eyes, she saw it then. Recognition. Silently, they shared a moment of mutual understanding.

'So . . . I've shown you the travel guides and the maps on the shelf – that little leather-bound telephone book over there is indexed alphabetically. If young Eddie asks you to call a plumber, an electrician or the local kebab shop, the number's in the book. *Everything's* in the book!' Matina insisted as if anyone would dare contradict her. Pointing to the tattered leather-bound book with a sharp finger, she carried on, 'I made sure of that. I'll thank you in advance for not knocking on my door all day for this and that, not unless you have to. I'm a very busy woman, Katie. You do your work and I'll do mine. I won't appreciate a great number of interruptions. So consult the telephone book first before knocking on my door. If you can't find what you need, whatever that is, ask Spyros here to help you.'

Spyros took a step forward like an eager schoolboy and nodded brightly as soon as his wife pointed to him. 'Yes, Katie. Feel free to ask *me*.'

'Spyros, I'll leave you and Katie to it. Stay with her tonight till ten as we discussed, but first, give her that little tour around the grounds.' Like a duchess on her way to a big gala, Matina spun around and walked away straight-backed. Stunned, Katie watched her till she disappeared inside her office, closing the door behind her.

'So! How about that tour? Shall we, Katie?' asked Spyros motioning towards the exit. Katie stared speechless for a few moments. The man seemed totally unaffected by his wife's patronizing tone.

'Yes, but . . . Is it all right if we leave the reception desk unattended?'

Spyros winked. 'No problem, Katie, it's a small hotel! We'll be back in a flash. This way. Let me show you the grounds outside first.'

They came out to the feeble afternoon sunlight, and Spyros waved his arms about a lot, greeting people and flashing big smiles. The beach was busy at this hour. Many guests came and went, in and out of the hotel, and others lounged on the lawn. Spyros motioned to Katie to follow him down to the beach. 'As you can see we have our own sun loungers and umbrellas here. If you see anyone who's not a guest using them, please tell Eddie. The loungers are his responsibility. Every night he stacks them and chains them together, then lays them out in the morning.'

Katie nodded happily and Spyros pointed at the jetty a little further away. The fishing boat was still moored there. It had an engine at its stern.

'This is my pride and joy,' said Spyros, bright-faced, as he pointed to it.

'That's nice. You take it out fishing?'

Spyros nodded eagerly. 'You bet!' I use it as often as the weather and my obligations here permit. Now you're here, I hope to be able to do this more often!' He winked and let out a little squeal of delight. Katie felt happy for him, guessing it must be a precious getaway from his oppressive spouse. Beckoning frantically, he led Katie back towards the hotel entrance but then turned right onto a side path. He opened a low wooden door to a secluded garden, and

Katie gasped when she laid eyes upon it. Decorated in white and blue it was an idyllic setting, so typical of the Cyclades that Sifnos was part of.

A dozen blue round tables stood in the midst of a paved courtyard, a vine trellis hanging overhead. A stainless steel buffet table stood a few paces away, half-hidden under a large sheet of canvas. On one side of the yard there was a line of fruit trees that offered a generous shade. Along the external wall of the hotel, large pot plants brimmed over with geraniums in various shades. There were a couple of windows on that wall but only one door, which was closed. Katie saw the extractor fan whirring away high above it, thick smoke spilling out to rise into the air.

'Eva is busy cooking dinner at this hour,' said Spyros. 'I expect you saw the lounge area on your way to the kitchen for lunch today?'

'Yes, I did. And Eva made sure to show it to me as well.'

'As you may have noticed it includes a small dining area.'

'Yes, I did notice. It's a quaint and comfortable space. I love the large TV on the wall, by the way. I expect the guests enjoy it.'

'Yes, they do. Lots of satellite channels available. You're welcome to watch too in the evenings, Katie.'

'Oh, this is kind, thank you, Mr Spyros.'

'Not at all. Anyway, what I meant to say was, we don't use that indoor space as much in the summer for serving food. Once it gets warm enough, our guests come out here to enjoy their meals.' He waved his arms about as they stood in the midst of the quiet yard. 'It doesn't look like much now, but I assure you, at the height of summer it's pleasant to eat out here.'

'I'm sure it is,' said Katie, taking a few steps to explore further. A bright red bougainvillea draped over the back fence. In the far distance, the view of Asimi was breathtaking. Katie turned to her left to admire the vibrant colours of the geraniums again. Above them, a line of quaint, antique lanterns hung from the external wall. In the distance, two sparrows perched on a branch busily tweeting to each other.

Katie closed her eyes, the sweetness of the bird song amplifying. *This is heaven. I love it here.*

'Eddie and I took the buffet table, and the tables and chairs out of the store room only this morning,' piped up Spyros, causing Katie to open her eyes with a start. 'As of Monday, if the good weather holds up, we hope to start serving breakfast outside, maybe even lunch. It's late May, after all! It's been windy recently, not a big surprise for this part of Greece, of course, but we expect the weather will be gentle on most days from now on.' His eyes lit up. 'Oh! I forgot to say, the staff cannot have their meals out here, but we do the odd BBQ for our guests in the summer, and the staff are welcome to dine with the guests then.' He winked and gave a bright smile. 'Occasionally, we even do a bit of dancing!'

Katie made appreciative sounds, mirroring his cheerful expression. She couldn't help but notice again what a different man he was when his wife wasn't around.

Spyros walked up to the kitchen door and opened it. With a gallant gesture, he motioned to Katie to walk in first.

Eva was standing in front of the stove frying meatballs.

'Mmmm! Divine!' said Spyros, taking a meatball from the platter. He gestured to Katie to follow suit but she declined politely. Spyros chomped away, rolling his eyes, making dreamy expressions.

Eva giggled. 'Thank you, Mr Spyros! Katie, are you enjoying your little tour of the hotel?'

Katie gave an easy smile. 'Yes. I love the courtyard.'

'It gets very crowded on Saturday nights in the summer. I think I still have a hangover from the last time I partied out there,' said Eva with a guffaw. She held her head with two hands, crossed her eyes and pretended she was wavering on her feet.

Spyros gave her a pat on the back, then took another meatball. 'Mum's the word . . .' he whispered to Eva, then gestured to Katie to follow him out of the kitchen. When Eva gave a giggle he stopped at the doorway and added in a fake-dread tone, a playful glint in his eye: 'The missus has me on a diet again.'

###

The moon was high in the sky when Aggelos opened his eyes to find himself on top of the hill. The first thing he registered was the magnificent view stretching out before him. Then, he took in the semi-dark rooftops of Asimi below, the highway that cut through the barren terrain near the water, and the sea, velvety and gentle. Aggelos was surprised he could hear everything – the sea sighing with every wave that retreated from the sand, the leaves on the trees rustling in the breeze. The blades on the windmill behind him made a soothing sound as they spun slowly as if waving a perpetual greeting to the heavens.

Aggelos put a hand on his forehead. 'I'm going to have to get used to this. And fast. Got a little dizzy just now.'

Esmera patted him on the back, her expression amused. 'You will. Trust me.' They were surrounded by a dozen others, all of them young. No one spoke. They were watching the view as if enchanted. Esmera cast her gaze upon them all, her lips curling into a smile, then turned to Aggelos again. 'I'm so glad you could join us here on the island. Now, our team is complete.'

'Sifnos is so beautiful. I'm delighted you placed me here.'

'Good to know. And well done on apprehending the pickpocket on the ferry. Although, Katie Pavlides didn't exactly thank you for it!' She let out a howl of laughter.

Aggelos shook his head. 'It's all right. I had my luggage so I changed into another t-shirt. No big deal.'

'How are you getting on with . . . you know, the human condition?'

'No problem. It's easier than I thought. And I enjoy it a lot more than I expected.'

'That's good. I hope you won't enjoy it too much, though. Remember, this is a temporary thing.'

'Of course, I understand.'

Chapter 11

Katie was standing behind the reception desk, tidying up, when Spyros came through the archway from the back, his face exuberant. Katie gave a big smile. He was carrying his fishing rod and a hefty backpack. 'Good morning, Mr Spyros. You're going fishing, I see!'

Spyros stopped before her and winked. 'Try to stop me, as they say!'

Katie giggled. He was so easy to talk to. She hadn't seen his wife yet but knew she was in her office. Eva had told her Matina starts her work days at seven a.m. and can spend hours in there without a break. That suited Katie just fine.

Spyros rested an arm on the desk and tilted his head. 'So? How is the first morning coming on?'

'Just fine, thank you, Mr Spyros. It was very kind of you to help with the couple who checked in earlier. Now I know how you want things done, I'll be fine with the next ones. I learn fast, you don't need to worry.'

'Oh, I don't worry at all, Katie. Your CV is very impressive. So, if there's nothing else you need, I'll be off.' He slung his backpack over his shoulder and waved, then hopped down the steps light-footed like a schoolboy.

Shortly, Julia came down the stairs, Eddie trailing behind her. They were carrying dirty linen in baskets. Katie had met them earlier when they'd arrived for work.

'You okay there, Katie?' asked Julia, stopping short, sweat glistening on her brow.

'Fine, Julia. You? Hard work, is it?'

Julia put down her basket, then chuckled. 'I'll tell you one thing, Katie. We Albanian women are tough. I was working in the fields as a teenager back home. Believe me, that was hard work. This is fun in comparison, even though I'm in my forties now.'

'Really? As a teenager?'

'Oh yes!' She stretched out her arm and patted Eddie on the shoulder. 'I make sure to tell my boy all about that whenever he complains. Life is easy here. That's why I came to Greece. For a better future for me and my children. A more comfortable life.'

Eddie's eyes twinkled as his mother spoke, but Katie noticed he cringed a little too as if the conversation embarrassed him. He hadn't spoken to Katie yet, and she wondered if he was shy. Jutting out her chin, she decided to encourage him. 'Anything fun to do around here, Eddie?'

Eddie brightened up and, having put down his basket too, he took a few steps towards her, then stopped short in the middle of the reception hall. 'There's a café and a taverna in Asimi but nothing else.' He curled his top lip. 'No bars and no clubs here.' But, if you have your own transport, you could go to other villages nearby. There are more choices down the beach, at the village of Pefki, for example.'

'Pefki . . . I'll remember that.' Katie gave him an encouraging smile and was delighted to see he responded with a huge grin. She knew what it was like to grow up in a small place where there was nothing to do. She'd been shy all her life but moving to Athens had helped her become more sociable and open.

Instinctively, she stroked the amulet with her fingertips and felt a strange consolation. She'd almost believed Esmera that the amulet had magic powers and wished it were true. Sometimes, she felt only magic could help her, because in this mundane world she'd tried everything else and, so far, all had failed.

By the time Katie snapped out of her trance, Julia and Eddie had gone off to resume their duties. She looked up, startled. *Did someone just talk to me? Damn it! Stop daydreaming, Katie!*

A man was standing at the desk in front of her, a wide grin spread across his face. *Wait a minute, that's not just any man. That's . . . that's . . . oh hello!*

Aggelos stared back at her, wide-eyed. 'It's you! Oh, hi! Fancy meeting you here. Is this where you work?'

'Hi! Yes . . . that's right.' Katie gave a demure smile, feeling smitten by his gorgeous looks. Panic gripped her when she realized she was blushing.

Aggelos pretended not to notice the flaming colour of her cheeks. 'You must be busy so I'll just have my key and I'll be on my way. Number twenty-seven please.'

Katie stared for a few moments, blank-faced. 'Excuse me? Your key?'

'Yes, my key. I'm a guest here.'

'Are you?'

'Yes. I arrived yesterday, well, obviously, since we met on the ferry.' Without meaning to, Aggelos pointed to his t-shirt. It was the one her fruit juice had soiled, but he had washed it and it looked brand new. As soon as he pointed to the t-shirt, he saw the red colour on Katie's cheeks deepen. 'So sorry . . . I didn't mean to remind you.'

Katie waved her hands frantically in front of her face and avoided his eyes. 'No . . . no problem. I'm glad to see I didn't ruin it completely.'

'So . . . about my key?'

Katie's apprehension about her strict employer made her paranoid. *What if he's a scammer? Should I ask for ID? How come I never saw him here yesterday?* She knitted her brows. 'What time did you arrive at the hotel, if I may ask?'

Aggelos leaned forward, put both elbows on the desk and cradled his head in his hands. Katie almost gasped at the sight. He looked drop dead gorgeous, and so relaxed as if he had all the time in the world to talk to her.

Aggelos' lips curled into an easy smile, his eyes dreamy as he gazed at the ceiling. 'Well, let's see . . . I got off the ferry, had a look around Kamares, grabbed a bite to eat, then came straight here. Say, around three o'clock?'

Katie's eyes lit up. 'That's why I didn't see you. I started work at five o' clock yesterday. So, Mr Spyros, the owner, must have checked you in.'

'Uh-huh,' replied Aggelos with a cute grin that made him look simply adorable.

Arriving at this conclusion helped Katie to relax, her face blooming with ease like a flower. She saw his eyes widen then, but it was only momentary.

He looked away, then gave a chuckle. 'So, you just started working here?'

Katie nodded happily. 'Yep, my first full day today.'

'Great. Wish you all the best.'

'Thanks.' She stared into his eyes again, those perfect, deep blue eyes. His dark hair was reaching down to his neck where a vein had popped out. Her gaze wandered to his broad shoulders and muscly arms. The sight was irresistible, rendering her transfixed as she continued to play with a pen between two restless fingers. She started to feel woozy and got so carried away that when she heard his voice again, her shoulders jumped.

'So? Room number twenty-seven?'

'Of course!' Katie snapped out of her trance and turned around. There were pigeon holes on the wall for the mail as well as a wooden board where all the keys hung from nails. 'Well, look at that!' she exclaimed, picking up a shiny golden key that was in stark contrast to the others. 'All the other keys are rusty and old, and yours looks like it's never been used before.'

Aggelos winked. 'Lucky me!'

Katie handed him the key and he thanked her. As he took it, her fingers touched his. They felt warm, shooting an arrow of heat down her spine. The hairs on the back of her neck stood on end. She gave an awkward smile and whispered, 'Oh . . .'

'What is it?'

'I got goosebumps. Just now.'

Aggelos smirked, his eyes sparkling. 'Well, who knows? Maybe an angel just brushed past you.'

Katie gave a giggle. 'Nah, no such luck. I'm probably sitting in a draught so I'd better get used to it. This is the Cyclades, after all. I hear it's very windy here.'

Chapter 12

Matina came out of her office and walked up to Katie. 'Oh hello, Katie. So sorry I didn't come out sooner, but I've had a busy morning. Everything okay? Have you had any problems?'

'Everything's fine, Mrs Matina. It's been an easy morning.' She looked at the clock on the wall. It was a quarter to one. She was getting hungry, in time for lunch. 'May I ask, who will man reception at the end of my shift?'

Matina had taken off her glasses and was rubbing the base of her nose, her eyes closed for a few moments. Then, she put her glasses back on and heaved a long sigh. 'Don't worry, Katie. I leave my office door open from one till five. This way there's always someone to man the fort.' She gave a sweet smile then, and it took Katie by surprise. This woman could be sweet if she wanted to. A tiny hope nestled in Katie's chest. *Not another Roula then. Hopefully.*

A breezy greeting echoed from the entrance and both women turned their attention there. It was Spyros, back from fishing. He was holding a basket full of fish. He glided towards them, his chest puffed up, his voice reverberating off the walls with vibrancy. 'Look at this mackerel! And red mullet! A great catch today!'

'Bravo, Spyros!' said Matina, her face lighting up. Another surprise for Katie. *Maybe this guy isn't so much under the thumb. Or, he's allowed at least one little pleasure in life.*

'I'll take them to Eva to prepare for cooking. And if she's too busy, *I* can do it. Thought we could have the mullets fried for lunch? We have boiled broccoli left from yesterday, don't we?'

'Sounds great, Spyros, but leave it for dinner instead. I'm running late with work.' Matina gave a little wave, then stifled a yawn. 'You go ahead and have lunch on your own today. I'll have a sandwich at my desk or something.'

Spyros shook his head forlornly and patted her shoulder with a gentle hand. 'You work too hard, my darling Matina.'

Matina threw Katie a furtive glance, then shot a stern look at her husband and stiffened, causing him to clear his throat and jerk back from her as if scalded with hot oil.

Matina set her jaw, her eyes vacant. 'Well, Spyros, you know the work gives me joy. It's good for me, and it's good for the community.'

'Of course, of course,' mumbled Spyros and disappeared down the corridor without further ado.

###

By the time Katie went to the kitchen for lunch, Spyros had already cleaned and washed the fish. He was standing by the sink, salting his catch in a big bowl, whistling a happy tune. Eva stood ruddy-cheeked at the kitchen island, taking cheese pastries out of a baking sheet. They'd just come out of the oven, judging from the warmth and the delicious aroma hanging in the air.

'This smells phenomenal!' said Katie coming to stand beside Eva.

'Just another day in the kitchen of Hotel Asimi,' replied Spyros. 'It's our Eva who's phenomenal. We still thank our lucky stars she came to us for work.'

'Oh stop, Mr Spyros,' said Eva with a huff, then leaned over to Katie pretending to whisper, 'He's only buttering me up because he's after the muffins.'

Spyros' eyes widened. 'You didn't! The coffee and walnut ones? My favourites!' He approached the island in a flash, looking and sniffing around like a K9 on duty.

Katie giggled. She loved the camaraderie between these two. They were like schoolkids in a sandpit. Eva removed the foil from a large platter to show a dozen muffins sprinkled with icing sugar.

Eva pointed at it with a flourish. 'Here you are. Baked them while you were fishing.' She shook a finger at him. 'But don't have them all in one go. Matina saw me bake them. If she checks tomorrow and there's only two left like last time, I'm not taking the heat for you again.'

'Scout's honour!' Spyros made a move to pick up a muffin but Eva slapped his wrist. 'Eeew! You've been handling raw fish!'

Spyros turned around to wash his hands under the tap but then they all heard footsteps. Guessing it was Matina, he dashed to the sink in record time, aiming to put as much distance as possible between himself and the muffins before she walked in.

Matina poked her head around the door. 'Eva? Are the cheese pastries done yet? They've been torturing my sense of smell in the office for so long. I'm dying for a bite.'

Eva giggled, grabbed a dish from the cupboard and put three large pastries in it before handing it to Matina.

Matina rolled her eyes. 'There goes my waistline! But to hell with it. I'm ravenous. You're such a blessing to us, Eva.' She picked up a pastry and bit into it, her expression dreamy.

'So, I hear,' said Eva, her mirthful eyes darting to Spyros. He was wiping his hands with a towel by the sink, looking uninterested in the generous display of yummy food in the centre of the room. It was so obvious he was putting it on that Katie placed a hand over her mouth to stifle a snigger.

'Speaking of waistlines, go easy on the pastries,' said Matina, serving Spyros with a stern look. 'And don't you think I don't know there are muffins. I'm counting them this time!' she warned in a light-hearted tone, amusement lighting up her tired eyes. Without further ado, she spun around and vanished to the sound of Spyros assuring her he was going to be good.

###

Katie, Eva, and Spyros had just finished their lunch of cheese pastries, fried sausages, and salad, and were now sampling the delicious muffins. Spyros gobbled his up and was about to reach out for seconds when Matina appeared at the door again, causing Spyros' hand to disappear under the table with the desperation of a fish diving back into the water.

'Spyros, remember, the drain pipe in the backyard is hanging in mid-air. You haven't fixed it yet, have you?'

Spyros grimaced and gave a little wave. 'No, I haven't. It's the damn wind, I know. I'll fix it.'

Matina placed a hand on her waist and tilted her head. 'When?'

'I will, Matina. Tomorrow morning. I'll tend the garden with Eddie first, then I'll do the pipe.'

'Why can't you do it now? Goodness knows what time you'll finish with the garden tomorrow. You don't have anything to do now, do you?'

'I was hoping to have an easy afternoon. Get some shut-eye.'

'Spyros, it'll take you seconds. It's just a couple of brackets and a few screws. You'll be done in no time. We all know how forgetful you can be. I don't want to have to remind you again.' Her face softened, and she gave a sweet smile. 'If you do it now, then it'll be done, and I'll have one less thing to note down for you to do. All right, Spyros?'

Spyros gave a sigh. 'Oh all right! He stood reluctantly, shot a forlorn look at the muffins and left the kitchen in a hurry. When he reached the door, he stopped in front of Matina.

'Where would I be without you reminding me of this and that?' There was a tiny bite of sarcasm in his voice. It was so evident Katie bit her lip, hoping it wouldn't lead to a domestic. To her surprise, far from annoying Matina, Spyros' remark caused his wife to sweeten further.

'Thank you,' she purred at him, squeezing his arm in a fleeting, yet tender gesture. Spyros gave her a tight smile and left without another word. A moment later, Matina returned to her office.

As soon as they were alone, Katie turned to Eva searching her eyes.

Eva shook her head and looked out the window. 'Whoa,' she mumbled. 'That woman is something.'

Katie hesitated for a few moments but her curiosity was too much to resist. 'Is she like that all the time?'

Eva rolled her eyes, then smiled. 'Every single day. And, poor Mr Spyros, he takes it without ever complaining. He's a saint.'

Katie pressed her lips together. 'Yes, he's lovely. Mind you, Matina is not exactly bad either, just . . . well . . . a little overwhelming at times.'

'She is. But trust me, she's harmless. Mr Spyros knows that so he puts up with her bossiness, you know? Deep down she's an angel. And she means well.'

'Frankly, she's a bit of a mystery to me, so that's good to know.'

Eva looked Katie squarely in the eyes. 'Matina wasn't always like this, you know. But the few of us who know what happened to change her, are happy to humour her; Mr Spyros more than anybody else.'

Katie's eyes widened. 'Why? What happened to her?'

'Sorry, Katie, but it's not my place to say. Besides, I only know very little. It happened long before I came here. Just believe me when I say, Matina has more bark than she has bite. Just ignore her when she acts all stern and bossy. Her heart is one of gold and that's what matters.'

Chapter 13

On her first day off work, Katie visited the village of Asimi to explore. The stunning beauty of its picturesque paths and old, often decrepit buildings enchanted her. When she passed a small rent-a-scooter business near the main road, she decided to rent one and explore further. Visiting a series of quaint little villages she got as far as the island capital, Apollonia, a marvel of whitewashed yards and quaint shops. After a late lunch at a taverna in the generous shade of a dense vine trellis, she walked around a little more, then got on the scooter to head back to Asimi.

She was riding along the highway, marvelling at the ragged beauty of the sparkling coastline when she heard a loud noise, then the scooter started to veer along the road. She stopped at the roadside, frustrated to see her back tyre had been punctured. The culprit, a rusty old nail, was still lodged in the tyre. Panicking, she looked at the deserted road. It was late afternoon, but the sun shone brightly, scorching the world around her with fervour.

Katie laid the scooter down on the dusty roadside, beads of sweat dripping heavy from her brow. With a little effort, she managed to dislodge the nail from the tyre, and now, she was desperate. *What am I going to do?* Her eyes lit up when she remembered the paperwork the nice young man had given her at the shop. *I can call for assistance!* According to the last road sign she'd passed, Asimi was less than five kilometres away. She took the document and her mobile out of her backpack, but the smile of hope soon froze on her lips. *Damn. No signal.*

'Aaaargh!' Katie stood upright and pulled the scooter up holding it by its handlebars. She ran a hand through her hair, the rushing wind sending the long strands to twist and whip against her fluttering eyelids. Her eyes were gritty from the dusty ride and salty air, and that didn't help her spirits.

Grunting, she began to walk, holding the scooter, rolling it alongside her. It was a strenuous task, seeing that the tyre was now totally flat. She started to worry that moving the scooter could ruin the tyre totally but what was the alternative? Who knew when another vehicle would drive past? And even then, would they stop to help her? It was best to keep moving and to get to Asimi before the sun began to set. She had no idea how long it would take at such a slow pace but it was worth a try. A minute later she took the mobile out again to check for a signal, but to no avail. 'Aaaagh!' she shouted again, her lips twisting. 'Damn it! On my first day off!' She raised an indignant fist towards the sky. 'That's not fair. I need help and I need it *now*!'

'Hi!' came a jovial voice from the other side of the road, a mere moment later.

'What the—' mumbled Katie. The fields across the road were at a lower level and someone had just appeared to stand at the roadside, waving both hands at her. Katie squinted her eyes against the glaring sunlight. *Who is that?* It looked like a young man. He'd just repeated his earlier greeting and was now crossing the empty road, rushing towards her. She couldn't make out a face or even a clear frame through the glare and that made her grow numb as he came closer. *Please don't be a weirdo!* She gripped the handlebars, her knuckles turning white, but then they relaxed as she raised a hand to return the greeting.

'Hi, sorry, I didn't recognize you earlier!' she said with an open smile when the man stopped before her. It was the handsome guest from the hotel. She ran an urgent hand through her hair, her lips twitching. *I must look horrid in this darn heat!*

'What's happened? Do you need help?' Aggelos reached out with both hands and took the handlebars from her. Katie took a step back, admiring his strong naked shoulders. He wore a sleeveless top and khaki shorts, his fine hair dancing in the breeze, lips sweet like honey, eyes sparkling like diamonds. She stood there for a few moments, speechless, just thinking how weightless the scooter must feel in his strong hands.

Aggelos gave a frown. 'Are you okay, Katie?'

Katie gave an awkward smile. 'Yes, I—' Her lower lip twitched, eyes narrowing. 'How do you know my name?'

He shrugged. 'You told me yesterday.'

'No, I didn't!'

'Yes, you did.'

'If I told you my name, then how come I don't know yours?'

'Sorry.' He offered his hand. 'It's Aggelos. Pleased to meet you.'

'Aggelos?' she said with a titter.

'Yes. Why is that funny?'

'You know . . . because Aggelos means "Angel" and you turned up just as I needed help.' She gave a huge grin, her eyes twinkling. She was still quite sure she'd never mentioned her name to him but decided to let it go. After all, he was a guest at the hotel. Perhaps he'd overheard her name there.

'I see.' Aggelos scratched his jaw and rested his eyes, those sparkling lagoons of brilliant blue, upon her, causing her to stare helplessly back at him for a few more moments. The effect he had on her was indescribable. She felt dizzy looking into his eyes so she pointed at the flat tyre to take the attention away from herself.

'See? Totally flat. So glad you came. I tried my mobile but there's no signal. Could we try with yours please?'

Aggelos shook his head. 'Sorry. I don't own a mobile.'

Katie's eyes turned huge. 'What? How is that even possible?'

'I don't like them. Simple as that.'

'But what do you do if you want to call someone?'

'I use a landline, I guess.'

'And what about emergencies when you're out and about?'

'I count on the kindness of strangers.' He gave a chortle. 'You have a mobile. It didn't do much for you today, did it? But trust a kind stranger to always turn up.'

Katie let out a giggle and pointed at the scooter. 'So, kind stranger, any ideas about how I could get this thing back to Asimi?'

'Wish I could fix it for you but I don't know how. But maybe we could stop a car and get some help or a free ride.'

'That would be nice, except . . .' she stretched out both hands 'there's no one about.'

Aggelos gave a lopsided smile and laid the scooter down on the dirt. 'Oh, ye of little faith . . .'

Katie was about to give him a cute comeback about faith being one thing but the twilight zone another when she heard a horn-honking sound. She turned around and saw an open truck coming to stop in front of them. She turned again to face Aggelos. He had an arm up, signalling the man behind the wheel to move a little closer. The truck had come out of nowhere. She hadn't heard it coming. Speechless, Katie watched as a burly man jumped out of the vehicle and strode towards them.

'Hi, love! What seems to be the problem?' he asked, a benevolent smile spread across his face.

'Oh hi! Thank you for stopping. It's the back tyre. It has a puncture.'

The man dashed to his truck and, moments later, returned with a spray can to apply some kind of foam in the tyre.

'Thank you so much,' said Katie, then turning to Aggelos, 'I guess this is my lucky day!'

Aggelos gave a chuckle but said nothing. At the same time, the man stood back on his feet.

'This should fix it temporarily,' he said as he replaced the cap on the spray can. 'And it was nothing. Glad to help! Just ride the scooter slowly and carefully now. Where you off to?'

'Asimi. I'm returning it to the rent shop there.'

'You'll be all right then. Well, goodbye!' He gave a bright smile and hurried back to his truck to the sound of Katie's heartfelt thanks.

As soon as he left, Aggelos pulled the scooter up in one swift, effortless move, and Katie jumped on it, her face bright with relief. 'He was a helpful guy, albeit a little strange, don't you think? He never said a word to you.'

Aggelos sniggered and looked away. 'I don't mind. I stopped him for *you*, after all.'

Katie shrugged. 'So, what are you waiting for? Hop on! I'll give you a ride.'

Aggelos shook his head but Katie beckoned frantically. 'Come on, it's the least I can do to thank you.'

'But I don't need a ride. Besides, we don't know how safe the tyre is with the quick fix. You'd better ride alone.'

Katie raised her brows. 'Are you sure?' What he said made sense but she'd still risk it if he'd only change his mind. He was so delicious. The very idea of him riding the scooter with her, holding her by the waist, made her reel with the sheer desire to be near him.

'Yes, I'm sure.' He gave a dreamy smile. 'I was hiking through the fields when I saw you. Now I can pick up from where I left off.'

'You're hiking?' Katie's brow furrowed when she dropped her gaze to his feet. 'In sandals?'

'Yes,' he replied, deadpan. Katie put up a hand, pretending to rub her nose, but what she really did was try to suppress her amusement. He was adorable and she felt more drawn to him by the second. *He doesn't own a mobile and hikes in sandals through open fields?* His intricate quirks made her head spin, but even so, she found it all contributed to his charm.

'So, off you go. I'll see you later,' he said as he came to stand by the scooter, putting a light hand on her shoulder. A blast of warm heat bloomed inside Katie's chest, then coursed down her spine.

Reluctantly, Katie waved and left him behind. The scooter behaved well. As she rode away, she checked her mirror, over and over again, marvelling at his distant form. In the sweet, afternoon sunlight that bounced off the tarmac causing it to glisten, he seemed like a mirage of awesomeness. Already, she was daydreaming about their next encounter. *How fortunate was I that he showed up just as I needed assistance! A proper 'Aggelos', indeed!*

###

When Katie arrived back at Hotel Asimi the sun was slowly gliding towards the horizon against a pastel-coloured sky. She was strolling past the hotel's thatched umbrellas, making her way towards the entrance when her jaw dropped. Sitting on the bottom step was Aggelos. He was holding an orange juice carton, drinking through a straw thirstily.

Katie put her hands on her hips and gawped when she stopped to stand before him. 'Aggelos! How did you do that?'

Aggelos beamed at her and pulled a strand of silky hair back from his brow. 'How did I do what?'

'How did you get here before me? It was a good five kilometres out of Asimi where I left you. Did you hitch a ride?'

Aggelos pointed at his feet. 'Yes. On those babies.' He winked. 'I'm a fast walker.'

'But . . .' She scratched her head. 'You can't be faster than the scooter I was on, surely.'

Aggelos stood and scrunched up the carton, then hopped up the few steps to the bin. He tossed it inside and shrugged when he returned to her at the bottom of the steps. 'Nah, you've been gone ages. I bet you wandered around the village and lost track of time.'

'I did buy an ice cream . . . and lingered at the village square for a while,' she mumbled.

Aggelos tilted his head. 'See? Not Superman, after all.'

'I never said you're Superman. But, I *have* noticed you tend to save the day.'

Aggelos put up a finger. 'Now, that's a compliment and a half! Thank you, Katie.'

Katie heard the sound of her name on his lips again, and it made her knees weak. Earlier, when he was drinking his refreshment she couldn't take her eyes off his pouted lips around the straw. She'd tried to imagine there and then how it would feel to kiss them. Now, as he gazed at her, his wide smile exposing perfect pearly whites, she shifted her weight from foot to foot, wondering if she had it in her to ask him out. She decided it was too soon, and besides, she'd never done this sort of thing before. As she contemplated all that, Aggelos was telling her about the beauty of the places he'd explored that day. She kept nodding and making the odd comment and, all the while, marvelled at his perfectly sculpted features.

###

Matina came out of her office and walked up to Spyros, who was manning the reception desk. It was getting up to six o' clock and he'd just booked in a large group of tourists.

'Are you done for the day, Spyros?'

'Just booked in the last group and I'm wrapping things up. I tell you, I'm ready for a shower. Want to get to bed early tonight. Going off fishing early tomorrow.'

Matina nodded happily. 'Before you go, Spyros, can you help me with something, please? The printer's playing up again. Where is the phone number for the technician who fixed it last time?'

Spyros opened the telephone book to look for the number. Absentmindedly, Matina turned around and looked at the front entrance. Her eyes lit up to recognize Katie standing at the bottom of the stairs outside, but the sight intrigued her as well.

She took a few steps closer to the entrance and tilted her head, watching her employee. Moments later, she spun around and approached the desk again. Spyros handed her a scrap of paper where he'd jotted down the number she wanted.

Matina thanked him, then shook her head. 'I think our new employee is a bit loopy.' She pointed to the exit with her eyes.

Spyros craned his neck and saw Katie standing outside but nothing else that seemed strange. 'Why do you say that? It's her day off. She's entitled to stand outside if she wants to.'

'She's not just standing there, Spyros! She's mumbling to herself. Look! She's talking to the rosemary bushes! She nods at them and everything! You don't think she's one of those funny hippy types, do you?'

'I hear it's beneficial to talk to plants. Couldn't hurt them, you know.'

'Really, Spyros! Sometimes I think you'd give anybody the benefit of the doubt!'

Chapter 14

It was midday and the sun was hammering down on the world outside, but Katie sat blissfully in the air-conditioned lobby. After a week, she felt confident with her duties. There were idle intervals on any work day, but she was allowed to open a book or a magazine to pass the time. The guests were friendly and chatty, and so were her colleagues. As for Matina, she still spent all morning in her office, her printer whirring away, a good indication that she was engrossed in whatever she was doing and not likely to come out, which suited Katie just fine. Thankfully, Matina wasn't schizzy like Roula, just awkward, but it was enough to make Katie uneasy around her.

A cheerful greeting from the open door snapped Katie out of her thoughts. Aggelos raised his hand and gave a bright smile as he came to loom over her on the other side of the high desk.

Katie looked up, her eyes dancing. 'Hello, Aggelos! Did you enjoy your swim?' she asked, noticing his wet hair and damp t-shirt.

'Oh yes. Fantastic!'

Katie marvelled at his sun-kissed complexion that brought out the blue in his eyes. By now her heart palpitated whenever she laid eyes on him. Katie brought a hand to her chest as if to will her heart rate to return to normal. She brought the other hand to her hair and tucked a long strand behind her ear, her eyes seeking refuge at the open notepad before her. She fiddled with her pen, then looked up again to find his eyes smiling at her.

Aggelos seemed unaware of her discomfort. He gave a beaming smile, arms flailing about excitedly. 'I just love it here, Katie! I'm so glad I came to Sifnos. The more I see, the more I fall in love with it.'

'Me too! Do you still enjoy hiking?'

'Yes. But I'm also enjoying the sea sports. I went down to Pefki the other day and hired a jet ski. You should try it.' His eyes lit up. 'It's great fun!'

Katie couldn't help thinking how adorable he seemed, talking about the jet ski like a ten-year-old would talk about his new bike. 'Pefki? It's the next village down that way, isn't it?' She pointed vaguely to her left. 'Haven't been there yet,' she added when he nodded.

'Haven't you?' He rested his elbows on the desk, then leaned in, his expression turning serious, a spark igniting in his eyes. 'Maybe we can go together sometime. When is your next day off?'

Katie went rigid and blinked a few times. *Did I hear right? Did he just ask me out?* 'Um . . . next week. Monday.'

Aggelos wrinkled his brow and nodded suggestively. 'So, is that a yes?' He flashed a lopsided smile. 'I'd love to show you around.'

Katie mirrored his bright expression. 'Of course, I'd love to.'

'It's a date!' he said, winking. 'Thank you, Katie.'

'No need to thank me,' she said, waving dismissively. She should be the one saying thanks. He was dreamy, way out of her league. If anything, she should be paying him for taking her along. Top-notch hired escorts around the world had nothing on him.

Aggelos didn't seem to notice the looks of adoration she kept throwing him. 'No, really, Katie. It's a lonely business sightseeing on my own. So much beauty around and no one to share it with. So I'm glad you said yes. Look forward to it.' He tapped his hand on the desk to stress his last statement.

'Oh! I just remembered. It's just a technicality. I need to confirm your booking details and give them to Mrs Matina. She enters all booking information in a computer program, you see. Problem is, I can't find anyone named Aggelos in the register. But perhaps Mr Spyros only entered the initial of your first name. He does this sometimes.' She took the tattered register in her hands. 'What is your full name?'

Aggelos squinted his eyes for a moment or two, then looked up pretending to admire the wooden panelling on the ceiling. 'It's . . . um . . . Aggelopoulos. Aggelos Aggelopoulos.'

Katie gave a loud chuckle. 'Oh! I love your name!' He'd sounded so confident saying it, so suave, she wished she had a martini, shaken, not stirred, to hand it to him on the spot.

Aggelos offered another killer smile as his eyes locked with hers again. 'Thank you.'

Katie felt her brow grow warm and brushed it with an impatient hand. 'Let me check the register again.' To her dismay, she couldn't find his last name either. 'I don't understand, it's not here. Did you say Mr Spyros signed you in?'

Aggelos stood straight and put out an open hand. 'Can I have a look? I'm sure I can find it.'

Katie didn't have the heart to say no, even though she couldn't see the point of him looking. She handed him the register and gave a smirk. 'I'd be surprised if you found it and wouldn't put it past Mr Spyros to be the reason behind this. He can be a little forgetful at times. I expect he planned to put the details in the book but forgot to get around to it. But not to worry; if this is the case, I'll talk to him and we'll sort it out.'

Aggelos turned the pages in silence for a few moments. Then, he cleared his throat and placed two fingers on his lips, still looking at the register. 'No, don't ask him, Katie. He did write it in. I saw him do it.' He looked up at the antique chandelier that hung from the ceiling and pulled a face of frustration. 'I'm sorry. I can't see well in the electric light. Give me a minute.' Without waiting for an answer, he spun around and went to stand in the doorway.

Perplexed, Katie waited, staring at his back for a few moments as he seemed to scrutinize the pages. Moments later, he strode back to her, a triumphant expression on his face. 'There you go! Found it!'

Katie leaned closer over the reception desk, her eyes darting to the spot on the page where his impeccably manicured finger rested, pointing.

She scratched her head. 'How peculiar! I could swear it wasn't there just now.'

'Well, maybe you're tired. Natural light is so much better to read with, don't you think?'

Not knowing what else to say, Katie nodded and smiled again. Then, she spotted something was missing from the booking. 'Oh. The check-out date has been left open.'

Aggelos scrunched up his face and looked away. 'Yes . . . erm, it's because I don't know yet when I'm leaving. I'll be here a while.'

Katie felt delighted to hear this but had a little problem still. 'I'm afraid Mrs Matina likes to have a departure date on her computer, even if it's a tentative one. Would you mind?' She picked up a pen, expecting him to return the registry so she could write in it.

Aggelos gave a crooked grin. 'Is that so?'

Oh my goodness. He's absolutely gorgeous! Katie felt faint. She brushed an urgent hand across her forehead. *Is the air-condition failing? It's so warm in here!* She huffed, then fanned her face. 'So sorry for the trouble, but perhaps you could give us a random date? You can always change it later.' She pinned her eyes on him, her pupils dilating when he moved his face ever so slightly nearer to hers.

'Uh . . . I'm afraid I can't help you there.' Aggelos scratched his head as he looked down at the entry. 'You see, I'm here on business.'

Katie gave a frown. 'Business?' She couldn't help dropping her gaze at his swim shorts and flip-flops.

'Well, not on business as such. Let's just say, uh . . .' He raised his laughing eyes to the ceiling and back down '. . . that my employer has placed me here, and I can be called up anytime and ordered to leave.'

'Called up?' Katie's eyes roamed to Aggelos' broad shoulders and up and down his towering figure, despite herself. She swallowed hard, then met his gaze again. 'Like, in the military, you mean?'

Aggelos' eyes lit up. 'Yes! You can say that.'

Katie nodded, her eyes focusing far behind him for a few moments. *Now it makes sense. I knew he wasn't some nine-to-five office wimp!* She felt herself swoon. She'd always had a thing for men in uniform.

Aggelos pointed to the wall behind her. 'Say, Katie, can I have my key now?'

Katie snapped out of her reverie and literally jumped backwards. She snatched the key of room twenty-seven and handed it to him, once again marvelling at it like all the other times she'd taken it into her hands. 'Just look at it,' she said handing it to him, 'It's such a beautiful key. So shiny . . . all the others are dull and rusty.' She pointed to the mounted wooden board where a dozen or so worn out keys signalled mutely they'd seen much better days.

'Yeah, it *is* beautiful.' Aggelos shrugged as he held the key in his hands, turning it this way and that, causing it to catch the light. 'They probably replaced it recently or something.'

'I guess so,' said Katie and gave a little wave as he moved to go, a mischievous smile playing on the corners of his lips.

Chapter 15

Katie had a long refreshing shower at the end of her work day, then decided to take a walk down the beach before heading to Asimi for dinner on her own. Dressed in a patterned summer dress, her hair still damp from her shower, she came out in the soft light of the descending sun. When she stood on the top step of the hotel entrance, her breath caught in her throat.

The breeze came, cheerful and pleasant, to caress her cheeks, the sea's murmur pleasing her ears, the beauty of the landscape magnificent. With a big smile on her face, Katie headed for the sand, took off her sandals and began to saunter towards a protruding tongue of sand in the far distance that lapped thirstily at the water.

A dreamy smile made Katie's eyes light up. She loved the feel of the sand, cool and soft, under her naked feet at this hour. When she made out a familiar shape she shaded her eyes and, recognizing Aggelos approaching from the other direction, quickened her pace. *What's that?* She shaded her eyes again. *Are those seabirds?* Chuckling, she shook her head from side to side.

'Hi! What's so funny?' asked Aggelos when he stopped in front of her, dressed in a t-shirt and a pair of blue, knee-length shorts. Katie put a hand on her hip, the other pointing upwards. 'Are you aware you're being followed by a flock of seabirds?'

Aggelos looked up to see the birds circling over him, his face animated with surprise. He raised his arms and began to flail them frantically while jumping up and down. 'Shoo! Shoo!' The sight was hilarious. Cawing, the birds flew away as Katie began to giggle.

He shook his head and gave an awkward smile. 'Sorry. They're my minions. They tend to follow me around.'

Katie smirked and placed her hands on her waist. 'Is that right?'

'Yes.' He leaned closer and brought down his voice a few notches. 'Superman can't do it all by himself, you know. Minions are important. And this can be our little secret.' He winked.

Katie snapped her fingers, amusement lighting up her eyes. 'Now I get it. So it was the birds that let you know I'd broken down on the side of the road the other day.'

'You got me. Just keep it to yourself lest a whole bunch of damsels in distress will start calling out my name whenever they have a puddle to cross. And I'd rather dedicate my time to save *you* only . . . Katie.' His expression changed when he said her name. As their eyes locked together, rendering Katie mesmerized, Aggelos leaned in closer, moving his hand towards her forearm, but not touching. Katie darted her eyes at his hovering hand, wondering what he was doing. When his palm touched the tiny hairs on her arm ever so slightly, a jolt of static electricity crackled causing them both to jump back in astonishment.

'Oops – sorry!' said Aggelos, cringing.

Katie rubbed her arm and giggled. His clumsiness had helped her relax around him. She wondered if she had the nerve to ask him to grab a bite with her. They could go anywhere he wanted. She was still wondering if she should ask when Aggelos stiffened, his eyes focusing far. Katie turned around and saw a young girl rushing towards them, waving frantically.

The girl was gorgeous. Glamorous. She came to stand before them, a vision of female perfection dressed in skimpy khaki shorts and a white cropped tank top that barely covered her big boobs and flat tummy. She wore impeccable make-up, her long lashes stunning, her pouty red lips belonging to the cover of a fashion magazine. She looked like a 30s movie star thanks to her platinum blond hair that was styled in waves. Slim and ethereal, yet feisty-looking too, she was a cross between Ginger Rogers and a female commando. She was almost as tall as Aggelos.

With a huff, the girl flicked the fringe of her shoulder-length hair back from her eyes and, much to Katie's dismay, got hold of Aggelos' arm as if she owned him. Katie's heart sank. With her sparkling baby blue eyes and muscly arms the girl seemed perfect for him. Too perfect for it to come to any good. Katie was so downhearted by the girl's arrival, she didn't realize she'd been missing the conversation going on between the two for a while. The first thing she noticed when she focused on their exchange was the girl was now practically pulling Aggelos away.

'I said I'll come later. Go. Please!' Aggelos' expression had lost all its joviality.

'No! We need to go *now*. This cannot wait.' She darted her eyes at Katie for a moment, then back at Aggelos. 'Our . . . erm . . . *employer* awaits.'

Aggelos turned to Katie and his lower lip twitched, then he tucked it under his top one. Katie saw a tumultuous sea raging in his eyes, and the sight made her heart melt. She turned to look at the girl again, her brows knitted. *Who is she? Why does he let her handle him like that? Are they more than just colleagues? And what's the big urgency with their boss?*

Aggelos extended his arm towards Katie, the movement fluid, effortless. 'This is Katie,' he said to the girl.

Katie gave a faint smile. 'Hi,' she said to the girl, who was now checking her out from head to toe, her eyes narrowed. But then, she broke into a smile. It was forced, but at least it made her look more likeable. A little. She extended her hand and shook Katie's firmly, too firmly for a girl. 'Hi Katie, I am Elise.'

'Hi, Elise. Pleased to meet you,' said Katie, without meaning it, wincing. Her hand joints had made all sorts of cracking noises during her handshake with Xena the Warrior Princess. *So much for my plan to ask Aggelos out tonight!*

Elise pinned her eyes on Aggelos again and nodded suggestively, gritting her teeth at him, her fingers wrapped around his arm so tightly her knuckles had turned white. As stunning as she looked, she was acting like a bully. She'd arrived like a macho commando hell-bent to carry out her mission. Reluctantly, Katie admired the girl's glamorous hairdo and imagined a Rambo-style band around her head would be the perfect accessory.

Aggelos grimaced, then huffed. 'Oh, all right!' then turning to Katie, 'I'm sorry, Katie. I have to go. Catch you later?' He gave a feeble smile.

Katie put up a hand and waved, watching as the two began to walk away in a hurry. Elise wasn't holding Aggelos' arm any more but she was talking to him as they strode side by side, gesticulating wildly. Every now and then, she'd look over her shoulder to shoot daggers at Katie.

Katie watched, her jaw slack, her mind in a whirl. *What the hell?*

Chapter 16

After Aggelos and Elise had left, Katie grew so frustrated she abandoned her plans for dinner out in Asimi. Dragging her sandaled feet, she returned to the hotel and poked her head around the kitchen door. 'I think I'll eat with you this evening, Eva. Don't feel like walking to Asimi, after all.' Katie's eyes fell on the baking tray Eva was holding and her eyes grew huge. 'Oh my goodness, that looks divine.'

Eva gave a big smile and beckoned her in. 'Come! Just took the *biftekia* out of the oven. I made them with various fillings today. You like garlic potatoes, yes?'

Katie gave an open smile and breezed in. 'Yum!' she exclaimed as she stood next to Eva to marvel at the tray on the kitchen island. The potatoes were in there with the meat. 'I love garlic! What did you fill the *biftekia* with?'

Eva pointed with puffed up arthritic fingers. 'These have feta and tomato in them, those have peppers and mushrooms.'

Katie bent over the tray to take in the heavenly smells of garlic and herbs. 'Mmmm!' As if on cue, her stomach gave a loud grumble causing her to stifle a snigger. 'Looks like I'm starving and I hadn't realized.'

Ten minutes later, Katie had had a big plate of the delicious meal with a green salad but, as she often did in the evenings, instead of going off and doing her own thing after dinner, she stayed in the kitchen to help Eva and keep her company. Although Eva was in her late sixties and Katie was almost forty years younger, they found a lot to talk about. Today, Eva seemed chattier than ever and, before she knew it, Katie was telling her about Aggelos and how much she liked him.

Eva grew excited about it, even though they both found it strange she couldn't place him from Katie's detailed descriptions. He didn't look anything like the other guests. Being so tall and broad, and with his unblemished, porcelain-white skin Katie would have expected Eva to remember him, if anything, from serving him breakfast.

'How can you not remember anyone like that? He's been here a week,' said Katie as she turned over a batch of courgette patties in the frying pan.

Eva shrugged. She was flouring the next batch and putting the patties on a platter ready for the pan. 'Maybe he doesn't eat in.'

'What, *ever*? Not even breakfast?'

'Who knows? I've seen all sorts. Maybe he's an early bird and leaves the hotel in the morning before we open for breakfast. You did say he's here on business, after all.'

Katie scratched her jaw, her eyes two tiny slits. 'Yes, maybe,' she mumbled over the sizzling frying pan. 'Wait a minute!' She snapped her fingers and turned to Eva again. 'What about dinner? Surely he's tried it at least once now we serve it outside in the courtyard.'

'I can't say I remember anyone matching your description out there either. But why don't you ask Eddie? He does most of the serving out there, after all.'

Katie shook her head. 'No, I'd rather not.'

Eva chuckled, an impish gleam in her eye. 'Have a peek outside then!' She pointed at the door. 'See if you can spot him now and show him to me!'

Katie pressed her lips together. She was still downhearted from what happened earlier on the beach. The last thing she wanted was to talk about it and spoil the good mood. 'He won't be out there. He's going out tonight.'

Eva shrugged and resumed flouring the patties. That's when Spyros walked in from the courtyard. He and Matina had had their dinner earlier. Matina had retired to bed early with a bad headache so Spyros was entertaining the guests on his own at the courtyard tonight. He came in bright-faced and eager-looking, like a maid ready for a day's work. Once again, Katie marvelled at his demeanour. He seemed nothing like his spouse, and like his life was a string of sunny days where rain had zero probability.

'All okay in here, girls?'

'Yes, Mr Spyros, thank you,' said Katie. She'd just taken the patties out of the pan and was putting in the new batch Eva had brought her. They worked wonderfully together, like two synchronized watches that never missed a beat. Spyros came closer, his expression jovial, to pat Katie on the back. 'I'll make sure to tell Matina you're helping here again tonight on your time off. This is very kind of you, Katie.'

Katie gave a little wave. 'It's my pleasure, Mr Spyros. Besides, I don't see it as work. I enjoy spending time here with Eva.'

Eva made a cooing sound and put a hand on her heart. 'And I enjoy your company too, sweetheart.'

Spyros grabbed a patty from the platter and popped it in his mouth. He made appreciative sounds that echoed almost orgasmic, making the women giggle. When he opened his eyes again, he smacked his lips and reached over to Eva, giving her a kiss on the cheek. 'You're the best, Eva!' Then, he reached up to a high cupboard, opened it and pulled out a tall glass bottle. He put a finger to his lips. 'Not a word to the missus!' he burst out in a mock-dread fashion.

'I thought I smelled it in your breath just now. You started early tonight, boss!' joked Eva.

Spyros winked. He pulled three shot glasses out of the cupboard and placed them on the counter in line. 'This, Katie, is my very own, special *tsipouro*.' He tipped his chin and pointed to himself with a sharp finger. 'I make it myself. Old family recipe!'

Katie nodded, impressed, while Eva issued a knowing smile.

Spyros poured *tsipouro* in the three shot glasses and offered the women one each. They all raised their glasses.

'*Ya mas*!' said Spyros, his eyes twinkling.

'*Ya mas*!' said the women in unison. Spyros and Eva put it back in one go, but Katie was cautious, not sure how strong it would be, so she only had a little sip.

'Come on!' complained Spyros, '*Aspro pato*! Bottoms up! Let's see you drink it all! There's more to come!' He shook the bottle in his hand.

Katie did as she was prompted and put the glass back down, savouring the taste on her tongue for a few seconds before swallowing. 'It has herbs in it. And is that orange I taste?'

'Yes, well done, Katie. One of the secret ingredients is orange peel. But that's all I'll say.' Spyros tapped the side of his nose. 'I can't disclose the family secret or my great-grandfather will turn in his grave!'

They all laughed, then Spyros offered to show Katie his shed in the backyard where he made the *tsipouro*. As the two of them exited through the back door, Eva noticed Spyros was taking the bottle and their glasses with him. Chortling, she stood at the stove and began to take out the patties from the pan.

Chapter 17

An hour later, having visited the back shed, Katie and Spyros were sitting outside on two breezeblocks, their backs resting against the hotel's external back wall. They sat in silence, marvelling at the magnificent view of Asimi and the brown distant hills. In front of them, on another breezeblock, stood the bottle and two empty shot glasses.

Despite her best intentions to take it easy, Katie had had two more shots since coming out of the kitchen. Spyros had had about four and his speech had turned a little slurred when he last raised his glass. She could tell from the way he kept laughing to himself that he was in a happy place. Katie brought a hand over her mouth and stifled a snigger imagining he needed that *tsipouro* as much as he did his fishing escapades.

'It's nice to hear you like our little village,' he finally said pointing vaguely at Asimi. Katie was telling him earlier she'd found it enchanting with its quaint narrow streets, old buildings and lush, beautiful fields.

'Yes, it's paradise to me, having escaped the bustling city of Athens.' Katie wanted to say more, to talk of her own town in Epirus that had its own irresistible appeal, but the beauty that unravelled before her commanded her total attention and silence. The sun was about to set. The feeble last rays of the day caused the rooftops and the blue domes of the village church to glint softly as if signalling a distant greeting back to her. The sky, ablaze with hues of pink, yellow and orange, seemed to wait for the sun to go down to sleep, for the dramatic reds to take their place. Katie couldn't get enough of the sky at this hour. On many other evenings, she'd watched the sunset from her room's balcony.

'I may be partial to it, it being my birthplace and all, but I'll say it anyway,' said Spyros putting a hand on his chest, 'I wouldn't change Asimi for the world.'

Katie whipped her head around to face him. 'I'm sorry. I didn't realize you were a local. I thought it was Mrs Matina who was from Asimi.'

Spyros grimaced, squinting at Katie. He was so intoxicated he seemed to have trouble focusing his eyes. 'Why would you think that?'

'Oh!' Alarm flashed in Katie's eyes. She'd heard from Eva that Matina was the owner of the hotel, but she didn't want to say that. How could she admit to gossip? 'I . . . I just had this impression for some reason, that's all.'

'Actually, Matina is from Thesaloniki.' Spyros bent forward and poured himself another glass. 'You want one?'

'No, thank you. I've had enough.'

Spyros downed his drink and smacked his lips with relish. 'My Matina fell in love with this place at first sight.' He moved his arm in front of him in a sweeping gesture pointing at the ragged landscape. It seemed to shimmer now in the face of the setting sun. On top of the tallest hill in the distance, the blades on the windmill had started to turn ever so slowly. The sight was so serene it made your heart sing. Katie looked around her, her expression dreamy. Not a leaf stirred in the trees. Not a chirp echoed from the birds. Only the occasional squawk of the ravens raiding the fields broke the dead silence.

'And she fell in love with you, too, I presume?' asked Katie with a cautious smile.

Spyros smiled back and met her eyes. 'Yes, indeed, she fell in love with me too, just as intensely. Mind you, I was in my twenties then. Young and carefree. Damn, I miss those days! Even though I was a simple waiter then at an old taverna on this very beach.'

'Oh! Where is it? Is it still open?'

'No. It was demolished ages ago. But it was right here. The man who owned it was my great-uncle. When he passed away, Matina and I were planning to get married and looking for something to make for ourselves here. Her parents, well, they were comfortable with money. They wanted to build a house for us here, but we preferred to run a hotel on the beach and live in it. When my great-uncle's offspring put the old taverna up for sale, we bought the land with my father-in-law's dowry money and made the hotel here. The rest, as they say, is history.'

Katie took her eyes from his crouched figure. He seemed so deep in thought it felt like an intrusion to look at him. She turned her gaze towards the sky, caressing with her eyes the fluffy clouds that were edged with gold and pink. 'You must have had some wonderful years here,' she burst out before she could stop herself.

Spyros heaved a long sigh and looked at the sky too, his eyes focusing far, misty. 'We've had many happy days . . . but alas, bad times too.' He shook his head and that seemed to snap him out of his evident overpowering sadness.

He turned to Katie and forced a smile. 'Katie, the truth of the matter is, time and hardship change people. In case you're wondering, my Matina used to be nothing like the woman she is today. Let me tell you . . . That woman used to shine like the sun, so bright was her smile.' He was looking away again, but Katie could see he was smiling widely, at whatever cheerful memories had come alive before his mind's eye.

'Matina and I used to laugh so much, you know, chasing each other up and down the corridors on every floor back in there, giggling like idiots,' he said, pointing vaguely over his shoulder at the hotel building. 'We used to be so happy. So madly in love . . .' He shrugged. 'These days, we're still chasing each other in there, but now we're like two soulless Pacman figures, you know? Forever up and down corridors but never really getting along.'

Katie thought that was very deep and sad. She felt her heart contract with sympathy, but said nothing. What could she say?

Spyros turned to her then, an evident attempt to lift the mood in his expression. 'Sorry about all that, Katie. Don't listen to me, the old party pooper, talking of old woes.' He chuckled. 'Look at you, so young! You probably don't even know what Pacman is!'

Katie stared blankly at him, unsure how to respond, but then he laughed and offered her a drink. This time, she said yes out of sympathy. One more glass and then straight to bed. She was dog-tired but that suited her fine. It meant she wouldn't have to spend any time in bed tonight thinking of Aggelos, unlike every other night.

Chapter 18

'Enough!' shouted Esmera, causing Aggelos and Elise to whip their heads around to face her. Elise's fist had frozen mid-air, where she'd been shaking it with frustration as she tried to put her point across to Aggelos. As for him, he had his arms crossed over his chest, his lips tightly pressed together, a huge frown on his face.

Esmera heaved a sigh of exasperation and beckoned them to follow. Aggelos and Elise had been arguing for the past hour non-stop, driving her crazy. Finally, the pre-arranged meeting had ended. Everyone else had left but Esmera had ordered these two to stay behind and try to see eye to eye before leaving the hilltop.

Esmera gestured to them to sit on the ledge before the windmill. The pigeon-grey pavement felt deliciously cool to Aggelos when he sat as instructed. He stretched his long legs out in front of him, his calves resting on the soft soil. Then, placing both hands on his knees he looked up eagerly at Esmera, who stood before him. He seemed like a studious pupil waiting for the teacher to begin.

Elise sat in her khaki shorts beside him with her knees bent, having first dusted the ledge with her fingertips to avoid soiling her clothes. She rested an elbow on her knee and turned to sneer at Aggelos, about to utter yet another accusing remark, but Esmera saw it coming. She put up a hand that caused Elise to lower her head.

'What am I going to do with you two?'

'But, Mrs Esmera—'

'Enough, Elise! Don't try my patience! I heard you earlier. But I assure you, you have nothing to worry about. Why don't you let Aggelos see to his duties without interruptions? He's not stopping you from working on your own assignment, is he?' Esmera turned to Aggelos for confirmation.

Aggelos' eyes lit up in protest. 'Certainly not! I'd never do that. Besides, I don't even know what her assignment is.'

'That's a point. Elise, how did you know I left Katie Pavlides in the care of Aggelos? All the assignments are top secret. Who told you?'

Elise tutted and rolled her eyes. 'Mrs Esmera, it wasn't hard to guess. He chases that girl around like a puppy looking for adoption. It's totally unprofessional of him. I mean, what is he doing exposing himself like that? Making himself visible to her all the time? What happened to the discreet observation the Manual for Spiritual Guides and Guardian Angels talks of? I'm sure this is against the rules!'

Aggelos turned to Elise pointing a finger sharply. 'And what if I am interacting with her? What is it to you, huh?'

'Now, Aggelos, Elise has a point. I didn't know you've been interacting with the girl frequently after your arrival here.' Esmera tilted her head and took one step forward. 'What are you doing this for? You don't need to talk to her to protect her.'

Aggelos looked up to find his boss looming over him like a treacherous mountain. She was one big woman. Even though he was clothed in flesh and bone on and off these days, he felt relieved he didn't have to worry about physical damage like the humans do. That woman could be scary if she wanted to. The sheer volume of her alone made sure of that. 'Mrs Esmera . . .' he cleared his throat before continuing, 'I find it facilitates my mission, and that it makes for a deeper bond between my ethereal essence and her soul, if you like. I've noticed a heightened sense of joy and inner peace in her aura following our short exchanges.'

Elise rolled her eyes. 'Is that what you call it? Looks like common woman-chasing to me. And it's not like . . .' her eyes wandered to his groin and back '. . . you know what to do to close the deal.' She winked. 'If you know what I mean.'

'Elise! Don't be vulgar!' yelled Esmera causing the girl's leering smile to freeze, then disappear from her face. Esmera brought a hand to her forehead and scratched hard at the point where her thick eyebrows met. *That girl will be the end of me! Why do they send all the hard cases to me?* She drew a long breath and turned to Aggelos again. 'You were saying?'

Aggelos gave a soft sigh. 'I was saying, before I was so rudely interrupted,' he shot Elise a fiery glare, 'that I think talking to Katie is better than if I were to be a mere shadow she cannot see. And it's not like *everyone* in the hotel can see me. I only appear in front of my assigned human to aid her progress. Isn't this what you have commanded me to do? How I do it should be my own choice.'

Esmera tapped her finger on her chin a few times, then turned around, her eyes resting on the breathtaking view of the bay. Moments later, she turned to the two again. 'Elise, I want you to mind your own business from now on. It doesn't sound like Aggelos is doing anything unprofessional here. Concentrate on your own work. The training period will end before you know it, and I'll announce the two among you all who will get posted on this island. You're two of my best recruits. You could wind up posted here together, and I need to be certain you can co-exist in harmony. I don't want to see you again acting like two tiny schoolchildren! Sort out your petty issues, and don't bother me again with this type of nonsense! Do you understand?'

Aggelos and Elise nodded profusely, then hung their heads in shame and Esmera raised her chin, satisfied to have delivered a clear message. When she told them they were free to go, they jumped to their feet but before they could speak, Esmera vanished in a flash of clear white light. When that vanished too, a fine dusting of dark soil hovered in mid-air for a second in its place before settling on the ground.

Pressing her glistening red lips together, Elise turned to Aggelos, her expression sheepish. 'Okay, I'm sorry. Friends?'

Aggelos took her hand and shook it. 'Friends. Just stop being such a pain in the ass!'

Chapter 19

Matina opened her office door with urgency and stuck her head out. 'Katie!' she yelled when she didn't find her at reception.

Katie rushed through the front door, brushing her brow with an urgent hand. 'Oh, hello Mrs Matina!'

'I hope you didn't leave reception unmanned for long, Katie—'

'Oh no, Mrs Matina. I was out for just a few moments, and I kept my eyes on the lobby at all times. Mrs Sparks asked me to bring her a sun lounger. She wanted to sit on the lawn. There!' she said, pointing to a frail old lady in a burgundy one piece swimsuit and a floral beach skirt that exposed lean and leathery legs. On her head, she wore a bright pink turban and huge dark sunglasses. She was sitting on a sun lounger, facing a rhododendron bush, one gnarled hand on the tiny buds, murmuring something.

'Oh, I see. She's at it again, is she?' Matina gave a snort. 'She's as mad as a hatter, that one. She's a kind person though, and one of our oldest customers too. I hope you didn't mind me asking just then, Katie. But I need to be assured the reception desk is manned at all times.'

'Yes, of course.'

'Anyway, I'm going to leave my door open so you can go upstairs quickly. I need you to do something for me. I've sent Eddie on an errand so there's no one else.'

'Of course. How can I help?'

'Mrs Akrita called from number twenty-one. Her husband has a bad stomach. Can you make him a chamomile tea and take it up? Or get Eva to make it if she can manage it quickly?'

'Of course! I'll be glad to do it myself.'

Katie rushed to the kitchen and five minutes later she was climbing the stairs with a tray. Eva had given her a few dry rusks and a sachet of honey to go with the beverage. On her way up, she admired the antique paintings on the walls and the aged red carpet like she always did when she used the stairs.

As soon as she got to the second floor, she checked the signs on the doors across from her and made a sharp turn right to find number twenty-one. She delivered the tray and was on her way to the stairs when something attracted her attention at the end of the corridor. There, shining in bright gold was a door that didn't match any of the others. *How come I hadn't noticed it before?* Dazzled, she strode to it but, even before getting there, she knew which number it was. The door to room number twenty-seven was identified with a bright golden sign at its centre. It was unlike any other. *Just as shiny as the key that opens it! What the—?*

Cheerful conversation echoed from the lobby below, and it snapped her out of her intriguing thoughts. She identified the voices as Spyros and Matina and guessed he'd returned from his fishing, probably with another good catch to show off. She chuckled at the thought and spun around.

As soon as she came downstairs, Spyros rushed to show her his basket. He'd caught various kinds of small-sized fish and told her he'd be sharing some of them with her and Eva for lunch, much to her delight. In the meantime, Matina had returned to her office and shut the door behind her. Spyros was retreating to the kitchen with long strides when Katie burst out, 'Mr Spyros! Can I ask you something?'

Spyros turned around, a huge grin plastered on his face. 'Yes?'

'Why are the door and the key of room twenty-seven so shiny? They don't look anything like the rest.'

Spyros' face dropped, his expression vacant for a few moments. Then, his eyes lit up and he gave a thundering belly laugh. 'Looks like you've enjoyed my *tsipouro* last night. I'd have thought it'd have left your system by now, though, dear girl!' He winked and gave a snigger, then disappeared from view before Katie could stop him.

Chapter 20

Katie was tidying up her desk during her afternoon shift when Eva walked out of Matina's office. She'd just baked cookies and delivered some to her boss. With a wink and a cunning smirk, she invited Katie to the kitchen, and Katie followed her, bright-faced and eager. It was too early for dinner but she was starving. Coffee and freshly baked cookies sounded like the perfect choice.

As soon as they went through the kitchen door, both knew something wasn't right. The back door was wide open and no one was in. Everyone knew not to leave that door open; stray cats were forever lingering outside, looking for the odd scrap of food.

The two women exchanged glances full of panic, then set out to inspect the floor and the counters in search of feline intruders. Eva rushed to the kitchen island. Earlier today she'd baked *moussaka* and left the roasting pan on there to cool off. She had one look at it and let out an ear-piercing shriek causing Katie to hurry to her side.

A big chunk was missing from one corner of the pan. Beside it, a large spoon lay in a big splash of sauce. 'Cats don't use spoons,' mumbled Eva before diving behind the island like a well-trained Marine, in case the intruder hadn't had the chance to escape in time.

To her surprise, when she pinned her eyes on the floor she found a little girl crouched there. She was about six or seven years old and was looking up at her, with huge green eyes. She looked extremely cute, her heart-shaped face framed by long, curly hair. The sides of her mouth were smeared with sauce, and she held a fork in her hand, a piece of cooked potato hanging from its end.

'Hey!' yelled Eva, reaching out to grab the girl's arm, but the girl was faster. She jerked sideways, leapt to her feet, threw the fork to the floor and dashed out of the back door in a split second, her curly, flyaway hair dancing behind her as she went.

Katie and Eva ran outside but the girl was gone. Scratching her head, Eva gave a deep frown. 'Little devil! Where did she go?' Even though she'd run just a few feet, she sounded out of breath.

Katie, her brow wrinkled, shook her head. 'It's like she vanished into thin air! Do you know her?'

'No, never seen her before.'

'She's not a guest then?'

'Probably one of the local children. Plenty of poor families living there, unable to make ends meet.' Eva pointed at Asimi in the distance. 'I expect she was hungry and took advantage when she found no one in the kitchen. But it doesn't matter. She only had a small chunk from the pan. And I guess we gave her such a scare that she won't be coming back anytime soon.'

'But where did she go?' mumbled Katie, intrigued how the little girl could have disappeared like that. She still hadn't solved the mystery of the shiny door to room twenty-seven. To have another potential mystery on her hands felt simply unbearable.

Eva pressed her lips together. 'I don't care. If you want to look for her, be my guest. I got work to do.' Without waiting for an answer, she spun around and went back in the kitchen.

Katie stood alone in the midst of the backyard for a few moments and was now considering letting this go when, with the corner of her eye, she caught some movement. It came from the far end of Spyros' shed. Light-footed and advancing slowly, she neared it and stopped before reaching the far corner. Pricking her ears she heard a rustle, like feet on dry grass. Holding her breath, she took a single step forward.

'Gotcha!' she shouted, her eyes wide, as she pounced on what she hoped was the little girl. Thinking the child might be in for a little game of hide-and-seek, she thought it best to turn this into a light-hearted chase. After that, she intended to ask the girl why she was stealing food and what she could do to help her.

But alas, instead of seeing the little girl, Katie wound up with her face knocked against a wall of cloth and what felt like warm, firm skin underneath it. Shocked, she jerked backwards, then looked up.

'Aggelos?'

'Hey! We have to stop meeting like this.' He gave a cunning grin. 'What? No juice this time? I *knew* this was my lucky top!' he said pointing at the colourful t-shirt he wore.

Katie pulled a face of mock-dismay. 'Nice one.' She stood on her toes and peeked behind his shoulder, her thin smile fading. 'Wait. Where is she?'

'Where is *who*?'

'The little girl . . .' She looked down the narrow passage where they stood, between the shed's back wall and the low garden fence, and found no one.

'What little girl?'

Katie squinted at him, her jaw hardening. 'Wait a minute! What were you doing back here?'

'I was . . .' He looked away, his sparkling blue eyes seeking refuge to the stunning view of Asimi. His arm flew out to point. 'Just admiring the view to the fields and Asimi.'

'From back here?'

'Yes. From back here.' He drew a long breath and stood up straight. 'I'm allowed to wander around as a guest, aren't I?'

'Yes, sorry. Of course you are. But, are you sure you didn't see a little girl here just now?'

'No. What did she look like? If she's one of the guests I might know her.'

'She's not a guest. I don't think so anyway. Our cook, Eva, she says she's probably a local child from Asimi. We caught her in the kitchen stealing food. Eva says her family must be poor.'

The jovial smile on Aggelos' face faded. 'You mean she steals food because she's hungry? Really?'

'Yes, we think so. Anyway, this girl has green eyes and curly hair—'

'Green eyes, you said?' His eyes lit up. 'Long curly hair?' He shook both hands profusely by the sides of his head. 'Really wispy?'

'Yes, very. She's a cute little thing.'

'That's Chloe. Of course, I know her, but—' He put a hand over his mouth.

'What? What is it?'

'You saw Chloe? Just now?'

'Yes! Can you help me find her? I want to help her if I can. It broke my heart to think she was so hungry she had to steal food.'

'I see.' Aggelos turned around and began to shout, 'Chloe! Come out, my darling. It's okay. Katie is my friend. Don't be afraid.'

A frail voice echoed from behind a barrel in the distance. 'She's not mad at me?'

Katie giggled. 'No, Chloe. I'm not mad. Don't be afraid. I won't hurt you, sweetheart.'

Chloe came out from behind the barrel where she'd been hiding. She stood straight and flicked a long strand of frizzy hair behind her shoulder. 'You're not mad at me for eating your *moussaka*?'

'No, of course not.'

'I'm sorry. I couldn't help it. It's my favourite meal, *ever*!' She paced slowly towards the others, her face beaming.

Katie held out her hand and Chloe took it.

'Come. Let's go inside, sit properly, and I'll treat you to a big meal.'

Chloe scrunched up her face. 'Won't the other lady mind?'

Katie laughed. 'Mind? Chloe, her heart is even softer than mine!'

Chloe gave a big smile and followed Katie into the kitchen. From the doorway, Katie turned around to wave at Aggelos. He was still standing on the very spot she'd left him. 'Would you like to come in, Aggelos? I'll introduce you to our cook, Eva.'

'Sorry, Katie. Maybe tomorrow. I got to run.'

A shadow crossed Katie's face but she forced a smile to hide it. Uncomfortable thoughts about Elise, that horrible bossy girl, whirled in her mind still, on and off.

Aggelos kicked a stone with his shoe, then looked up, a lopsided smile curling his lips. 'So, are we on for that day in Pefki?'

Katie's face brightened. 'Of course! That is, if your job doesn't claim you in the last minute . . .' She wanted to mention Elise, hoping he'd volunteer some information about the kind of relationship they had. But, she decided not to. If she mentioned her, he might guess how much she minded her very existence.

'No, it'll be fine. No more interruptions from work. That's a promise. I apologize about Elise, by the way. She's a pain in the ass.'

Katie giggled despite herself, her face ablaze with relief. 'That's okay. What's up with her, anyway?'

Aggelos flicked his wrist. 'Long story.'

Chloe was getting restless, pulling Katie's hand and whining, itching to get reacquainted with the *moussaka* tray.

Katie patted the girl's hair. 'Come on, my darling, let's meet Eva, shall we?' She turned to Aggelos to wave goodbye and found him walking towards the courtyard at the side of the building. As he strode past flower beds and herb bushes along a tiled path, he whistled a happy tune, an evident spring in his step.

Chapter 21

When Katie's day off finally came, she and Aggelos met at the lobby in the morning and began to walk along the beach towards the neighbouring village of Pefki. During their stroll, they could hear nothing but the gentle splash of waves breaking on the sand. The shoreline between the villages bordered private fields and was rarely visited by tourists or locals. So alluring were those quiet moments that Katie and Aggelos were reluctant to make much conversation.

When they neared the first white-washed buildings and quiet tavernas at Pefki, Katie's eyes widened to find it was as enchanting as she'd imagined it; even more so than Asimi, simply because unlike Asimi, Pefki was built on the shore.

The village had a busy street with shops near the seafront while the main residential area was more inland on a hill, a scatter of old houses around a church yard. Everywhere you looked, sky blue and white, and ceramic pot plants: basil, spearmint, and geraniums more than anything else. Their rich aromas wafted in the breeze, mixing with the salty air. Grape vines and bougainvillea bushes crept up trellises and over paint-chipped fences.

People sauntered in the streets chatting excitedly; children played in the yards, while housewives and grannies sat nearby preparing fresh vegetables for lunch. Most of the buildings were small, one-floor high. The village church on the hill towered over them all. It stood at the edge of a small square, its sky blue dome glinting in the morning light. A stone's throw away, a hanging bell outside what looked like the village school echoed gently, half-hidden behind cypress trees, as the gentle wind tipped it this way and that.

Aggelos pointed at the edge of the headland where a small beach bar stood on the shore beside a sparse pine tree forest. He suggested to go there for a coffee and Katie nodded happily. The setting was enchanting. Some of the pine trees had grown near the water. Their gnarled trunks were almost horizontal to the ground as if trying to kiss the sand or to offer themselves as a bench for the odd passer-by to rest upon.

Katie and Aggelos found an empty table and leaned back in their chairs, heaving long sighs of delight as they took in the stunning sea view. A couple of boats sat on the sand before them. Four small children soon came to jump onto one of them, taking the oars to paddle, pretending they're out at sea. Their excited squeals as they played and fought over who would hold the oars next caused Katie and Aggelos to laugh.

The waiter came out to bring the chilled coffees they'd ordered. When he saw the children, he shooed them away. They jumped out of the boat and ran away, the oars landing on the sand with a soft thud as they dropped them in their haste.

After the waiter had left, Aggelos turned to Katie, his expression jovial. 'I'm so pleased you agreed to come along, Katie. It's great here, isn't it?'

'Yes, fantastic!' Katie looked around, but the easy smile froze on her face when she saw a busty blond approaching in a skimpy bikini top and hot shorts. *Oh-my-God! It can't be!*

'Elise . . .' said Aggelos, his tone of voice flat. Elise stopped in front of them with a hop, her boobs nearly skipping out of the bikini triangles, a happy grin on her face as if she'd done something worth receiving praise for.

Katie found it hard to be polite this time. 'Hey,' she said in lieu of a proper greeting.

'What's wrong, guys? Why so glum?' asked Elise with a playful frown. Before either of them could respond, Elise pulled a chair from a nearby table and sat between them, resting her elbows on the table, then flashed Aggelos an impish grin. 'If I didn't know what a good sport you are, I'd think you're not happy to see me.'

Aggelos forced a smile behind gritted teeth. 'Elise? What are you doing here?'

Elise took hold of a stray tendril from her silky blond hair and twirled it between two glossy red, long manicured nails. 'Just chilling. Same as you, I guess.' She shrugged and pouted her full lips, her eyes darting to Katie, then back to Aggelos.

Katie couldn't help noticing how irresistibly sexy Elise was. That nail colour matched her lipstick, and they seemed to be top class cosmetics. *Probably the kind of produce they use in makeover reality shows that can turn any girl into Marylyn Monroe . . . Either that or I'm deluding myself that it's all down to her make up.* Elise could seduce any man, present company included. Katie let out an inaudible sigh and slumped back into her chair.

'Actually,' said Aggelos to Elise, 'Katie and I were in the middle of a private conversation. So perhaps you could join us later. Or preferably another day? Now if you don't mind . . .' He grimaced suggestively and pointed to the beach.

Elise shook her head and sat back in her chair, crossing her arms. 'That's not very nice.'

Aggelos sprang upright and turned to Katie. 'Elise and I are going to have a little talk. Excuse me for a moment?'

Shocked, Katie watched as Aggelos beckoned Elise to follow. They went to stand a few feet away among the pine trees. Katie could see them but couldn't hear a word. They were both gesticulating, Aggelos shaking his finger at her while Elise had both hands on her waist, her perfectly styled hair bouncing in a mesmerizing way as she shook her head.

A couple of minutes later, they were back at the table. Aggelos sat and let out a laboured sigh, while Elise remained standing, patting her hair, her chin tipped when she said, 'I've decided to go meet some friends. I'll see you later, Katie.' With that, and before Katie could respond, Elise took the paved path that led to the village square, disappearing behind the taverna that stood on the corner.

'What did you say to her?'

Aggelos sniggered when he met her eyes, then looked away and brushed two fingers across his lips. 'Don't mind her. She's a nutcase. But trust me, she means well.'

'Is she really meeting friends?'

Aggelos gave a smirk, meeting her gaze. 'I doubt she has a single one on the island.'

'She seems to be fond of you.'

'I wouldn't say she's fond of me.' He raised his eyes to the thatched canopy over their heads, his eyes focusing far. 'I have the impression she feels protective of me for some reason. And she can be high maintenance. But she's a good girl. I guess that's why I put up with her.'

'You guys are colleagues, right?'

'Yes, that's right.'

'Just colleagues then?' It had come out before she could stop herself. Faking nonchalance, Katie looked away, pretending to admire three cute little girls that had just passed by eating ice cream.

Aggelos sank back into his chair, a curious expression on his face. 'What else could we possibly be?'

'Well, I thought maybe . . .' The suggestive nod she gave him told him the rest.

'What? Are you kidding? She's not even my type.'

'So why's she following you around?'

He gave a soft sigh. 'I'm not sure.'

'Aggelos, this is all very strange.'

'What is?'

'I don't know . . .' Katie hesitated, unsure how to explain. But, the truth was, it wasn't just Elise that presented a mystery. Everything about Aggelos caused her equal mystification. 'Well, there's something about you too that I find intriguing, but don't ask me what it is. I don't have a clue.' She gave a nervous titter. 'You're a man of mystery, Aggelos. I guess it's because I know virtually nothing about you.' She flashed him a smile, then looked away again, chewing her lip. *Oh God, I'm flirting and not even making an effort to hide it. Get a grip, girl!*

Aggelos leaned forward and gave a charming smile. 'But isn't this why we're spending this day together? To get to know each other better?'

Katie gave a beaming smile and finally relaxed.

'Come on!' exclaimed Aggelos and picked up his tall glass. 'Let's have our coffees, then hit the water before it gets too warm. Today it's going to be a scorcher, I can tell.'

Chapter 22

Katie and Aggelos spent all morning swimming and sunbathing, talking about their likes, and even though she told him a lot about her past, both in her hometown and in Athens, he was most economical with information. Katie appreciated he might be the quiet type and decided not to pose any questions. She was just happy to spend time with him. And he was gorgeous . . . Oh, so gorgeous.

They spent an hour on a rented canoe and, sitting behind him, Katie took advantage of every chance she had to touch his arm as they spoke and steered with the paddles. When a fishing boat passed at a close distance, leaving strong waves in its wake, they nearly fell off the canoe, but Aggelos reached behind him and grabbed her with a steady hand, holding her up against his back. Katie almost swooned when that happened. The sight of the lean muscles and flawless skin on his bare back were delicious enough, let alone the feel of them against her.

At lunchtime they visited a taverna on the seafront and sat outside in a cool elevated terrace. They'd just placed their order when the inevitable happened: Elise walked in, having spotted them from the street, and sat between them breezily as if the earlier awkwardness that morning had never occurred.

Aggelos rolled his eyes. 'Elise. What a lovely surprise.'

Elise put up a hand. 'Relax. I'm not staying. Just hiding from Babis, that's all. As soon as he goes, I'm out of here.' She turned to check the street, craning her neck to see through the thick foliage on the outside fence.

Aggelos gave a snorting laugh. 'Babis is here? Serves you right.'

'It's not funny!' Elise shook her fists like a wayward child, her brow deeply furrowed. Moments later, she relaxed and brought her voice down a few notches. 'Sorry, yes, maybe you're right.'

'Who's Babis?' asked Katie.

'Just another of our . . . erm, colleagues,' said Aggelos. 'Except Elise is not as keen to follow *him* around.' He gave Elise a knowing look.

Elise gave a mock-shudder, then screwed up her face with distaste. 'Let's just say he stinks.'

'What? Not a nice guy, you mean?' Katie leaned forward in her seat.

'No. I mean, *literally*, he stinks. The man perspires beyond control, and he cares naught for personal hygiene. In this heat, it's impossible to be around him. Plus, he smokes. A filthy habit.' Elise curled her upper lip and snarled like a mad dog.

Aggelos howled with laughter. 'Okay, since it's Babis you're hiding from, we'll let you stay for a while. But then you'll have to hit the road. This is a private lunch and you're not invited.'

'Fine,' said Elise, frowning.

Katie studied her for a few moments and, to her surprise, saw her in a different light this time. Her mind wandered to what Aggelos had said earlier about her having no friends. She turned to him, her features arranged into an expression of sympathy. 'Aggelos, perhaps Elise could join us for lunch?'

Aggelos raised his brows. 'Are you sure? I don't mind if you don't.'

'Of course, I'm sure.' Katie turned to Elise and gave her a bright smile. 'Stay, Elise, I insist.'

Elise's eyes widened. 'Really? You don't mind? Thank you!' She seemed like a little girl finding her Christmas presents under the tree. The big ones she had written to Santa about.

'Okay, Elise, but behave!' Aggelos shook a finger playfully at her.

Rubbing her hands together with delight, Elise called out to the waiter to bring her a menu when they heard a booming voice from the steps behind them.

'Hey! I thought I saw you guys!'

It was Babis. Big, chubby Babis, and the awful smell that followed him around like an invisible aura. As soon as he came to stand before them, his signature smell hit their nostrils like a mixture of rotten eggs and furry road kill, with some toxic waste thrown into the mix. It took the three all their self-restraint not to reach for their noses to save whatever sense of smell had been spared for future use.

With the corner of her eye, as she willed herself not to pass out from the overbearing odour, Katie saw the middle-aged woman at the next table dive for her napkin and tuck her mouth and nose under it. Trying to control a gag reflex stirring in the back of her throat Katie imagined what the woman did didn't help at all. *Perhaps a space helmet or a nuclear suit might be more helpful.*

Aggelos' feeble greeting to Babis brought Katie back from her reverie. As for Elise, she had frozen with her hand in mid-air since calling the waiter over. When he arrived before her, she mumbled her request for a menu just as Babis came to sit across from her, between Katie and Aggelos.

'Fancy meeting you here, guys! And just as I was getting hungry too!' Babis turned to face everyone, his gaze lingering at Katie. Yet, he had such kind eyes that she didn't mind.

Aggelos cleared his throat. 'This is Katie. She works at reception where I stay,' he informed Babis, causing him to offer his hand to her with an open smile. 'Pleased to meet you. Always a pleasure to meet a new huma—' Babis stopped short, panic igniting in his eyes.

Katie shook his hand and giggled. 'Did you mean to say "human"? That's hilarious!' she exclaimed. His odour wasn't so bad now. Either that, or maybe she'd got used to it.

'Sorry – bad joke,' he said, not knowing how to explain his mishap. He looked to the others for assistance only to receive sheepish looks which weren't really helpful.

'I had a friend back home who was a trekkie. He was forever talking like that, quoting Spock all day,' said Katie with a grin.

'Trekkie?' Babis gave a deep frown. 'And who's Spock?' He looked at the others, who seemed lost for words.

'You've got to be joking! "Live long and prosper"?' She gave a Vulcan greeting and chuckled loudly.

'Yeah, yes, of course,' said Babis shaking his head from side to side, then turned to Elise, eager to change the subject.

'Say, Elise, I must have followed you all the way from the village square. Didn't you hear me call your name?'

Elise turned to him, her face the epitome of innocence. 'No,' she said, deadpan, a hand surreptitiously hooked over her delicate nose.

'I saw you quicken your pace at some point. Thought you had heard and were doing it for a joke. You're such a sport!' He gave a snorting laugh and nudged Elise on the arm, and she gave him a humourless smile in response. As soon as he looked away, she rubbed her arm fiercely, screwing up her face with disgust.

Unaware, Babis went on, 'But then, I had to go into a shop to buy the essentials for the day.' He took a pack of cigarettes and a plastic lighter out of his pocket. As he busied himself lighting one, Aggelos and Elise rolled their eyes.

The waiter returned to the table, and Elise and Babis placed their orders. The meal was delicious – the table full of plates of succulent *souvlakia*, *biftekia*, *tzatziki*, grilled chicken, chips, tomato patties and Greek salad. It was so good, everyone got side-tracked and, for a while, forgot about Babis' unfortunate problem.

Afterwards, Babis placed a hand on his belly and rubbed it, his face blissful. 'Excuse me for a moment, I think I had too much beer,' he said with a wink, then dashed indoors.

As soon as he was gone, Elise turned to look at Aggelos squarely in the eyes, her expression pleading. 'You have to help me. What can I do to make him understand this is not going to happen?'

Aggelos patted her hand. 'Darling, there's nothing you can do. And you can't really know for sure what the outcome will be. You and I just have to hope for the best. In the meantime, try to be a little nicer to him. You never know. You two might wind up together, after all.' He gave a snigger.

Elise huffed, her eyes turning into slits. 'This cannot happen, you hear? So don't even joke about it. It's not funny!'

Aggelos rolled his eyes, then pressed his lips together.

Elise crossed her arms over her chest and looked away, her eyes dancing with annoyance.

Katie leaned forward. 'What is this about? Does Babis fancy you or something? I noticed he looks at you like a sick puppy. He seems nice, though.'

'Nice?' Elise screwed up her face and turned to Katie. 'Nice won't save my nose from permanent paralysis!'

Aggelos chortled. 'It's not just that he fancies her. Elise doesn't have a problem fighting off admirers. She gets that a lot. The problem is there's a possibility he might be her future partner. You know, in our . . . job.'

Katie knitted her brows. 'I see. And what is your job exactly? I meant to ask.'

'Sorry,' said Elise, 'it's a secret. We're not supposed to talk about it.' Her eyes darted to Aggelos.

Aggelos cleared his throat. 'Well, as I explained to you, Katie, you could think of our job as something similar to the military.'

'Yes, I remember you said that.'

'The thing is, it's top secret stuff. Our lips are sealed.'

Katie nodded. 'I understand, Aggelos. Anyway, I've already worked out it's not a soldier's job in the strict sense. It's more like a guard-and-protect kind of thing, like police work, isn't it?'

Elise widened her eyes with exasperation. 'Katie, you're asking again. What did we just say?'

Katie put her hands up. 'I'm only saying! If I'm right and your job resembles policing, you could always send Babis for doughnuts if he gets too much, then disappear for a few hours!' She gave a howl of laughter, causing the others to look at her with dismay.

Elise shook her head. 'It's not funny. Can you imagine me working with Stinky Boy all day?'

'So, what are the chances of that happening?' asked Katie sobering up.

'Fifty-fifty,' said Elise, regret heavy in her voice.

'Who's the other applicant then?'

'Elise's eyes flicked to Aggelos, who pulled a face of mock-dread.

Katie's eyes lit up. 'Oh.'

'That's right,' said Aggelos. 'It's either I or Babis that will get to be Elise's partner. Our whole team of, erm, soldiers, is here for training. Each one has their own assignment and two of us will get to be posted together here on Sifnos. This post is only offered to the best in the team.'

'Wait a minute,' said Katie scratching her brow, 'isn't there a possibility that Elise won't get the job? You could wind up with Babis, couldn't you?' she asked Aggelos.

'I doubt it,' he said, just as Elise nodded to agree.

'Why is that?'

'Elise is too good in her job. She has that . . .' he pointed at her with a sweeping gesture '. . . incredible charm, the Midas touch, if you like. That's important in our work so there's no way she won't get the job. Which leaves me or Babis to fill the other position.'

'And Elise wants you desperately to be her future partner as opposed to Babis.'

'Well done, Katie.' Aggelos gave a charming smile. 'Now you know why Elise keeps showing up. She likes to check on me, to make sure I'm doing well in my . . . erm, assignment. Also, she's nervous about bumping into Babis on her own because she can't get rid of him easily. He doesn't get it that she's avoiding him and, well, she's too nice to break it to him.'

Elise, who had been hanging her head in despair, looked up then, but only to cringe visibly as she spotted Babis returning to the table.

Chapter 23

It was mid-morning. Eva brought a snack to Matina, then stopped at reception to have a quick chat with Katie.

'Oh! Lovely day today,' she said when she stood in front of the desk and looked outside.

Katie gave a breezy smile. 'Sure is. Although, for you and me, the weather outside doesn't matter much.'

'True. But still, life is easier in the summer. For one, I make more money than I do in the winter when the hotel is shut. And there's also the weather. I'm like a new person in the summer, but in the winter . . .' Eva tutted and shook her head from side to side. 'Bones don't need much to start complaining when you're in your sixties.'

Katie chuckled, then her eyes lit up when she saw Chloe rushing in. She was in a t-shirt and shorts and wore a Minnie Mouse baseball cap over her shock of flyaway hair that made her look extra cute.

'Hello, my darling!' said Katie.

Eva put an arm on the little's girl's back, bent over and squeezed her lovingly against her. 'Hello, my little Chloe!'

'Hi Eva, hi Katie!'

Eva pinched Chloe's cheek. 'I say, is it me or is there more meat on your bones these days?'

'You certainly feed her a lot,' said Katie. The three of them had been having all their lunches and dinners together for a few days.

'Anything for my darling angel!' said Eva, who had developed a soft spot for the little urchin. Katie felt just as happy they could feed Chloe every day, even though it was unnerving, having to do it under their bosses' noses.

It wasn't that they didn't want to tell them. But when they'd insisted Matina should know, the girl had started to cry. She'd become so upset they didn't know what to do to calm her down. In the end, she made them promise not to tell her anything. She said she had her reasons. It was all too mysterious, especially as Chloe refused to say who her family was. All she said was that she was from Asimi. At least, they knew she was a local.

Since they hadn't met her until recently, they surmised she and her family had lived somewhere else before, or perhaps it was only now they got to be so poor that the child resorted to coming to the hotel to find food. The thought of the first day they'd met Chloe still broke their hearts, and they tried not to dwell too much on it.

'So, what are you doing out there today? Did you bring any of your friends to play with you? We've never seen you play with other children. How's that?' asked Katie.

Eva watched, her brow furrowed. Every now and then, they took turns to throw a surreptitious question at Chloe, trying to find out more about her, but it was always to no avail. Today was no exception.

Chloe shrugged and pouted her lips. 'I don't need to bring any friends along. All my friends are here,' she said with an irresistible smile that revealed tiny gappy teeth.

Katie smirked. 'Yeah, like who?'

'Other than you two?' asked Chloe readily.

'Mm-hmm . . .' said Eva as Katie chortled.

'Aggelos is my friend. And his friends are nice too.'

Katie was intrigued. She wondered if Chloe knew Elise and Babis. But how could she? She'd never seen them at the hotel. She opened her mouth to ask but Eva spoke first.

'Excuse me,' said Eva looking unimpressed. 'Am I the only one who hasn't yet met this handsome, freakishly tall Adonis?'

'Who?' said Chloe.

'Never you mind,' said Katie giggling, slapping Eva's shoulder playfully. 'So, what were you saying? Who else do you know around here? Have you met Mrs Matina and Mr Spyros yet?' she added with hope.

Chloe's chin hardened, a shadow crossing her face. She looked away. 'No. But Mrs Sparks is nice. She speaks only a little Greek so we mostly play chess. I let her beat me, but I think she knows.' Chloe screwed up her face cutely, then pointed outside.

Mrs Sparks was lying on a sun lounger on the grass in her favourite spot by the rhododendron bushes. Today she wore a long sarong with a Hawaiian-style print. Its colours were greens and blues and clashed with her pink turban. Her bikini top was bright red. If she had breasts somewhere in her past, they'd shrunk back to nothing over the years. Her chest was flat, tanned and leathery.

Katie shook her head and wondered if the woman was blind on top of everything else. Her choice of clothes was two colours short of a rainbow. Either that or she did it on purpose to blind everybody else.

As if contributing to her thoughts, Eva tittered and said, 'Mrs Matina says she's certified, you know? Something about her parents committing her to an asylum when she was a young girl.'

'Really?' asked Katie. 'But how would Mrs Matina know that?'

'Mrs Sparks has been coming here for over ten years. Mrs Matina has had many long conversations with her from time to time. And I think Mrs Sparks is a loner. Not many friends back home. Or family. Which is why she opened up to her. Told her everything about her past.'

'And you think she's crazy?'

'Hello? Can't you see for yourself?'

'Oh, I think it'll take a bit more than a few clashing colours for me to think someone's mad.'

'Well, obviously it's not just her dress sense. Apparently, she sees things!' Eva gave a mock shiver. 'Spirits. The unseen. That kind of thing.'

Katie fell silent and watched Mrs Sparks for a few moments, who lay blissfully on her sun lounger reading. To her surprise, she then saw Chloe approach the woman. Eva noticed at the same time. Caught up in their conversation as they were, they hadn't realized the child had left their side. They watched now as Chloe took out the travel chess game that lay under Mrs Spark's sun lounger. They placed the board between them and began to play, little Chloe resting an elbow on the sun lounger as she sat on the grass, her heart-shaped face deep in concentration before making her first move.

'Such a delightful child!' said Eva, then turning to Katie, 'So, when am I going to meet Aggelos? Sounds like you two have hit it off. What are you waiting for before introducing me to him? The wedding invitation?' She nudged Katie on the arm.

Katie let out a giggle. 'Hardly.'

'Have you guys kissed yet?' She leaned closer and squeezed Katie's shoulder playfully. 'Come on, you can tell Auntie Eva.

Goodness knows, being a widow for so long, I need some excitement in my life, even if it involves the love stories of others.' She let out a howl of laughter.

Katie gave a demure smile, then shook her head. 'No, sorry to disappoint. We haven't even held hands yet, let alone kiss . . .' Katie stopped short when she felt her heart leap, then bloom, just at the possibility of a romantic moment alone with Aggelos. A soft sigh escaped her lips, causing Eva to giggle wickedly.

Katie cringed in response. 'Anyhow . . . But he's very nice, and I believe he likes me too. We had a great time in Pefki the other day.' She raised a shoulder. 'We shall see. From what I know he's not leaving anytime soon. *Que sera sera*, as they say.'

'Good. Has he asked you out again?'

'Yes. We're going out this evening. He's taking me for a walk around Asimi, then for dinner at the taverna on the square.'

Eva smiled encouragingly to that, then they both looked out over the garden again. Chloe wasn't in sight any more, and Mrs Sparks was alone on her sun lounger now, but it wasn't that that made them both gawp in perfect unison. Mrs Sparks was totting a tiny perfume spray bottle, spraying the air around her with such fierceness, as if her life depended on it. Her face was scrunched up like a *Thassos* olive, and ablaze with disgust.

'What the—?' asked Katie.

Eva crossed her arms and grinned. 'Like I said . . . *certified*!'

Chapter 24

At the end of her work day, Katie made a beeline for her room. She had a quick shower, then spent hours trying on different clothes for her evening out with Aggelos. In the end, she settled for a flower-patterned summer dress that complimented her flat stomach, tiny waist, and shapely long legs. She combed her hair, piling it high with a large diamanté pin, leaving a few short strands to caress her forehead and the sides of her face.

She applied discreet make up on her cheeks and soft brown eyes and accentuated her lips with a pink coral lipstick that matched her dress. After a coat of lip gloss on top of that, her lips looked fuller. *Kissable.* 'There,' she said to herself as she stared into the mirror, satisfied. 'If he doesn't kiss you tonight, he never will.'

They met on the beach upfront, just as they'd agreed. They lingered there for a moment, exchanging pleasantries and laughing as they watched two children playing with their dog in the shallow water. The children stood a fair distance apart, tossing a tiny yellow ball to each other, the dog paddling from one to the other, trying to get the ball, causing them to giggle. After a few passes, they finally let their pet have it, and the dog began a war against the yellow ball, biting and growling at it fiercely. The sight was hilarious.

Grinning widely, Katie and Aggelos turned to look at each other. Katie was about to ask him if he was ready to go when she spotted Matina walking past. The woman ran like clockwork. Once more, she was dressed in her usual, unimaginative office attire and was carrying her attaché case, as expected. Katie had seen her once fill it in her office with a stack of printouts. She had no idea what she was doing with those. All she knew was her boss went off in a hurry with that case three times a week, always at this hour.

As Matina walked past them at a distance of a few feet away, Katie raised a hand in greeting. She opened her mouth to speak, about to point to Aggelos and introduce them in case they hadn't met, but Matina never broke her stride. Instead, she put up a hand and grimaced. 'Sorry, Katie. Whatever it is, it has to wait. I'm running behind today.' With that, she trotted away, raising puffs of sand behind her as her high heels dug into it.

Katie shook her head, unbelieving, then turned to Aggelos. 'That was my boss, in case you didn't know. And it was terrible, the way she ignored you completely just now. I apologize on her behalf. She can be rude sometimes, but I'm told she's a nice person underneath that cool façade.' She tipped her chin. 'I'm still to see it, though. For now, I just think she's very strange.'

Aggelos put a hand on Katie's shoulder, taking her by surprise. His blue eyes, intense, yet kind, caught the soft evening light, sparkling like stars in the making. Katie felt her breath catch in her throat, the world suddenly shrinking . . . shrinking . . . until there was nothing else than the look in his eyes and the touch of his hand on her shoulder.

Aggelos shook his head ever so slowly from side to side, causing her to snap out of her reverie. 'Katie, trust me when I say, there's no such thing as strange people, just people whose path in life you do not understand.'

###

When they reached Asimi, Aggelos, who had been walking beside Katie looking pensive, stopped short and pointed at one of the old stately buildings that lined the street before them. It stood on a corner at the entrance to the village and had an impressive set of marble steps on its façade unlike all the other buildings that had concrete ones. Its large French windows on either side of the imposing entrance looked welcoming, the sky-blue shutters wide open. Behind thick white curtains that swayed softly in a subtle breeze, they could just make out the figures of small children chasing each other indoors, playing. Then, a woman spoke, her voice heavy with command, and the children hurried to take seats, a deadly silence ensuing.

Katie and Aggelos couldn't see any of that, but it was easy to imagine everything by the dragging sounds of chairs being pulled with urgency. Then, they heard the woman speak again, but in a steady rhythm this time, softly and lovingly. Katie's eyes widened, her lips parting, and she let out a gasp that was barely audible. 'This sounds like . . . What is this place?' she mumbled.

Aggelos gave a firm nod as he stood beside her. 'Yes. It's Mrs Matina. She comes here to teach the children. Their parents bring them from many villages in the area. This is the community centre of Asimi.'

'Really? And what does she teach them?'

Aggelos shrugged. 'Whatever she knows. And whatever she doesn't know, she researches the Internet and shares it with them. Not just the children, but their mothers too. She's committed to enhancing their lives, to educate them, and to entertain as well.'

'What does she do exactly?'

'Various things. She does painting classes, reads children's stories, and gives cooking lessons to the mothers from time to time. Occasionally, she brings whatever teachers she can source from Apollonia to give dancing, music, and even language lessons here. In return, she offers the teachers free accommodation in Hotel Asimi for their weekend breaks. These days, seeing that the crisis has made life here harder for the locals, she has dry packets of food delivered here for the poor families by local businesses that are willing to donate.'

To hear those words made Katie ashamed for what she'd said earlier on the beach about Matina. Stunned to silence, she moved closer to the window that stood high above her head. She placed her open palms on the wall, trying to stand on tiptoe like a curious child that wasn't invited. She knew the curtains wouldn't allow her to peek inside but hoped to have a better listen. Aggelos followed behind her and stood under the window with her, listening.

'And so . . . the dwarf decided to visit the castle again, but this time, he went on his horse and loaded it up with two sacks of gold. In his pocket, he hid a small satchel filled with the magic coins the witch had given him. There was no way he was going to let the wizard take him for a fool again . . .'

'A fairytale!' exclaimed Katie with delight, trying to keep her voice down.

'Yes. Her own.'

Katie's eyes widened. 'She writes?'

'One of her many talents. This reading has been long-standing now for three straight weeks. I wish you could see, Katie. You can't drop a pin in there. Every child is accompanied by its mother today.

They don't miss the next episode of this tale for anything. It's one of her most popular ones ever.'

'But how do you know all these things?'

'I just know, okay? Let's just say that my eyes can see a little more than yours can.'

Katie turned to face him and tilted her head half-jokingly. 'Are you calling me short-sighted?'

'No, I—'

'Relax. I'm not serious. And even if you meant to call me that, I'd deserve it. I feel ashamed now, calling Matina rude and strange earlier on the beach. I'm so sorry.'

'Well, if you're sorry, don't say it to *me*.'

'Who should I say it too? I can hardly say it to *her*. She doesn't know what I think of her.'

'Doesn't she?'

'Of course not. She's not a mind reader.'

'Katie, *everyone* is a mind reader. Haven't you ever heard of body language? Pregnant pauses? Hunches? Impressions? Chemistry?'

Katie's eyes widened as their eyes locked together. She certainly knew all about chemistry.

Aggelos took a step closer and leaned towards her. He was so much taller than her that it overwhelmed her to be under his gaze at such close proximity.

Aggelos smiled sweetly, helping her to relax. He knew he had succeeded when he flicked his eyes to the amulet and saw the aura around it had stopped pulsating as erratically as before. Even its colour had turned softer, a light pink spreading around it, silky and tender like the first roses of spring. He was the only one who could see that aura.

Tilting his head, he locked eyes with her again. 'Take *us*, for instance, Katie. Isn't it obvious that I like you? And yet, I've never told you. And I know you like me too.' He was so close now, his soft breath was tickling her face.

'What?' Katie was shocked by his directness. She couldn't believe this was happening. *Is he going to kiss me now? Here? With my boss' voice in my ears? As nice as she turned out to be, no thank you. I want waves, I want moonlight. Lots and lots of stars.*

Aggelos saw the aura around the amulet flash a deep blue for a moment, then back to pink. *What on earth was that? And why does she look so dazed? Is she okay?* 'Katie?'

Katie shook her head and looked up at him again. 'Sorry, you were saying?'

Aggelos took two steps back and smiled brightly. 'Anyway, I just proved my point, didn't I? And as for Mrs Matina, I hope you learned a lesson today. Don't take everything at face value. Not everyone is what they seem. Try to remember that.'

'What?' she mumbled, a deep frown on her face.

'That's right, Katie. Try to see people with your heart. Give them the benefit of the doubt. It'll make your life so much easier. It's obvious you have issues with authority figures.'

Katie gazed back at him, her jaw slack. She had hardly heard a word of all that, her mind in a whirl. *Hello? What just happened? Did I phase out and miss something? Did he kiss me or not? Should I ask?*

'Oh Katie!' Aggelos brushed two fingertips across her cheek, as if complimenting a small child, and then began to walk away without warning, leaving her behind. He stopped after a few steps and beckoned her. 'Come on then! Aren't you getting hungry? I'm starving!'

Numb, and with her mind swimming with questions, Katie moved to his side. Aggelos beamed at her, and they began to walk uphill, side by side, along a quaint paved path. Behind them, the sound of children's laughter burst out through the windows of the community centre. They turned a corner into a wider lane, and cool air from the mountains began to caress their cheeks. It carried sweet fragrances of wild herbs, and jasmine from the yards. A cockerel crowed nearby, and the faint cry of ravens echoed in the distance as the sun sank low on the horizon. Katie glanced at Aggelos, who walked beside her none the wiser, and felt her heart sink too. *What's wrong with him? Can I try any harder?*

Chapter 25

'I cannot believe you guys parted last night without as much as a kiss on the cheek!' said Eva rolling her eyes. Katie had just joined her in the kitchen at the end of her work day to have a quick snack. Eva gave a frown. 'Did you get a hug at least?'

Katie took another *kefte* from the platter in front of her and huffed. 'Are you kidding? He said goodnight at my door and left without even registering my stunned reaction.'

Eva squinted her eyes, her head tilted to the side. 'Wasn't this your second date?'

Katie shrugged. 'Well, yeah, if you count the day in Pefki as well. But it was crowded that day, if you know what I mean.' She gave a knowing look.

'You mean his two strange colleagues?'

Katie nodded, chewing her lips. 'It's all very strange . . . Somehow, I can't see how these three can be in the military. They're acting like a bunch of schoolkids. Especially Babis. He seems so naïve, like a teenage boy.'

Eva chortled and leaned towards Katie as she sat beside her at the table. 'At least you don't have to worry about the blond. She doesn't sound like she's out to get your man.'

'No, she's just worried she'll wind up with Babis in that new post they're all after, whatever that is. That's why she's on Aggelos' case all the time. She wants to make sure he doesn't screw things up.'

'In what way?'

'Beats me! Look, can we talk about something else? Just thinking about Aggelos gives me a headache.'

Eva was about to speak when Chloe ran through the door. 'Hurry! Go to Mrs Matina! She needs help!' Her eyes were wild.

'What is it, my darling?' said Eva springing upright. Katie followed suit. 'What happened, Chloe?'

Chloe rushed to them and tugged Eva by the hand. 'She's in her office crying. It's Mr Spyros!'

'What about him? Is he back from fishing already?' asked Eva. She and Katie hurried out of the kitchen with Chloe in the lead. Chloe was mumbling now, and the women couldn't understand what she was saying. All of a sudden, Chloe stopped dead in her tracks, turned on her heels and ran back towards the kitchen. Stunned, Katie and Eva watched, then they saw Matina running towards them from the other end of the corridor.

They saw the frantic look on her face and knew whatever this was, it was serious. Katie realized the child ran away so Matina wouldn't see her. It made sense. They still hadn't told Matina or Spyros about Chloe.

Matina reached out and grabbed Katie and Eva's arms. 'Quickly! The Port Police! We need to call them!'

'Whatever for?' asked Eva.

'Haven't you seen outside?' Matina flailed her arms about, her eyes glazed over. 'It's whipped up a nasty wind out there in the past hour. I just checked the weather online. It doesn't look good!'

Pulling them both by their arms, she practically dragged them to the indoor dining area where she stood with them at the window. In the courtyard, the wind was giving it some. Several of the wood chunks stored under the BBQ stand had fallen off the tall piles and lay scattered on the floor.

One large herb plant had fallen over in its pot. A plastic napkin holder lay on its side on the ground. Reams of napkin paper flew across the yard, dry leaves from the trees and the bushes dancing around them like whirling dervishes. The wind howled and screamed as it rushed through the trees and the fencing.

Eva brought a hand over her mouth, her eyes wide. Katie turned to her boss, her brow creased. 'Mrs Matina, is Mr Spyros still at sea?'

'He's not back yet, Katie. And he forgot to take his mobile with him again! I can't even phone him. I'm so worried!' said Matina, the corners of her mouth turned downwards, chin trembling. Tears sprang from her eyes before either of the women could respond. Both of them had this image of Matina as someone who always acted cool and formal. Seeing her like this was a shock. Even her hair, that was always piled up in a tight bun was all over the place now. Stray strands had come loose, dancing around her face as she whipped her head left and right.

'Calm down, Mrs Matina! It'll be all right . . .' Eva put a gentle hand on her boss' shoulder. 'Come with me to the kitchen; let me make you some chamomile tea,' she soothed, then turning to Katie, 'Will you please call the Port Police and let them know Mr Spyros is out there?' She waved in the direction of the beach with a frantic hand.

Katie muttered a reply and dashed out of the room, then ran down the corridor. When she got to reception she found Chloe sitting on the chair behind the desk, waiting for her. 'Finally, you're here! Please, let's go get Aggelos!' Chloe's eyes were pleading.

Katie's first thought was one of mystification. She'd seen Chloe rush back to the kitchen just now. How did she get to reception? *She must have come from the backyard around the perimeter to the front. That girl runs like a gazelle!* With a shake of her head, Katie brought her attention back to the emergency at hand. 'Aggelos? No, Chloe. I'm calling the Port Police! Out of the way, please, I need to get the number from the phone book.' Katie moved to slide past the girl, but Chloe clutched her arm. 'Please! Listen! Aggelos knows how to fix this! There's no time!'

'Knows how to fix *what*?'

'The weather, of course!'

'What?'

'Chloe clenched her teeth, then seized Katie's arm. 'Trust me! Let's go and knock on his door *now*!'

'Chloe, he's not in. He told me he's got work to do tonight. Whatever your plan is, it won't work. Now, if you'll excuse me—' She tried to take the phone book but Chloe twisted her hand away.

'No! You're wrong, Katie! All you'll have to do is call his name, and he'll come running! I know it!'

Katie opened her mouth to speak, to tell the child that she wasn't making much sense, but Chloe seemed determined. Although Katie knew her only a little she was well aware of her stubbornness. So, it made sense to humour her. It would take a few seconds to rush upstairs on a fool's errand. Then, she'd be able to call the Port Police without having to deal with the child's incomprehensible protests. Katie nodded and bolted upstairs, Chloe rushing behind her.

As soon as they got to the second floor, Chloe began to shout. 'Aggelos, Aggelos! Come, *now*! Katie, call him, *please*!'

'Okay,' said Katie, rolling her eyes. 'Agge—' The moment the two syllables left her lips, she felt a tap on her shoulder. Turning around, she saw Aggelos standing at the top of the stairs. 'What is it? You guys seem distressed!' he said, panic colouring his face.

Katie did a double take, then her eyes went from Chloe's wide grin to his expression of mystification, then back to Chloe. 'How did you know?' she asked, then turning to Aggelos, 'Where the hell did you just come from? Because you didn't come up the stairs; that's for sure!'

Aggelos flicked his wrist and half-closed his eyes. 'Of course, I did.'

'Never mind!' snapped Chloe. 'No time for that! Aggelos! Mr Spyros is in danger! He's out fishing. Please help!'

Aggelos' eyes lit up, his smile turning into a frown. 'What? Out in this hellish storm?'

'Yes! Please can you go to your room and, erm, you know . . . fix it?'

'Sure, sure!' said Aggelos.

'Wait! How can you . . .' Katie made air quotes '. . . "Fix it" and exactly fix what and how?'

'Um, you know . . . change the weather a smidge. Satellite technology. Military, secret stuff!' he said readily, but his eyes were looking over her head, focusing far.

Katie narrowed her eyes. 'Secret stuff?'

'Yes, Katie. So don't ask, okay? Just let him go and do his thing! Hurry, Aggelos!'

'Wait! You have equipment for that kind of thing in your room?'

'Katie! Please! Let him go! There's no time!' shrieked Chloe.

'Trust me, Katie. I can fix it,' Aggelos placed a reassuring hand on her shoulder. Under her stunned gaze, with a flick of his wrist, so swift, so smooth, his sparkly room key appeared in his other hand. It was a gesture any magician would be envious of.

'What the—? How did you—?' Katie pointed at his hand, her jaw slack.

'Never mind that!' he said, then opened his door in a hurry. He closed it behind him so swiftly Katie didn't have enough time to take a peek inside, let alone say another word.

Chloe seemed hopeful when she grabbed Katie by the hand and led her back downstairs, then out through the hotel's front door.

Katie stood on the top step with Chloe gazing at the deserted beach, her eyes half-closed in the tumultuous wind that blew, hitting the world like a merciless whip. The bushes and flowers in the garden were taking a harsh beating, sand rising and twirling madly. The sun loungers were stacked and chained by the umbrellas for the night, and Katie felt thankful Eddie had already done it. Her heart went out to Mr Spyros being out at sea in this storm. There was no one about. She imagined the guests must have retired to their rooms, waiting for the storm to pass. When she'd left her post at five, it had been rather windy but nothing like this. It was crazy how quickly the weather had worsened. As if sensing her growing distress, Chloe put her arms around Katie and rested her head against her torso, snapping her out of her thoughts.

'Don't worry, Katie. Aggelos will fix it.'

'I have to call the Port Police now . . . okay? Just in case?'

'Do what you want now. But you'll be wasting your time and theirs,' said Chloe, a knowing smile playing on her lips.

Katie opened her mouth to speak but then saw something unbelievable. Just like that, the wind died down. It was like the world outside was nothing but a room where a big fan had just been switched off. Everything that was flying mid-air settled on the sand: leaves, plastic bags, cigarette butts. Everything succumbed to the power of gravity at the same time.

Katie gasped, her eyes seeking Chloe's. The little girl smiled like a Cheshire cat. 'Told ya . . .'

Not a minute later, with the thunder clouds gradually clearing, the horizon became visible and, oh sweet miracle, Spyros' little boat came into view. Katie rushed to the kitchen to let Matina and Eva know. By the time they were all out at the edge of the shore, Spyros had steered his motor boat to the jetty, then jumped out dizzily on shaken legs.

'Oh my God! Matina!' he said as she rushed into his arms, not minding he was drenched to the bone, smelling like fish.

'Spyros! My love!' she shouted, tears of joy streaming from her eyes.

'I nearly drowned, Matina! Thought I was a goner!'

'Please don't talk like that, Spyros. I can't bear the thought of it. What would I do if I lost you too?'

As soon as Spyros and Matina entered the hotel, holding each other tight, Katie, still standing on the sand, turned to Eva. 'That was close.'

Eva shook her head. 'Poor Matina . . . She looked half-dead from worry back in the kitchen.'

'Eva, what did Mrs Matina mean when she said to Mr Spyros just now, "If I lost you too"? Who else did she lose?'

Eva bent her head and pressed her lips together. Then, with a soft sigh, she said, 'Her child, Katie. She and Spyros lost their daughter many years ago. A little girl. I never met her, but I know it's been hard for them. The pain of her loss pulled them apart at first, nearly got them separated. Somehow, they managed to stay together, but neither of them has been the same ever since.'

'Oh, I can imagine . . .' said Katie, then moments later she looked around, her brow furrowed. 'Where's Chloe?'

'Huh!' Eva chuckled. 'That child is like a church mouse. So good at hiding. It's no surprise Matina and Spyros have no idea she hangs out here, let alone that they've been paying for all her dinners!'

Sharing a laugh of relief after all the distress, the two women sauntered back to the hotel, their giggles rising into the cool, fragrant air.

Chapter 26

'*Aaargh*!' came a shrill cry from the first floor. At the time, Katie was munching a biscuit behind the reception desk. She froze and pricked her ears.

'*Oh dear, what shall I do*?' came the words from upstairs and, this time, Katie recognized the straggly voice. She jumped to her feet and dashed to the bottom of the stairs but then Matina opened her office door and stuck her head out. 'What is this racket? Who's shouting, Katie, do you know?'

'I think it's Mrs Sparks. I was on my way up to check.'

Matina raised her brows. 'Whatever's the matter with that woman?'

'*Ooooh! Come back here you rascal*!' Mrs Sparks' voice rang heavy with distress.

'I'd better go! She might be needing help!' said Katie, without waiting for a response.

Katie rushed upstairs more curious than she was alarmed. It would be unlikely Mrs Sparks was facing an intruder or an attacker in this small family hotel. She rushed to Mrs Sparks' door and knocked on it with urgency. Not a moment later, the old lady appeared before her, her brow beaded with sweat, a hand on the small of her back. For once, she wasn't wearing her pink turban. Her hair was short and dyed bright orange. Katie brought a hand to her lips to stifle her amusement.

'Oh! Katie! Thank God you came!' piped up the old lady, shaking both arms theatrically mid-air.

'What's the matter, Mrs Sparks?'

'It's my hamster. It's got out of its cage, the little scoundrel!'

'Oh no!' Katie entered the room and closed the door behind her. Mrs Sparks had bought the hamster a couple of days earlier after spending a morning in the capital, Apollonia, going around the shops. She'd come back to the hotel that early afternoon sporting the hamster in a cage with poise as if holding the latest creation of Prada. Katie had had to stifle her laughter when the old woman brought it in at reception. Then Mrs Sparks had a word with Matina and asked if she could keep it, saying she'd been a loyal customer for many years and, at that, a lonely one, who needed the company.

Matina hadn't had the heart to refuse her and, besides, what was the alternative? She could hardly expect her to go back to Apollonia to return it or to set it free in the fields. So, just like that, Mrs Sparks now had a new roommate but, as it turned out, their co-existence had just brought them to the first ugly bump down the road.

'I opened its cage for just one moment to pet him and he nipped at my finger. Look!' said Mrs Sparks, putting out a gnarly hand with long manicured nails. Katie bent over to inspect it but saw nothing.

'See? Such a nasty bite! Who would expect they could be so vicious? They look so cuddly, don't they?'

'Mm-hmm,' mumbled Katie, looking around her feet. She wasn't crazy about pets that could nip, no matter how little, especially ones that resembled mice, even remotely. She brushed her forehead with an urgent hand. 'So, where did it go?'

'It was behind the curtain a moment ago, but then it scurried under the bed when I tried to catch it.'

Katie went to the wide open French windows and closed the glass pane. As much as she wasn't crazy about the idea of being in the same sealed room with a hamster, she was eager to avoid further distress to the dear old woman. Despite her eccentricities, she was a lovely old lady. Wincing, Katie knelt on the tiled floor and looked under the bed. The moment she did, the hamster rushed out from the other side.

'*Eeeek!* There it is! Hurry, hurry, let's get it!' said Mrs Sparks rushing to chase the animal that hid behind the drawer cabinet this time. Mrs Sparks stood in front of the tired-looking piece of furniture, a shaky hand on her brow. 'Katie, we need help!'

'Yes, we do, but—' Katie was about to agree, but also point out what they needed was a butterfly catcher and a thick pair of work gloves, when an urgent rap on the door made both women whip their heads around. Mrs Sparks opened it a smidge, just enough to see who it was. 'Oh, just in time! You look like a man who can do the job!' She opened the door wide open to reveal Aggelos.

He looked incredibly tall the way he stood there, barely missing the top of the doorjamb, and oh, so deliciously muscly. Katie dropped her gaze to his massive hands. They seemed hard and strong enough to handle nips from hamsters that cannot be found. 'Thank goodness you're here!' she blurted out, brightening up.

'I heard you shouting so here I am.' He looked amused. 'You know me, always ready to come to the rescue. So, how can I help you, ladies?' The lopsided smile he gave then made Katie weak at the knees. When she stopped fluttering her eyelids back at him, she noticed Mrs Sparks had got hold of his arm with both hands, an open smile plastered on her face. *Is she blushing? Are her hands feeling up his biceps?* Katie shook her head and decided her infatuation for the man was starting to play tricks with her head. She wasn't the jealous type. *What's the matter with me? And if I should get jealous, isn't it a little odd I don't mind Elise but feel threatened by a frail old lady?*

'Katie!' she heard, snapping out of her ridiculous thoughts, realizing that Mrs Sparks and Aggelos were done talking and were now waiting for her to do something. She turned and saw Aggelos gazing into her face, his cheeks flushed, blue eyes twinkling. *Oh, how beautiful he is!*

'Katie, can you please go to the other side of the bed? I'm going to move the cabinet in an attempt to make the hamster come out this way,' he pointed to the right of the cabinet, 'but if it goes the other way, then I want you to be there to shoo it so we can get it to return back to me. Okay?'

'Sure, sure,' said Katie nodding profusely, feeling stupid for letting her internal monologue get the better of her earlier for the umpteenth time. She gave Mrs Sparks a furtive glance. Being thin and heavily wrinkled she looked like a twig of a person, not the alluring diva she might have to compete with to get to Aggelos' heart. It still bugged her he hadn't tried to kiss her goodbye after their dates. He seemed attracted to her in every other way, so what was the problem? Still, this wasn't the right time to let her pressing questions bother her. *We have vermin on the loose, for Pete's sake, get a grip, girl!* Katie went to the other side of the bed and knelt down.

'Ready, Katie? We'll do it on the count of three, okay?'

Katie flashed Aggelos a thumbs up, then stooped low. Under the bed, she could see Aggelos' loafers, and Mrs Sparks' sandals. Holding her breath, she waited.

'Ready? One . . . two . . . *three*!' cried Aggelos. The dragging sound of the cabinet moving away from the wall reverberated loudly in the small room. Katie gasped, her eyes wide. The hamster ran halfway under the bed towards her, stopped short, sniffed the air, and turned around, dashing to . . . *What? Aggelos' loafers?*

Just as the hamster neared his footwear, Aggelos bent over, reaching down with one arm. His open palm touched the floor and the hamster got on it with an effortless hop, then started nibbling at some kind of food it found there. *Wait a minute. Is that cheese? What the heck?*

Katie sprang to her feet, her brow knitted. 'Aggelos? You have cheese?' She walked around the bed and went to him as he slowly stood up, the hamster still in his huge palm, nibbling away at the unexpected treat.

Mrs Sparks came to stand beside him just as Katie did too. 'Oh, the little darling! Look how cute it is!' said Mrs Sparks putting her hands together over her heart.

'Little darling?' huffed Katie, not even knowing why she felt so annoyed. 'You were calling it a scoundrel just moments earlier, Mrs Sparks.'

'Oh! It wasn't its fault, bless its little heart! I probably startled it, that's why it bit me. I can be so clumsy sometimes!'

'You're not clumsy, Mrs Sparks,' said Aggelos flashing an irresistible smile. 'It was just an unfortunate moment. This little creature won't bite again, I guarantee it. Here, take it!' Aggelos placed the hamster gently in Mrs Sparks' open hand. The old woman cooed with the kind of fervour that would put any doting mother to shame.

Katie turned to Aggelos, her voice reduced to a whisper. 'Well done for saving the day . . .' she twisted her lips, '. . . again! But may I ask, how did you know to come prepared for the job?'

'I didn't.'

So you just happened to have cheese on you, did you?'

'Yes,' he replied, deadpan. 'I was just nibbling some cheese and crackers when—'

'Save it!' Colour rose in Katie's face, then she hooked her arm around his and turned to Mrs Sparks. She seemed to be overjoyed, in a world of her own. She had put her pet back in its cage and was chattering away to it, seemingly oblivious to their presence.

'Glad it's all fixed; we're going now,' said Katie without waiting for an answer.

Behind the closed door, she turned to Aggelos, her eyes narrowing into slits. 'I know there's something sinister about you, Aggelos. You can fool everybody else, but you can't fool me.'

Aggelos shrugged. 'What are you talking about? I—'

Katie put up a hand, her expression impatient. 'Don't! You work for the military. I get it. You like to keep quiet about yourself but you seem to know everything about others. And you always appear ready for every emergency situation. It's all down to secret intelligence, isn't it? Come on, admit it! You have an ace up your sleeve. You can't be turning up every time, and always happen to carry the very article required. The other day, when the light bulb blew out at reception and I'd forgotten to order spare ones, you happened to have one in your room; unused, in its box! And what about the pack of painkillers you pulled out of your shirt pocket that evening when I mentioned I had a migraine and the pharmacy was shut?'

Aggelos hung his head for a few moments, then locked eyes with her again. His gaze wandered to the amulet around her neck. Its aura had turned a stark red. It was important to calm her down, to return her heartbeat to a steadier rhythm.

He took a step closer, causing her to retreat, her back slamming against the wall. He brought his voice down a few notches, and it echoed velvety as the next words left his lips. 'You got me, Katie . . .' He planted the palms of his hands on the wall on either side of her head, leaned even closer, and gave a slow, confident smile.

Katie gazed at the delicious corners of his lips, and the dimples that popped up there, mesmerizing her. Her world began to whirl as he continued to smile, as his eyes twinkled at her, his biceps bulging, causing her to hyperventilate. It was all she could do to dig her nails into her flesh as she stood with both hands closed into fists at her sides, even though she wanted nothing more than to swing them up and around him, squeezing him into a close hug, before her lips could finally claim what they've been thirsting for.

At such close proximity to him, she found it impossible to fight the effect he had on her. A trickle of sweat streamed down her forehead, and she put up a hand there to brush it away. She puffed, then fanned her face, looking away, at the end of the corridor where the view was indifferent, allowing her to breathe.

Aggelos was unaware of her discomfort but pleased to see the aura around the amulet had softened to an orangey red. He gave a soft sigh of relief and took hold of her hand that fanned her face. Tenderly, he held it in mid-air for a moment, then let it fall limply to her side. Taking a slow breath, he leaned even closer, impossibly closer, then placed a light finger on her lips. 'Katie, I'd love to tell you my secrets, but I can't. So, if you have any ideas about what's going on, please keep them to yourself . . .' He tilted his head, his expression pleading, taking her by surprise.

She perked up and met his eyes again, a faint smile on her lips. 'Sure, I can do that. But if I guess the right answers and tell you about them, will you admit to the truth then?'

'Why are you so curious, Katie? Why can't you just be happy that I'm here to help? For the little time that I can be here to do that?'

Katie opened her mouth for a crazy, split second. She wanted badly to tell him she was happy, but that she wanted him to stay for good. Yet, she couldn't say that. She had no idea where the military would take him in future. And besides, who was she to tell him what to do? She was just a girl, one of many that he must have taken out on dates. Based on his lack of interest in her, she imagined he was just playing anyway. For her, it was different, though. For days now she'd started to fear she'd fallen for him.

Aggelos let out a soft sigh and stood straight, allowing her to breathe freely again. He retracted his hand from the wall and gave her an awkward smile. 'Katie, just promise not to share with anybody any ideas you might have about me and what I do. Please?'

'Only if you own up to one thing. Tell me, was it really you who saved Mr Spyros? Do you really have instruments in your room that can control the weather? Because I'm prepared to believe anything now, Aggelos. I saw what happened outside with my very own eyes. The storm subsided moments after you returned to your room. Mr

Spyros is convinced it was a miracle that saved him from the clutches of death.'

Aggelos shook his head, his lips pressed together. He looked almost upset when he met her eyes. 'Katie, please let it go.'

'So, it *was* you. You *did* save him.'

He let out a long sigh. 'All right. Yes, I did. Or rather, my boss did. Now, will you please promise not to tell anyone?'

Katie huffed. 'Fine. Besides, who am I going to tell? Hardly anyone in this hotel seems to know you're here. Mr Spyros included.'

'Just don't tell your friends. Like Eva, for instance. I know you talk together a lot, over lunch for sure.' He winked, a lopsided smile on his lips.

Katie's eyes turned huge like wagon wheels. 'What? How do you know that?' She gulped, her mind in a whirl. *How does he know we talk in the kitchen? Eva hasn't even met him!*

Aggelos chortled, turned around and walked away, whistling a happy tune.

As she watched him disappear down the stairs, realization dawned on her. She chewed her lips, her gut twisting into knots as she brought both hands to her head. *'Oh God! Somehow, he's had the whole damn hotel bugged and he knows! He knows I'm attracted to him!'*

Chapter 27

By the late afternoon, Katie had somewhat calmed down. It helped that Aggelos was nowhere to be seen and that it was a busy afternoon. New guests kept arriving to be checked in. Her work day was winding down towards a quiet end when Eddie stopped at reception to have a chat.

'Phew! It's a scorcher today, isn't it?' He placed an elbow on the desk, raising his free hand to wipe his brow. 'It's almost six o'clock and still as hot as it was in the morning.'

'Sure is,' said Katie with an easy smile. 'Then again, I have the benefit of working in an air-conditioned room, unlike you who runs around all over the place all day.'

'You can say that again! When I was helping my mother in the rooms this morning, the sun was hammering on the window panes from nine o' clock. And I won't even describe what it was like replacing broken ceramic tiles on the roof an hour ago!'

Katie pulled a face of sympathy and leaned back in her chair. 'You poor thing. But cheer up, at least you're young. It must be harder for your mother than it is for you working in the heat.'

A cunning grin spread across Eddie's face. 'She doesn't change ceramic tiles, *I* do!' He giggled, and Katie slapped him on the wrist with a magazine. Eddie smirked and opened his mouth to speak but heard footsteps and turned around. It was Sarah, a young English girl who had arrived a few days ago with her parents.

'*Yasoo! Ti kaneis*?' she said in broken Greek.

'*Yasoo, Sarah!* How was your swim?' asked Katie and then registered something very interesting. The English girl smiled politely, but her eyes seemed hasty to move on to Eddie, who stood there smiling at her. And did he seem nervous? Either that or he had bugs in his shoes – he kept shifting his weight from foot to foot while hopping on the spot. It was most peculiar.

'*Yasoo . . .*' said Sarah to him and as he returned the same brief greeting, Katie saw the unmistakable signs of flirting in the girl's body language. Sarah raised a hand to touch her hair while holding Eddie's nervous gaze for a few moments. He looked away first, clearing his throat, and she looked away too, biting her bottom lip and smiling faintly. It was such loud body language it made Katie cringe for them both. *Ah! Not missing my teenage years. How awkward things were back then!*

Katie didn't have the chance to ponder on that long enough because then the girl hurried up the stairs. Eddie placed both elbows on the desk, his head cradled in his hands, a dreamy expression on his face. 'Oh, if only I could speak English even a little . . .' he muttered.

Katie gave a frown. 'Don't you speak English? I thought you did.'

Eddie shook his head. 'I wish! But I never paid any attention to the professor in English class. Now I see what an idiot I've been.'

'Now? Why now?' said Katie. Surreptitiously, she put a hand over her mouth to hide her amusement. She didn't need an explanation but couldn't help teasing him.

'Isn't it obvious?' He waved vaguely towards the staircase. 'I'm crazy about her! And I can't say a word to her. She'll probably go away tomorrow, and all I'll have said to her will be a few boring hellos.'

Katie leaned forward, her face sombre. 'Would you like me to teach you?'

Eddie's eyes flashed as if mirroring a lightning bolt. 'Really? Oh, could you?'

'Of course!' She gave a happy grin. 'And you don't need to worry she'll be leaving tomorrow. According to the register, you have about a week to master a few phrases before she departs.'

'What can you teach me?'

'I don't know. What would you like to say to her?'

Eddie raised his eyes to the ceiling and sighed. 'That I would give her the stars if I could . . .'

Katie fell silent for a few moments. She had forgotten how sensitive and romantic teenagers could sound sometimes, even boys, at that age. 'How old are you?'

'Seventeen.' He heaved another sigh, a deeper one this time.

'You make it sound like a curse.'

He shrugged. 'Isn't it?'

'What makes you say that? Aren't you happy living here on Sifnos? I don't suppose things would have been easier for you, your mother and your little sister had you stayed in Albania. From what I know, your mother wouldn't think so.'

He ran a rushed hand through his hair. 'Oh, I don't know. Don't mind me. I'm just a moron. Or . . .' He gave a deep sigh, then shook his head. 'Maybe I'm just missing my father.'

'I'm sorry to hear that. Is he in Albania?'

'No . . .'

He seemed reluctant to reply. Katie thought the worst. 'I'm sorry. Did he . . . has he passed away?'

To her surprise, Eddie gave a guffaw. 'For my mother, he's as good as dead.'

'Forgive me, I don't understand.'

'They're divorced and . . . he lives in England now.' The sorrow in his voice towards the end of the sentence was so palpable it made Katie's heart constrict with compassion.

'Oh, I see. It's hard to visit him there, I expect. But maybe, now that you work, you can save some money and go there to catch two birds with one stone.' She nudged him playfully to lift the mood. 'See your dad *and* Sarah!'

Eddie looked away and snorted, then gave a firm nod but stayed silent.

It was then that Katie realized this was a more painful subject than she'd imagined at first. She gave a soft sigh. 'How about the English lessons then? Do you still want me to help?'

Eddie, whose eyes had been staring out into the distance, far beyond the glass panes of the hotel's façade, turned to her, his high spirits restored. 'Yes, thank you, Katie! When do we start?'

###

And start they did, the very next morning. As soon as Eddie finished helping Julia upstairs, he came down to reception and sat with Katie for their first lesson. He had about forty-five minutes to spare, before having to water the garden and then go home with Julia for their midday rest.

During their lesson, Matina came out of her office. 'Eddie, what are you doing here?' she asked, one brow raised.

Eddie sat up in his chair, alarm flashing in his eyes. 'I hope you don't mind, Mrs Matina. My mother and I finished earlier upstairs, and it won't take a moment to water the garden. Katie was helping me learn a little English, you see.'

'Yes, Mrs Matina. I'm also idle at the moment. So I trust this is okay with you,' said Katie.

Matina came closer and, with an inquisitive expression, inspected the scribblings Eddie had made on his notepad. Her hard mouth broke into a faint smile. 'No, of course I don't mind. Education is of paramount importance. Good for you!' She flicked her eyes back and forth between Katie and Eddie as she nodded firmly. 'I had no idea you needed help with your English. I could have helped you all this time. Why didn't you ask me, Eddie?'

'Oh no, Mrs Matina. I couldn't possibly impose on your time.'

'What nonsense! As you know, I spend three evenings weekly to help the children in our community. How could I say no to help *you*, one of our own? You're part of this hotel, Eddie. This makes you part of the family.' Matina placed a tender hand on the boy's shoulder. It took both him and Katie by surprise. It wasn't often that she broke into heartfelt gestures of this kind.

She has changed recently. So much. How did this happen? Katie couldn't imagine how, but it was evident that Matina had, in fact, changed a lot, both in her appearance and manner. She wore brighter colours these days, she smiled more, her voice rang softer, and no longer scolded Spyros as much as before, especially about his notorious forgetfulness. She'd even changed the way she wore her hair. No longer piled up in a tight bun, she'd often let it hang loosely over her shoulders, except on the hotter days, like today, when she'd pull it into a ponytail.

A smattering of loose strands hung on both sides of her face this morning, bouncy and soft, giving her a careless, more casual look that matched the patterned summer dress she was wearing. Katie's eyes scanned Matina's form lower as her boss continued to give praise to young Eddie. Katie made a conscious effort not to gasp when her eyes stopped at Matina's toes peeking out of her elegant leather sandals. *Painted toenails to match her fingernails? Another first!*

'Thank you, Mrs Matina,' said Eddie, forcing Katie to snap out of her reverie. 'I appreciate that. And I'll keep it in mind in case I need your help later on. For now, Katie's doing such a great job!'

Before Matina could respond, footsteps echoed from upstairs, and they all turned to see young Sarah and her parents coming down the steps. They were in their beachwear, carrying large beach bags and a thermos flask.

'You seem ready for a whole day out!' said Matina to her guests in impeccable English after the initial exchange of greetings. Sarah's father informed her they were planning to rent scooters so they could explore the island further. They wanted to visit the Monastery of Chrissopigi before heading over to Platis Yalos for a swim and a lunch. In the afternoon, they were hoping to explore the picturesque Kastro on their way back to Asimi.

'That's a busy schedule! I hope you've had a hearty breakfast!' said Matina with a roaring laugh, and Katie was amazed once more by how different her boss seemed in the presence of her customers. Being a true professional, Matina was able to hide perfectly in their presence the vague shadow of grief that still crept up on her face from time to time.

Katie imagined Matina's sorrow was related to the loss of her child years ago. Somehow, the thought brought to mind her previous boss, Roula, back in Athens. Could that hysterical woman have been hiding behind that hard façade a misery she never let anyone see? Then, she remembered what Aggelos had told her - that there are no strange people, but just people whose path in life you don't understand. She wondered how much truth there was in that and if, somehow, she'd been having the wrong idea about Roula too, the way she had misjudged Matina at first. That's when she heard howling laughter, which broke her deep thoughts.

'I'm telling you, Mrs Matina, we only find them on Sarah's pillow!' said the girl's mother.

'And Sarah finds a red rose on her pillow *every single morning*?' asked Matina, amusement igniting in her eyes.

'Yes. Without fail. It started about four or five days ago. We can't work it out.'

'Well then,' said Mrs Matina sweeping her arms theatrically, then clasping them together before her chest. 'Sounds like your Sarah has a secret admirer!' She turned to Sarah, 'Be easy on him – whoever he is, sounds like he's really in love. I hope you'll treat him gently.'

'Do you think it's one of the staff?' asked her father, looking just as amused as Matina did.

Matina waved dismissively. 'I was only joking earlier. I know who it is. Only our lovely maid from Albania, Julia, has access to the rooms. But don't worry. They do this in her country. It's a gesture of hospitality. She does this occasionally for some of our guests. I wouldn't worry about it. She's a darling. She means well.'

'Oh! I didn't know that. We should make sure to tip her a little extra when we go,' said Sarah's mother to her husband as Matina began to usher them to the exit. Walking behind her parents, Sarah looked over her shoulder, her eyes darting shamelessly at Eddie to serve him an open smile. It made his eyes sparkle and she giggled, satisfied with his response, before walking away.

As soon as she was done waving them goodbye from the entrance, Matina turned around and strode back to Katie and Eddie, who still sat side by side looking stunned. 'Right! Carry on with your lesson, Eddie. Now I see why it's so important to you.'

She winked, then made to go, but stopped again to pin her eyes on Eddie one last time as her mirthful smile continued to play on her lips. 'And, Eddie, as of tomorrow, do make sure to get *three* roses from the front garden on your way in as opposed to one. We can't have them thinking your mother's choosing favourites now, can we?' Katie and Matina burst into hysterics, the deep crimson on Eddie's cheeks only causing them to laugh harder.

Chapter 28

Katie was still giggling at the memory of Eddie's embarrassment earlier. It was five minutes before the end of her work day and she was looking forward to a cooling shower and a hearty dinner. Somehow, the mirth of the episode and seeing Matina act so differently had made her feel more relaxed than ever before in the hotel. Today, she felt like she finally belonged, the fuzzy feeling settling delightfully inside her like warm, comforting soup on a cold day.

By now, she'd even set aside her sense of discomfort since her last encounter with Aggelos the previous day. Yet, when he walked through the front door, her teeth clenched with discomfort. *Yikes! Here we go. Play it cool, Katie. Like we said. He may have overheard you tell Eva how much you fancy him. So, whatever you do, make him think otherwise.*

'Hi, Katie!' said Aggelos raising his hand in a casual greeting, as if that awkward exchange had never happened between them the previous day.

'Hi,' she said, throwing him a furtive glance, then setting out to tidy up her desk. With just a handful of stationery accessories, one notepad and three magazines available to her the task ended mere seconds later, which left her feeling frustrated for something to do to ignore him. Annoyingly, instead of leaving, Aggelos had stopped at the desk, his forearms resting on top of it, watching her. She could feel his eyes drilling into her skull. With a huff that caused a strand of her hair to fly upwards, then land flat on her sweaty forehead, she looked up, her eyes dancing with annoyance. The tone of her voice was curt, heavy with impatience. 'Can I help?' *Yes, that's right. I'm annoyed. Learn to live with the new Katie, my friend!*

'Whoa!' he said, his brows shooting up, as well as both his arms. 'What's the matter with you? I only said, hello.'

She chewed her lips. 'Sorry. I'm about to end my shift and I'm tired.' She tilted her head and attempted a faint smile. *Professionalism first.* 'Is there something I can help you with, Aggelos?'

He surprised her when he shook his head, then gave an easy smile. 'Nope! I just stopped by for a chat, see how you are.'

What's wrong with him? He was basically toying with me yesterday, telling me HE KNOWS. Doesn't he? What if he doesn't? No, of course he does! If he doesn't know then how come he told me about Eva? 'Well, I'm fine, thank you,' came her tight response.

'I was just wondering, there's a live *bouzouki* band playing in a club in Pefki tomorrow night. How would you like to come along?'

'*Bouzouki*?' Katie didn't know what stunned her more. The fact he liked this kind of music, or that he was asking her out again. *If he overheard me talk about him in the kitchen, then he knows I'm desperate. Don't desperate women put men off? What's with this guy? He's driving me nuts!*

Aggelos leaned forward, his face hovering over hers at close proximity, forcing her to look into those eyes again, those eyes that looked like fresh mountain ponds. They caused her to stare.

'You look very intense today, Katie. What's the matter? Bad day?' He gave a frown, the look in his eyes sincere.

She shrugged. 'I'm a bit tired, yes. But I'll be fine once I've had a shower.'

'So?'

'So, what?'

'How about the *bouzouki* night? Would you like to go?'

'Oh! It's just that I had pinned you down for a Rock-music-kinda-guy. You know, being so tall and muscly.'

'What? Is *bouzouki* music for the short and thin? I didn't know that.'

'No, no. I was just saying—'

'Katie, is there a reason why you're avoiding to answer? Because if you don't want to come, it's okay. I'm a big boy, I can take it.'

He gave a smile, one of those irresistible ones that made her heart leap. And leap it did, so high in fact that she had trouble pushing it back down from the base of her throat. She managed a smile, then ran a hand through her hair. 'Well, it's not that I don't want to, it's just that . . . well, I can't tell from now. Something else might turn up till then. Can I answer you tomorrow morning?' *That's it, Katie! Act like you don't care. He deserves it for torturing you like this, playing mind games with you! How dare he? Just because he looks so cute . . . oh, so DAMN cute!*

Aggelos shook his head, his eyes narrowing, but he never broke his gaze. 'Phoarrr! Katie, you sure act strangely today.' He waved both hands dismissively before his face. 'And of course, of course, you can answer tomorrow. Say, what's that?' he asked when he dropped his gaze to see the handwritten notes on the pad in front of her. 'That's not your handwriting.'

'You're right, it's not,' said Katie, tipping her chin, 'but I'm not going to tell you who wrote it; you can't know *everything* around here.'

He winked. 'I bet you I can guess.'

'Really?' She squinted her eyes. 'Did you tap the reception as well as the kitchen then?' she said, mocking him, even though she suspected the joke, as always, was on her.

He placed a hand on his chest, looking hurt, but that didn't surprise her. She supposed a part of his basic military training must have involved utilising any natural acting skills he might have. They must come in handy to soldiers when they get caught by the enemy so they can lie convincingly if they electrocute them or something.

Aggelos let out a long exhalation. 'Have I done something to offend you? Because if I have, Katie, you should tell me so I may apologize. I surely never meant to cause you any offense.'

'Huh!'

'What does that mean?'

'Come on, admit it! Why would you tell me you know about me and Eva talking over lunch unless you wanted to make a point?'

'A point about what? I just mentioned a fact, which is that you made a friend. Someone to talk to. Friends are important. Same with you and me. I enjoy being with you, Katie. Why would you think badly of me for that?'

'Huh?'

'Really, Katie, sometimes I don't get you at all.'

'You? You don't get *me*? That's a joke!'

Aggelos threw his hands in the air. 'What is that supposed to mean? Katie, all I did was ask you out and you're at my throat. What exactly have I done wrong?'

'Nothing. Okay, just nothing. And if you must know,' she added, desperate to change the subject, 'Eddie wrote on the pad. They are English phrases. He asked me to teach him. He picks it up fast.'

'Oh, that's nice.' He gave a benevolent smile, his demeanour perfectly relaxed, his eyes soft as if the tension of moments ago had never come to pass.

Katie gazed into his face, unbelieving. *What a mystery you are!*

'Oh!' exclaimed Aggelos, breaking her thoughts. He slid a hand into his shorts pocket and handed her a little book of Greek and English phrases. 'Give that to him. I'm sure it'll help.'

Katie gawped at him for a few moments, her jaw slack. 'You know, I'm not even going to ask this time. And if anyone asks me, I'll tell them you're Inspector Gadget. That would be more believable than any excuse you might have for having one of those in your pocket.'

'Yes, I just happened to—'

'Like you happened to be munching cheese when a hamster was on the loose.'

'Yes,' he replied matter-of-factly.

'Right,' said Katie, shaking her head, before handing him his shiny golden key. He took the hint the conversation had ended and walked to the stairs looking deep in thought.

###

Aggelos and Elise stood on the hilltop looking at the momentous beauty of the scenery before them. At that hour, after the sun had set, the sky would always fire up with an explosion of pastel colours, some more dramatic than others, but all making up a live painting of unsurpassable beauty that changed by the second.

Aggelos and Elise stood there, watching it unravel and deepen into perfection while breathing in the crisp evening air so fragrant of mountain herbs it was impossible to feel anything but elated and glad to be a part of Existence. And yet, Aggelos seemed down-hearted. Elise had noticed earlier, when everyone was still around, performing their daily evening ritual. When Aggelos asked her to stay behind so he could ask her something, she knew there was something wrong.

'So, what is it you wanted to ask me?' Elise led him to sit beside her on two ancient stones that time and weather had ground flat to perfection.

Aggelos exhaled audibly. 'I think I've messed up.'

'Mm-hm.'

'It's about Katie.'

Elise rolled her eyes. 'I hate to say I told you so.'

'I never thought I'd mess things up so badly. I don't know what happened. We were fine, and I was being helpful as I was supposed to be, but now I seem to annoy her every time I do it.'

'A-ha . . . how do you mean?'

Aggelos told her everything that had happened from the hamster incident onwards.

Elise shook her head. 'You utter *moron*!'

'What is it? What have I done wrong?'

'Had you listened to me and not made yourself visible all day, had you worked your magic surreptitiously, as angels are supposed to, you could have avoided this fine mess!'

'Can I fix it? Just tell me how. But first, can you tell me what I've done wrong? I can't work it out.'

'Of course you can't work it out! You're such a rookie! But you're hard-headed too. I tried to protect you but you wouldn't listen.'

'Can you stop preaching and actually help me?'

'Aggelos, you're the only one among us who doesn't have much experience on Earth as a human. When you died you were just a little boy, remember? The Divine graced you to serve in Heaven as an angel instead of returning you to another body. You've been in Heaven ever since, until you were posted to serve on Earth. Esmera granted you, as you asked, the physical looks you'd have had in your late twenties had you not died. But, you have none of the experience that would have come with it. You just don't know the complexities of the adult world.'

'Okay, so what do I miss? Can you teach me?'

Elise did cartwheels with her hands, her eyes skywards. 'Where do I even start? You know nothing about dating, the guessing game . . . this girl is in love with you! And you are with her! I tried to tell you. It won't work, Aggelos. I told you it would mess up your assignment and your career on the earthly plane!'

'Don't say that, Elise! I don't want to go back to Heaven. I loved it there, sure, but now I'm here, seeing so much beauty and enjoying myself so much, I couldn't leave again. You have to help me, Elise! You have to help me stay.'

'Did you hear what I just said? That the girl's in love with you and you with her? Do you even know what that means?'

'It means we want to be together all the time. So what?'

'So what? It's not that simple, Aggelos. When you feel like that for someone, it's not like when you're kids. You don't just want to hang around together. You want to do more stuff. Things that adults do. And you're not cut out for that. You're confusing this girl. From what you told me, she must think all sorts of bad things about you.'

'Like what?'

'That you're playing with her, for starters. That you're only pretending to like her, plus that you know she likes you and you're mocking her for it.'

'But how can she think all that? I only mentioned her talking to Eva. Why was it bad to mention they are friends?'

'Just think, Aggelos. You're not even supposed to know Eva. The woman's never seen you, has she? Only Katie and very few others can see us. Of course, we may choose to be visible sometimes, when we need to interact with others, but you haven't done that around Eva, have you?'

Aggelos chewed his lips, his brow creased. 'You're right. I've never shown myself to Eva. I haven't even visited the kitchen. I only imagined they must be talking and sharing while they eat . . . I know people like to do that. And as for listening in on Katie's conversations with Eva, I never did that. I only saw them talking at reception a couple of times but I was on the beach, too far to hear. I—'

Elise put up her hand. 'It doesn't matter. What matters is the wrong impression you gave her. She probably confided in this lady about her feelings for you and now she feels exposed, thinking you've been listening in on their conversations. You'll be lucky if she doesn't think you're a stalker.'

'What? No!'

Elise patted his shoulder and gave a thin smile. 'Relax. We'll think this through with a cool head and we'll fix it.'

'Oh Elise, can you teach me? The way of the adults, I mean? So I don't make more mistakes? I don't want to lose her, Elise! I love her!'

'Aggelos, you're not listening to me. You're an angel. You're not human, remember? What are you hoping for? Even if Esmera never finds out what you've done and even if you get the job here on the island, you'll receive a different form, one Katie will no longer be able to see. It won't cater for much of a relationship then. Face it, my friend, it's hopeless.'

Aggelos stared mutely back at Elise for a few seconds, his lower lip trembling, his eyes glassy, and then, something incredible happened. Tears started streaming down his face. He wiped them with his fingertips then stared at his wet hands, unbelieving. 'Tears? How's that even possible?'

Elise growled with frustration, but then her eyes lit up. 'Okay, give me some time to think about it. I may have a way to help you.'

His eyes widened. 'Really?'

She put up a hand. 'Don't get too excited. I didn't mean I can help you get the girl. That's not possible, and you know it. But I can try to help you a little so that Katie and you can part ways on friendly terms, at least. You do realize that if Esmera finds out you've caused this mess, she'll send us both back to Heaven faster than you can say hallelujah.'

'But why would she expel *you*?'

'For not telling her sooner, of course. Don't you think she'll guess I've known for a while the way I've been watching you closely?' She shook her head forlornly. 'There I was, worrying I'd wind up with Stinky Boy and instead, I'm about to leave Earth again just as I'd begun to enjoy myself.'

'Sorry, Elise. I never meant to—'

'I didn't say it so you can apologise, you fool!' She shook a sharp, manicured finger at him. 'But you'd better say nothing to Esmera about you and Katie. Or Babis even. We don't know him that well and he might spill the beans to make sure he gets the job instead of you or me. Do you have plans to see Katie again?'

'I asked her to come with me to Pefki tomorrow night. There's a *bouzouki* band playing in a local club. She said she'll give me her answer tomorrow.'

Elise rested a tender hand on Aggelos' arm, a cheerful smile spreading across her face. 'Don't worry. She's just keeping you on your toes. Of course, she'll come. I'll be sure to be there too. She and I are going to have a nice girlie chat.'

Chapter 29

When Aggelos and Katie arrived in Pefki, the sun was slowly descending on a clear horizon ablaze with pastel pinks and yellows. Katie kept stealing glances at Aggelos as they ambled along the shore. He seemed to be in great spirits, asking her again about her life back in Epirus, her family and school years. As always, he revealed nothing from his own background. Still, she was happy to answer any questions he had.

His stay at the hotel would be over sooner or later. She'd given up on any romantic dreams she may have had about him and was just happy to spend time with him as a friend. That didn't stop her heart from beating frantically, though, every time he pinned his eyes on hers, his gorgeous lips spreading into that huge grin that lit up his face like a Christmas tree.

'How about a stroll down the market before we head to the club?' he asked when they neared Pefki, causing her to come to.

Katie nodded happily, knowing he meant the busy street that was lined with shops on both sides and was a delight to visit. Most shops sold souvenirs and local produce, but there was also the odd patisserie or bakery. Half way down the street, they neared a popular café that served delicious *bougatsa.* People came from all over the island to enjoy the creamy, aromatic dessert with the crusty pastry that was being served straight out of the oven in large batches all day. Sprinkled with generous amounts of icing sugar and ground cinnamon it was one of the things worth tasting at least once in your life.

Katie and Aggelos were instantly captured by the tantalizing smells of warm custard and cinnamon. When Aggelos proposed to sit at the café Katie accepted gladly. They found a table in the shade of a huge plane tree and were soon enjoying their *bougatsas* while watching the world go by.

Suddenly, Katie did a double take. She sprang upright and walked up to a woman that had just passed by. 'Excuse me,' she said causing her to turn around. 'Esmera! I thought it was you!' she exclaimed, placing a gentle hand on her arm.

Esmera stared at her mutely for a few moments, then broke into an awkward smile. 'Oh, hi! Katie, right?'

'Yes, that's right. And guess what I'm doing here! Oh Esmera, you were right about everything! I found a job here just like you said I would. You must be psychic – I thought you were just one of many who read coffee grounds to pass the time, but you have a gift!'

Esmera chuckled, looked at the road behind her, then back at Katie. She looked uncomfortable and it hit Katie as strange. 'I'm sorry, Esmera . . . I hope I didn't embarrass you. But when I saw you, I had to tell you. You and your beautiful gift have changed my life. I've never been happier!' She caressed the amulet around her neck, her face beaming.

Without meaning to, Esmera's eyes flew to Aggelos, who sat at the table, staring mutely back at her, looking like he wished the ground would open and swallow him whole. Esmera narrowed her eyes, then looked away from them both, fanning her face to gain a few precious moments. 'Phew! Amazing how hot it is at this time of day.'

'Would you like to join us? My friend and I have just had a *bougatsa* each. Have you tried them? They're out of this world. Come on, my treat! The least I can do—'

Esmera put up a hand and gave a thin smile. 'This is very kind, Katie, and I'm so pleased to see you again, and to hear you're happy now, but I really must go. I have a pressing appointment.'

'Oh, that's okay. Maybe I'll see you another time.'

Esmera patted Katie gently on the shoulder and made to go, when a booming voice echoed from behind her.

'Esmera! Hi! I didn't know you guys knew each other!' Babis came to stand before them, his hands on his hips, a goofy smile spread across his face.

Katie gave a frown. 'You know Esmera?'

'Of course, we *all* know her. Elise, and Aggelos too – Oh! Hi, Aggelos! I didn't see you there!' Babis chirped with a nod of his head when he spotted him standing up and rushing towards them. As he waited for Aggelos to come over, Babis wiped his sweaty forehead, then wiped his hand on his t-shirt, causing Esmera and Katie to cringe at the same time.

As always he sweated heavily, being such a big guy, but at least there was a novelty today. *No nasty smell.* Katie leaned towards him surreptitiously and sniffed, to confirm a pleasant woody fragrance emanated from him.

Babis grinned at Aggelos when he came over, offering his hand to him for a high five which Aggelos was happy to indulge him in. Then, Babis turned to Katie, a benevolent expression on his face. 'Where was I? Oh yes! We all know Esmera. She's our—'

Aggelos banged his open hand on Babis' back. It was a fierce blow that seemed to beat the air out of the guy's lungs.

'Hey! Take it easy, my friend! You don't seem to know your strength these days!' Babis balled his hands into fists and started to air-punch Aggelos playfully. He was just a big baby, Katie thought, but at the same time wondered if Aggelos' intervention was meant to stop Babis from completing his sentence. She decided that was definitely the case but didn't have time to dwell much upon it, because then Esmera put up her hands to get everyone's attention.

'Well, anyway, lovely to see you all. Glad you're all well, but I really must go. It was great seeing you again, Katie. Glad it all worked out for you. Bye now.'

With a wave of her hand, she was gone, lost in the crowd in a second, before Katie could do as much as raise her hand and mumble a goodbye. Then, the boys made sounds about heading over to the club before the best tables were taken. Mystified still, Katie followed, lost in her thoughts as the boys monopolized the conversation on the way, comparing notes about the best places for a meal or a swim after their extensive exploring around the island.

The *bouzouki* club was on the beach, a medium-sized one-floor building that, as Aggelos informed the two, also served as a reggae club. At the height of summer, tourists and locals visited from all over the island to dance the night away to the cheerful music of UB40, Shaggy, and Bob Marley. Tonight though, as the three made their way in, a melancholic *rebetiko* song by Tsitsanis was blasting from the speakers.

As soon as they entered, Elise, who'd been waiting inside, rushed towards them dressed in a gorgeous white dress made of silk and lace. She looked stunning as always. Her blond hair was piled high, eyes sparkling with glee, her discreet make up flawless.

They all greeted her and then Babis resumed a previous conversation with Stamatis. Katie turned to Elise with a wide grin. 'I'm so glad to find you here, Elise. Did you know we were coming?'

'Yes, Aggelos had mentioned it, so I came here early to get a table for us all.' Elise led them all to a table and sat next to Katie, the boys sitting across from them, still talking to each other.

Katie and Elise stayed silent for a while, just looking around. The club had begun to fill up fast with large groups of youngsters and families. Elise leaned towards Katie, bringing her voice down to a whisper: 'You don't mind me and Babis sitting with you guys tonight, do you? If you do, just say. I'll take Stinky Boy and we'll be out of here at once.'

Katie giggled. 'Don't be silly. It's lovely to see you again.' She was being sincere. Elise was a godsend tonight. Katie was downhearted that things with Aggelos hadn't worked out. Judging from the fact that he kept conversing with Babis and ignoring her, she assumed she had no hope left. Katie chased her sadness away with another smile. 'Actually, Stinky Boy's not so stinky any more. Have you noticed?' she whispered in Elise's ear.

Elise rolled her eyes and whispered back, 'Yes! He actually gave me a hug when he said hi and I didn't feel the need to vomit. Miracle of miracles, right?'

Katie let out a guffaw and Elise joined her, causing the boys to whip their heads around and stare blank-faced.

Chapter 30

Everyone enjoyed their delicious meal of pork chops, *biftekia*, roast potatoes, salad, *tzatziki* and *spanakopita* to the sound of cheerful bouzouki music. The band played popular songs that could be danced in the *syrtaki*, *hasapiko* or *zeibekiko* style and the dance floor was busy. Everyone had a stab at it, even Aggelos, who surprised Katie when he said he'd never danced to *bouzouki* music before in his life.

He found it hard to follow the steps she showed him during a *hasapiko* song, but he seemed to enjoy the simpler *syrtaki* steps a lot better. After watching a few Greek men dance the *zeibekiko*, a couple more glasses of wine gave him the encouragement to try it himself. As the other three watched from the table, Aggelos twirled around in a frenzy on the dance floor causing the girls to giggle. Babis brought his hands to his eyes, claiming the sight was too painful, and the girls howled with laughter even harder.

At the end of the song, Aggelos returned to the table, his arms raised, a triumphant look on his face. He was flushed, his eyes twinkling and glassy, a sure sign that he was intoxicated and enjoying every moment of it. As he came to sit beside Katie, Elise and Babis rushed to join the line-up and dance to a popular *syrtaki* song.

Aggelos put an arm around Katie and gave a long exhalation, locking eyes with her as he did so. 'Katie? Why aren't you dancing? Aren't you enjoying yourself?'

Katie stared at him aghast for a few moments. The feeling of his strong arm around her shoulders had beat the wind out of her lungs. It felt amazing. *What's he up to now?*

'What is it, Katie? Why don't you dance?'

Finally, Katie broke out of her trance. She looked away. She had to do that so she could form an answer. The effect of his eyes on hers was indescribable. She shook her head and managed a smile. 'I'm not much of a dancer.'

'Nonsense! You danced the *syrtaki* with us earlier. Let's do it again! Come!'

'I'd rather not. I'm tired. But you can go if you want.'

'What is it, Katie? Talk to me.'

Katie gazed back at him, melting. She could smell his aftershave and, from this close distance, could see tiny specks of green for the first time in his eyes. She felt light-headed, elated. It took all her self-restraint not to lean in and bury her face against his torso to breathe in deeply the smell of his warm skin. The white polo shirt he wore accentuated the dark tan he had acquired in the past few weeks and showed off his shapely body. It hurt her physically, down to the core, to be so close and not be able to open her arms and squeeze him against her.

'What?' he said with a delightful tilt of his head. He looked so much like a little boy trying to coax a lazy pet dog to have a walk with him. 'Why won't you dance, Katie? It's not something I did, is it? I haven't upset you again, have I? I can be an idiot sometimes, I know that.'

She shook her head. 'No, of course, it's not something you've done. Okay, let's dance,' she replied, jumping to her feet and taking his hand. Cheering, he followed her to the dance floor and they danced with their friends in a long line-up for the rest of the song and for two more after that. When a young man came to claim the space between Katie and Aggelos, Aggelos gave him a stern look, but let him break the connection he had with Katie. They continued to dance but Aggelos kept turning to check on the man, who held Katie by the shoulder as the *syrtaki* dance called for.

Katie noticed and wondered what Aggelos was doing. Every time he turned to stare at her shoulder, where the man's hand rested, he seemed more vexed than before. Further down the line-up, Elise, who had been watching too, broke away and came to claim the space between Katie and the man. Now that the stranger was holding onto Elise's shoulder instead of Katie's, Aggelos finally calmed down. As soon as the song ended, Aggelos broke away and took Katie's hand in his, then led her back to the table. Mystified, Katie followed him eagerly. On the dance floor, Babis made sounds about sitting down too, but Elise held him back, convincing him to stay and dance some more.

At the table, Aggelos brought his chair right next to Katie's and sat with her. He never let go of her hand and now held it on his knee, caressing her fingertips.

'Aggelos?' she asked, her voice a mere whisper. She was stunned and didn't know what she really wanted to say. But she called his name to catch his attention. He seemed engrossed in caressing her hand in his, staring down at his lap where their hands were now entwined. He snapped his head up when he heard her, and when his eyes found hers, they seemed bright, feverish.

'Are you feeling all right, Aggelos?'

'Never felt better, Katie.'

'You're a mystery, you know that?'

'No, why do you say that?'

Katie shrugged. 'I don't know. It's just that you tend to give out mixed signals.'

'In what way? I don't understand.'

She shook her head. 'Forget it. I'm just being silly.'

He leaned closer then, impossibly closer. So close now, that when he spoke, his breath tickled her ear and caused the tiny hairs on her temple to shiver. 'No, you're not. You can never be silly. You're too beautiful for that.'

Katie turned to face him, amazed. He still caressed her hand, his fingertips shooting arrows of warmth up her arm and into her heart. 'You think I'm beautiful?'

He nodded, a faint smile playing on his lips.

'But . . . but I thought you . . .'

'What did you think, Katie?'

'Well, all this time, I thought you didn't . . .' Katie swallowed hard, hesitating. *How can I put it? I'm not even sure what it is that's been confusing me.* She turned to face him again, only to melt like an ice cube tossed into the fire.

Aggelos gazed into her impossibly large, innocent eyes, then his gaze dropped to her neck where the amulet returned a silent greeting. He saw the angel depicted on it, where he was attuned to, listening to her every heartbeat day and night, picking up her vibes, making sure she was happy and safe. When he was first assigned to her, in those early days, all he could do was see the colours of the aura around the amulet and try to interpret them. At first, it had been hard to read her. But over time, he had got better at guessing her mental state and her feelings. It had made things a lot easier between them. Finally.

A beam of white light emanated from the centre of the amulet, taking him by surprise. It mushroomed into a strong flash of light that blinded him in an instant. He squeezed his eyes shut, then opened them again to register her bewildered expression and, at once, he knew. Katie loved him too. The pure feeling of adoration she'd just emitted had been too intense to misinterpret. He had nothing to fear.

With one swift move, Aggelos got hold of her face with both hands and kissed her hard, the way he didn't even know he had it in him to do. He drank from her lips desperately, as if he had been suffocating and only she could give him the oxygen he needed to survive. When they pulled apart, she brought a hand to her mouth, her eyes wild.

'I'm sorry, I didn't mean to . . .' he said when he saw in her expression that she was about to burst into tears. He thought he had upset her, but only Katie knew the kind of joy that consumed her.

'No, don't worry. It's okay,' she mumbled, then gave a sweet smile.

He let out a sigh, a crooked smile spreading across his face. 'You don't mind me kissing you then.'

'No, of course not,' she said before his lips sought hers again in the semi-darkness. He kissed her passionately, as they held each other tight, oblivious to the crowd partying around them.

###

By the time Elise and Babis returned to the table, Katie and Aggelos were sitting in each other's arms, enjoying the *chalva* dessert that the waiters had just served everybody. Babis, who had been oblivious to the developments between the two while he danced, sat and, without delay, began to devour his dessert. On the contrary, Elise had been watching all this time. She'd seen them kissing and holding each other, whispering sweet nothings in each other's ear.

'Katie? Can I talk to you in private please?' she asked, and Katie followed her eagerly through the front door. The two young girls exited into the warm night and sat on the cool sand. A waxing moon hung high in a velvety sky that was strewn with bright stars. The music was still blaring from the club, but the breeze carried it away. Within seconds, their sense of hearing had grown accustomed to the silence. Now, they could hear crickets in the distance, and the sea that whispered its lullaby as feeble waves caressed the sand.

'Katie, I hope you don't mind, but I'd like to give you some advice about Aggelos. I realize this is none of my business, but I know him better than you do, and I'd hate to see you get hurt.'

Alarm ignited in Katie's eyes. 'Hurt? How do you mean?'

Elise chewed her lower lip. 'Listen, Katie, Aggelos is not like other men. As you know he's in the . . . military, but he's not what you'd expect. If I could compare him to something that could make sense, I'd say he's more like a small, innocent child.'

Katie tittered, then brushed a hand through her hair, still elated by Aggelos' kisses and the warmth of his embrace. 'Oh, I think not.'

'Katie, we hardly know each other, but you seem like a good girl. I see you as a friend and that's why I'm trying to warn you.'

'It's kind of you, Elise, but I think I'll be all right.'

'You don't understand, Katie. Aggelos is going away soon and you won't be seeing him again. It could happen overnight. You may not even have the chance to say goodbye. I'd hate for you to get hurt when that happens.'

'Elise, I appreciate that. And I half-expected this may be the case, what with the military you're all involved with and all that. But I've been waiting for a breakthrough with him for such a long time. Tonight, finally, it happened. Why would you spoil it for me? Who knows what tomorrow brings for anyone anyway?'

Elise gazed at her for a few moments, spent. It was crystal clear Katie was in love with Aggelos just as much as he was with her. In the end, she decided to let things unfold. At least, she tried. But there was another thing she needed to discuss. She'd promised Aggelos she'd try to clear the air between them after the recent misunderstanding he'd caused. Not that it mattered much now, seeing that these two lovers were as happy as can be, but she felt she should do it anyway. Elise gave a big sigh. 'Suit yourself, Katie. You're both adults . . . well, *you* are for sure.'

'What's that supposed to mean? Aggelos doesn't seem immature to me.'

'That's not what I meant. Listen, Katie, Aggelos has not even one wicked bone in his body. He never spied on you, he hasn't bugged the hotel, and he certainly cannot control the weather—'

Katie sat up straight, her brows knitted. 'How do you know all this?'

'He and I are friends. We tend to share. And, I . . . I confess I feel very protective of him.'

Katie gave a frown. 'How come?'

'Let's just say I see him as my little brother or something. It's hard to explain.'

Katie chuckled. 'What? He's bigger than you and me put together!'

Elise rolled her eyes. 'Anyway, I assure you, Aggelos never spied on you or listened in on your conversations with anyone. We don't do that. Let's just say that our job is a little more decent than that.'

Katie scoffed. 'If your job is so decent then why can't you tell me anything about it? I don't know about you and the rest of your colleagues, but Aggelos has been doing some weird stuff, knowing things he's not supposed to, and saving the day in strange ways. How can it all be possible without the use of some kind of surveillance method?'

'Katie, you're wrong. Our job is noble. It's about protecting, about allowing the good and the innocent to lead a safe life.'

Katie shook her head, then brought a hand to her brow. She'd had a lot of wine, they all had. Which, of course, had caused them all to lose their inhibitions tonight. She felt thankful for that but also confused. She turned to face Elise. 'Can you tell me, what are a bunch of soldiers doing on a touristy island anyway? Why is Aggelos staying in Hotel Asimi as opposed to some barracks somewhere? Come to think of it, nothing about all of you, not just him, makes sense to me. And what about Esmera? How do you guys know her?'

Elise's eyes widened. 'Esmera?'

'Yes, Esmera! We bumped into her at the market before we came over. And don't tell me you don't know her. Babis said you all do. Can you at least explain that? I know the island is small but it's not *that* small! How come you all know some gypsy woman I happened to meet in Athens before I arrived here? I'm not paranoid normally, I assure you of that, Elise, but I can't help thinking we're all connected somehow and that there's something I'm missing. How can we all meet up here, as a big circle of friends? What's going on?'

Elise bit her lip and looked away. In the complete silence that followed, Katie waited, listening to the soothing susurrus of the sea as she tried to calm down, forcing her exasperation to subside.

Finally, Elise stood slowly and placed a hand on Katie's shoulder. 'Come, Katie. Let's get you back to Aggelos. He'll be wondering where we've gone to.'

'You haven't answered my question. I don't think I can handle any more mystery from you guys. Why don't you tell me the truth?' Her eyes were pleading when she tipped her head back to face Elise.

It's not up to me to tell you anything, Katie. You decided to open your heart to Aggelos, despite me trying to warn you. What happens from now on has nothing to do with me. If you want to know what Esmera is doing here, and how come we all know her, you'll have to ask *him*.'

Chapter 31

It was the wee hours of the morning when Katie and Aggelos began to saunter back to the hotel along the beach. Elise and Babis had said goodbye outside the club and then went off, as per Elise's suggestion, to have an early coffee and a cheese pastry at one of the early-opening cafés. Seeing that he smelled pleasantly still, she had no trouble giving the others some privacy, and Babis, being hungry after all the hours of dancing, jumped at the chance.

The sun had just risen, filling the sky with orange and yellow hues, the feeble sun rays bringing in with them the joy of a brand new day in paradise. Katie squeezed Aggelos' hand in hers and gave a bright smile.

In response, Aggelos stopped walking along the quiet shore and took her in his arms. 'Katie, I want you to know something. I haven't been very honest with you. And even though I can't tell you much, I feel I should at least let you know that, soon, I will . . . I mean . . .'

Katie brought her fingertips to his mouth and gave a faint smile. 'I know. But it's okay. There's a lot I don't understand about you, but I also realize your job calls for this kind of obscurity. I'll take what I can, while we're still together.'

Aggelos flinched at the sound of these words. 'So . . . you do know that I'll be leaving soon.'

'I'd rather not talk about it, Aggelos. I'm just happy you're here now. Kiss me again. That's all I care about right now.'

With an irresistible smile, Aggelos leaned in and kissed her for what seemed like an eternity. The fervour of their embrace caused their hearts to race and their knees to buckle. Before they knew it, they were lying on the sand, him on top of her, his hands running, demanding, up and down her torso, seeking her breasts with a want he didn't know he had.

Katie moaned with pleasure, a fire igniting in her belly, and just as she wondered if this was the right time and place to give him all she had to give, he pulled away to stare at her with wild eyes as he gasped for breath.

'Katie, I'm very sorry . . .' he mumbled and rolled over to sit up beside her. Leaning forward, he placed his elbows on his knees, his hands on his head.

Katie sat up, alarmed, putting out a tender hand to rub his back. 'What is it? Did I do something wrong?'

He shook his head and turned to face her, his expression troubled. 'I'm sorry. I just . . . I've never done this before. I . . .' He stared down at his groin. 'My body is acting strangely.'

Katie noticed the bulge in his trousers, which was no surprise, but what really mystified her was the sheer panic on his face. 'What is it, Aggelos? You can talk to me. Are you worried about . . . you know . . . have you had problems in the past? Is that it?'

'Problems?' His eyes darted to his groin again, then back to her. 'No! No, I haven't! I mean, I don't know. I've never done any of this before.'

Katie's jaw went slack. After a few moments, her voice came out cautious, in no more than a whisper. 'So, you're a virgin. It's okay, Aggelos. Actually, I think it's nice.'

'You do?'

'Yes! And this explains your reluctance in the past. You know, your hesitation to show your attraction to me. So, thank you. Finally, I can understand you a little better.' She gave a sweet smile.

His face exploded with relief, a huge grin spreading across his face. 'Oh thank goodness. I'm so glad you don't mind.'

'Of course, I don't mind. Actually, I have a confession to make.' She eyed him cautiously, her lower lip twitching. 'I'm a virgin too.'

His eyes lit up. 'Really? Oh that's wonderful!' He leaned in and drank from her lips, now more thirstily than before.

As soon as they parted, Katie giggled. 'I must say, for a virgin, you're one hell of a kisser.'

Aggelos shrugged with modesty, then said, 'I confess, I like movies, and I guess that's how I picked up a thing or two. There's plenty of kissing there. I spend most nights in the hotel lounge watching movies with the other guests.'

'Oh, pity I never saw you there. But I don't watch TV much these days. I'm exhausted most nights; I read a page or two in bed and go out like a light in no time. Sometimes I don't even get to close the book first.'

They shared a giggle about that and stood. Soon, they were walking again, holding hands and gazing into each other's eyes as they chatted, their faces warm and bright.

###

The next morning, Katie was half-asleep at her post. Aggelos had left her at her door with one last passionate kiss. She'd had only two hours of sleep. Still, the memory of him lying with her on the sand kissing, just hours ago, was enough to keep her going. As she greeted the guests, she had a dreamy look in her eyes and a goofy smile plastered on her lips.

At midday, she made a grilled toast in the kitchen and decided to have it on the beach during her short break. When she didn't find Aggelos outside she wasn't surprised, thinking he'd still be sleeping. Mrs Sparks was lounging on the lawn in her usual spot and Chloe was with her. Grinning widely, she went over to say hello.

Once more, the old lady had brought her hamster in its cage for company. It often attracted the odd stray cat, but today there seemed to be none about. Chloe was sitting on the lawn and feeding the hamster a slice of cucumber through the cage bars. She was smiling from under a wide-brimmed straw hat, her dimples making her incredibly cute. Mrs Sparks was giggling as she watched her pet munching with puffy cheeks.

'Oh! To be a hamster!' joked Katie as she flopped down on the grass beside Chloe. 'Is it me or is it getting bigger? It'll blow up one of these days, Mrs Sparks. I don't think hamsters are meant to eat all day.'

'Oh, you should say that to Babis!' said Mrs Sparks, huffing. 'He's the one feeding it *koulourakia* from the local café.'

Katie swallowed her last bite from the toast and gave a frown. 'You mean Aggelos' friend? The big guy?'

Mrs Sparks shrugged. 'Of course.'

'How do you know him? I haven't seen him at the hotel.'

'It's a small island. Everyone knows everybody, dear.' The old lady gave a little wave, her other hand shooting up to smooth her bright pink turban.

Katie put out a hand and caressed Chloe's hair. It was shiny and soft like silk but fell in a tangled mess on her shoulders. She wondered why the girl's guardians didn't bother to manage it a little better. 'Would you like me to pull your hair into a ponytail? Or make a nice plait?'

Chloe screwed up her face. 'What? No way!'

'But why not? Isn't it uncomfortable falling on your shoulders in this heat? Doesn't it make you sweat?'

Chloe never looked up from feeding the hamster. 'No, it's fine.'

'Hello!' echoed a breezy voice and Katie looked up to find Aggelos standing before her. With a huge grin, he sat beside her and planted a peck on her lips.

Katie grinned, but inside she cringed a little. She wasn't sure the guests should know whom she was dating, but it was too late to hide it now. She glanced at Mrs Sparks and then Chloe, to find them both smiling widely back at her. Aggelos squeezed her in his arms and she felt the warmth of his love. It made her heart swell. *The hell with it!*

'What is it, my love? You seem dazed. Did you not have enough sleep?' He cooed at her as he caressed her cheek.

Katie's heart leapt. *My love? Oh!* 'I'm a bit sleepy, yes.' She gave a bright smile and brought her voice down a few notches. 'But I'm also happy. So very happy . . .' she whispered in his ear.

He squeezed her hand in his and opened his mouth to respond, but Chloe sniggered and beat him to it. 'We can hear you, you know! Aggelos loves Katie! Aggelos loves Katie!' she began to chant causing Mrs Sparks to break into a hysterical giggle. Katie and Aggelos gave thin smiles, and Chloe resumed feeding the hamster under Mrs Spark's mirthful gaze.

Moments later, Katie checked her watch and was about to say it was time to return to her post when Aggelos jolted upright. Stunned, all three watched as he stripped off his jeans without saying a word. He was wearing his swim shorts underneath. Katie gave a chuckle and was about to ask what he was doing in such a hurry when he broke into a sprint and dived into the water, swimming away as if his life depended on it.

Katie exchanged stunned glances with Mrs Sparks and Chloe, then the old woman asked the child to return the hamster back to her room. Chloe took the cage and left, and the two women sat silently, looking out at the shimmering water and wondering what had made Aggelos do that.

The sea was swarming with people. As much as they both tried, they couldn't spot him in the water. The morning haze and the glare of the sun made it impossible.

Mrs Sparks gave a deep sigh, causing Katie to turn and face her. She found her gazing out to sea, a dreamy look on her face.

'What is it, Mrs Sparks? Everything all right?'

'Ah, Katie . . . Aggelos is such a fine young man! Quite a catch! You're so lucky.'

'Why, thank you, Mrs Sparks.' Katie turned away, eager to hide her amusement. She hadn't pinned Mrs Sparks down as someone who ogled handsome young men. Her deep sigh had echoed particularly amusing.

'He's just wonderful,' continued Mrs Sparks, 'always so helpful. Mrs Matina ought to give him a raise.'

Katie whipped her head around, her brow deeply furrowed. 'Mrs Matina? But Aggelos is not staff, Mrs Sparks.'

'Of course, he is!'

'You're mistaken, I assure you. He's been here a while, I can see why you may have mistaken him for staff. But he's just a guest here, just like you.'

'Katie, it is *you* who is mistaken. Aggelos is helping out Chloe on behalf of Mrs Matina. He's working here, just like you are.'

'What? This can't be right! Mrs Matina doesn't even know Chloe. Let alone employ Aggelos to mind her, if that's what you mean. And why should she? Chloe is not a guest here. Just a local girl who visits every day.' Katie gazed at Mrs Sparks' wrinkled up nose and shaking head, wondering if the old lady had been losing even more marbles than she'd thought.

Mrs Sparks pouted her lips, then tipped her chin. 'I didn't want to tell you, Katie, but you're making me. I've seen Aggelos and

Chloe enter Mrs Matina's office plenty of times. I'm telling you they have some kind of secret arrangement for the child's benefit.'

Katie pressed her lips together, barely stopping herself from responding that this was simply preposterous. She was about to respond with something non-committal when she spotted Aggelos at last. He had just come out of the water but he wasn't alone. In his arms, he was holding a middle-aged woman that seemed unconscious.

'Oh my God!' she exclaimed in a shaken-up voice and ran towards him, forgetting all about Mrs Sparks and her ridiculous notions.

Chapter 32

When Aggelos got out of the water and laid the woman down on the sand, a pandemonium ensued. The woman's husband and adult daughter rushed to his side, the latter wailing, all the bystanders rushing over, some out of concern, others out of sheer curiosity. Katie had joined Aggelos early on, so she was able to witness it all, before a big circle of onlookers solidified around them.

Luckily, one of the guests who knew mouth to mouth came forth and soon enough the woman came to. When she opened her eyes and spewed out water there was a round of sighs of relief from everybody. Within a couple of minutes she and her loved ones were put in a private car and whisked off to the island's Medical Centre.

When the crowd had dispersed, Katie sat under a thatched umbrella with Aggelos, feeling spent. She reached out and patted his shoulder. 'You're amazing, you know that?'

'I did nothing. I just happened to be there, that's all.'

'I don't think so. I saw what happened, Aggelos. You rushed to get in the water before the woman even began to need assistance. I never heard her call out for help. Do you have some kind of sixth sense? Are you psychic? Because that would explain a lot.'

'Psychic? What are you talking about?'

'Aggelos, don't lie to me, okay? There's a huge mystery about you. I'm having trouble dealing with it. It's bad enough having this between us. Don't add lies to the mix.'

'I'm sorry. I keep disappointing you, don't I? I'm trying my best, Katie. Can I just have the option not to answer then? You keep asking me the most difficult questions.' He pulled a sweet smile that made her heart melt. She wondered for how much longer he'd stick around for her to witness it. The very thought pained her. She shook her head. 'I just heard that you and Chloe meet with Mrs Matina in her office. Is that true?'

He gave a deep sigh. 'Please . . . no more questions, okay?'

'Aggelos, why don't you trust me? I promise, if you tell me what's going on, I won't tell.'

He leaned towards her and took both her hands in his. 'Will it suffice to tell you that I'm doing something good? Nothing I do can ever hurt anybody. Is this not enough, Katie?'

Katie shook her head, then glanced at her watch. She gave a shriek and jumped to her feet. 'It'll have to do for now. I must return to my post. But this is not over, Aggelos. You can't just pile the mysteries on me and expect me to not ask for a single explanation.'

###

It was early afternoon and Eddie was over the moon as he relayed to Katie all about his progress with Sarah.

'Really? She said she's in love with you too? That's wonderful, Eddie!' said Katie as she sat beside him behind the reception desk. Their English lessons had been going well, and Eddie had learned a lot in a really short time.

'Yes, and I owe it all to you, Katie. To your lessons and this amazing phrase book! I couldn't have managed to talk to her otherwise.' In his hand, Eddie held the phrase book Aggelos had produced from his pocket. That day it had seemed brand new. By now, many of its pages were dog-eared. Katie cast a forlorn gaze at it as Eddie continued to thank her. She imagined that phrase book was one of a multitude of good deeds that Aggelos must have done without ever expecting praise. She guessed he didn't expect the book back; which was just as well. It was so out of shape that she doubted it would be in one piece by the end of Sarah's holiday.

The door of Matina's office swung open, and she came out with Spyros, their faces beaming. 'Can you get your mother please, Eddie? And Katie, could you call Eva? Spyros and I have an announcement to make!'

Mystified, they rushed to get the others. A minute later all four stood before Matina and Spyros, bright-faced. Whatever this was, it was a big thing. Spyros kept rubbing his hands together, and Matina had a huge grin on her face.

'Whatever is it?' asked Eva, unable to contain her excitement any longer.

'We're having a BBQ this Saturday night! And seeing that we have more guests this year, we're planning a large affair. The whole village has been invited!' Matina spread out her arms like a large bird about to take off.

Everyone cheered, including Spyros, even though he knew already.

'Oh! That's wonderful! And I love our BBQs! I was wondering when the first one was happening this year,' said Julia. 'My boy loves them too, don't you, Eddie?'

Eddie nodded fervently. 'Whatever you need, Mr Spyros, just let me know.'

Mrs Matina gave a sweet smile. 'Eddie, you'll be happy to know we were initially planning it for the following weekend, but seeing that Sarah is leaving on Monday, I didn't want you to lose your chance to dance the night away with her before she goes.' Mrs Matina's words brought on a round of cooing sounds from everybody.

After everyone had had a chance to tease Eddie, including Spyros who delivered a play punch to the boy's shoulder, Matina raised her hands to get their attention. 'Listen everybody, I've been planning this for a few days now, and I want it to be a great success. We've had a few wonderful business weeks. We continue to be full and the bookings are looking great for the rest of the season too. To mark the occasion, we want this BBQ to stand out and to make a statement to our village. For this purpose, we're planning to invite the Stratos Band from Apollonia to perform for us!'

Everyone cheered, even Katie, who had never heard of the band before, but from what she gathered from everyone's response, she guessed they were famous on the island. Matina put up her hands again and everyone fell silent.

'The band said they were available for Saturday, and we've agreed on the fee, so they're just waiting for me to give the final confirmation for the booking.' She turned to Katie. 'Would you mind making the phone call, Katie? I have so much to do!'

'Of course,' said Katie, 'Can I have the number please?'

'It's in the book, I expect,' said Matina dismissively, then began to wave her hands about. 'That's it, everyone. Iron your glad rags and polish your dancing shoes. This Saturday will be a blast! Now, back to your posts!'

As soon as Matina disappeared behind her office door, Spyros turned to Katie. 'I know for a fact that number's not in the book. But not to worry. Leave it with me, Katie. I have it in my room. I'll make the call a little later, once I'm done with my chores.'

Chapter 33

On the big night, the courtyard outside the hotel was transformed into a whimsical dining space. The tables were set with crisp white linen, a tiny lantern at the centre of each, their delicate flames flickering in the breeze. Fairy lights twinkled overhead, tied from tree to tree, and lit torches hung on the surrounding walls. Three buffet tables were laid out with a multitude of serving platters that Eva, Julia and Eddie had just brought out. They all had their lids on, in an attempt to preserve the heat a little longer. They contained fried and baked delicacies that Eva had prepared the previous day, putting in the task all her mastery.

A little further, the coal on the BBQ was burning, waiting for juicy marinated steaks and herb-scented *biftekia* to be thrown on the grill by the dozens. On the BBQ stand, Eva had left a few stacks of tiny *pitta* bread ready to be baked too, and a large bowl of lemon juice, olive oil and local oregano for the basting. The hosts and staff had it all planned to perfection; the few guests that were already seated kept looking around them with evident appreciation.

Dusk rendered the scene picture-perfect as the sun began to set against the backdrop of a calm, alluring sea. Soon, more guests arrived to be seated and to be greeted cheerfully by Matina and Spyros. Both were dressed formally for the occasion - Matina in a green evening dress with a flowing skirt, and Spyros in an elegant shirt and trousers combo with a green tie that was in the same shade as Matina's dress. That little touch had been her idea. They looked like the perfect couple tonight, and happier than ever, flashing their best smiles as they made small talk with the guests.

Katie couldn't help noticing all of this as she stood by the buffet tables rather awkwardly, watching the scene. Beside her, Eva and Eddie were busy decanting wine into crystal bottles and cutting up bread. Katie ran a hand through her hair and gazed beyond the courtyard fence at the vast sea that murmured its eternal song. The breeze felt warm on her skin as the cawing of birds delighted her ears.

She couldn't grasp exactly what it was, but in those moments she felt a happiness she couldn't explain. More than anything, she felt her heart soar with a feeling of being perfectly in place. She had recently decided Matina had a much nicer character than she'd initially thought. Spyros was adorable, her colleagues lovely, the guests a joy to interact with, and the man she loved, even though he was leaving soon, was here still, and that, for her, was enough.

She kept throwing impatient glances at the front gate, waiting for him to emerge. She had decided to take him as he was from now on, without questioning him or his actions. It sufficed he'd shown to her his love and that she could trust him, beyond any doubt.

At last, Aggelos appeared from around the corner and walked through the open gate, a wide smile on his face. He was wearing a navy blue polo shirt and jeans, a light touch of gel in his hair, and a dashing smile that made her swoon when their eyes locked together. She ran to him and left a peck on his lips.

'You look absolutely gorgeous tonight,' said Aggelos, leading her to the side, out of the way of the stream of guests that kept coming in looking for a place to sit. Beside them, a large geranium plant was generously displaying its blooms in vivacious pink and white hues. Aggelos cut one off and offered it to her, causing her eyes to widen with sweetness of feeling. 'Aw! No one has ever offered me a flower before.'

Aggelos gave a wide grin and tilted his head, about to pay her another compliment, for she looked truly stunning in her plain white dress, her skin tanned and smooth, her eyes luminous more than ever, rendering him mesmerized for a few seconds. He never got the chance to express his admiration though, because Eva materialized from behind the crowd to tap Katie on the shoulder.

Katie gave a start, so transfixed was she while gazing into Aggelos' face. 'Eva!' she exclaimed when she recovered. 'Finally, let me introduce you to Aggelos!' She made the introductions and Eva shook hands with him, then made appreciative sounds. 'I see why it took Katie so long to allow me to meet you. I'd be keeping you to myself too for as long as I could. You're a dreamboat!' Eva winked, a mischievous gleam in her eye.

Aggelos didn't know what a dreamboat was but flashed a beaming smile nonetheless, and it made both women melt. Katie looked around, searching to find Aggelos a table to sit, when she noticed Spyros a few feet away, gesturing frantically to her to approach. She excused herself and went to him.

'Yes, Mr Spyros?'

'Katie, what time is the band coming? Matina asked me to check with you; she's getting a little worried. You know how she is.' He chuckled and rolled his eyes.

'The band?'

'Yes, my girl. The Stratos Band. From Apollonia.' Panic flashed in his eyes and his next words came out rushed. 'You did call them to confirm like Matina asked you, right?'

All colour drained from Katie's face in an instant. *Oh God!* 'But, Mr Spyros, don't you remember? You told me not to worry, that you were going to call them *yourself!*'

Spyros stared back at her mutely for a few, terrible split seconds, then his eyes turned glassy, and he brought both hands to his head, cringing. 'Oh no! Oh my God! Matina's going to kill me!'

'Oh come on, Mr Spyros. I'm sure she'll understand. These things happen.'

'I'm telling you, she'll have me for dinner, then spit my bones out one by one by morning! She's forever telling me off for my forgetfulness. There's no shutting her up now. Oh goodness me, what shall I do?' As he carried on mumbling to himself, Spyros kept squeezing a kitchen towel in his hand and pulling it from side to side, his knuckles snow white. Perspiration glowed on his wrinkled forehead.

Katie felt bad for him. She put a hand on his shoulder, but he kept staring at his shoes now, shaking his head, trying to think and finding no solution to the problem. He didn't seem to register Katie's touch, and she felt increasingly sorry for him. She decided there was only one solution and was about to tell him about it when she saw Matina approaching.

'Spyros, Katie, have you any news?' Matina raised her brows, a tight smile on her lips as she kept flicking curt glances at the sitting crowd.

Spyros looked up, his eyes darting from Matina to Katie and back, so full of apprehension that they resembled those of a hunted animal in the middle of a forest. Once again, Katie's heart went out to him.

'Actually, Mrs Matina, I have some bad news. I'm afraid the band won't be coming.' Katie jutted out her chin and let the pregnant pause hang in the cool evening air for a moment.

Matina cocked her eye at her. 'Not coming? Whatever do you mean, Katie?'

'Well, I admit it's all my fault. The thing is, I . . . I forgot to call them. I'm so sorry.'

'What?' piped up Spyros and Matina in unison.

'You forgot?' said Matina, ignoring her husband's equally stunned reaction.

'Yes, I apologize. It completely escaped my mind. I take full blame for this.' Her eyes wandered away from Matina's bewildered expression to gaze at the multitude of guests who'd arrived for a night of dancing to live *bouzouki* music. Clearly, this was not going to happen.

'Matina . . .' piped up Spyros.

'I do admit this is most unfortunate,' said Matina, rubbing her jaw as she looked around her too.

'I don't know what to say. As I said, I'm very sorry. If there's anything I can do—'

'This is nonsense! Katie, I can't let you—'

Matina put up a hand. 'No, Spyros, it's all right. Katie has proved to be a wonderful employee. But she's only human. We have to make do without the band and that's that! We have a stereo inside. We'll get Eddie to bring some CDs from his house. It'll be fine.'

'What?' said Spyros. 'You don't mind then, Matina?'

'Really? You don't mind?' asked Katie.

'Of course, I mind! Are you joking? What are we to tell all these lovely people who came here expecting live entertainment? I mean, look at them! I don't suppose either of you knows how to play the *bouzouki*?' She let out a chortle, causing them both to gasp. She saw their expressions and placed her hands on their shoulders, squeezing them playfully. 'Calm down now. There are worse tragedies in life than this, right?'

'Matina, you never cease to amaze me. Look, I was going to come clean anyway, but your reaction makes it easier now to fess up.'

'Come clean? Fess up? What do you mean, Spyros?'

'Katie took the fall for me, and as noble as this is . . .' He turned to Katie and mouthed a heartfelt thank you, 'the truth is that it was *I* who messed up. I told Katie I was going to make the call. It was *I* who forgot to confirm the booking. I'm so sorry, Matina.'

'You? *You* did this?' Matina's face contorted into a hard mask of disdain. She huffed, her squinted eyes sparkling under the fairy lights. 'You and your notorious forgetfulness! I don't believe you, Spyros! I've had enough of you and that Swiss cheese of a brain you seem to store year in and year out *needlessly* between your ears!' Before Spyros could respond to that, she left in a huff, her high heels clicking loudly on the cobblestones.

'Wait a minute! You were laughing just now thinking it was Katie's fault! That's not fair!' Spyros rushed off behind her. Gesticulating wildly, he followed her into the hotel through the kitchen door that closed behind him with a bang. The sound caused a few heads to turn, being loud enough to rise over the bustle as people chatted, eagerly awaiting their meal and the party to begin.

Chapter 34

'I've had enough, you hear? I can't trust you with anything! It's like you don't care!'

'Of course, I care!'

'Really? But you expect everything from me! I swear, it's like you're not even here!' yelled Matina behind the closed door of her office.

'Seriously? And there I was, thinking I've been doing all the plumbing, the watering, the hammering, the painting, and goodness knows what else all day around here! You're ungrateful! That's what you are, Matina! There, I've said it! You take me for granted!' Spyros' shouting echoed just as angry behind the closed office door. Eva could hear them all the way from the kitchen as she prepared the last two serving platters. When Katie walked in reluctantly, her face alight with concern, Eva beckoned her eagerly to follow.

The two women stood near the closed door of Matina's office and whispered to each other. Eva suggested they find an excuse to knock on the door and stop their employers from fighting. She was worried the guests might hear and imagined if they interrupted them, somehow, their anger might subside and they could come out again soon. Yet, no matter how many ideas they threw at each other they couldn't find an excuse to knock on the door. It was hard as it was to think, with the yelling that never stopped inside.

'All these years, I've done nothing but put up with your terrible bossiness!'

'Bossy? Me?'

'That's right. I put up with a lot, Matina. You speak to me in a way that suggests you don't respect or value me, often in front of the staff and the guests!'

'I certainly don't!'

'Yes, you do. You act like you're the owner, and I'm just an employee, your bloody helper! But, of course, that's exactly what you think, isn't it?'

'Oh no! Not that crap again! Spyros, the money my father gave us may have been my dowry but it was for both *of us! The hotel is yours just as much as it is mine!'*

'You know very well this is not so. I asked you years ago to pack up and leave this place, to see if it could help our marriage, and yet you wouldn't have it. As always it was your *choice, like* everything *else is!'*

A pause ensued for a few moments, and then, Matina spoke again, her voice echoing broken, upset this time. '*How can you bring that up again? You know very well I could never leave . . . this is where we lived with our little girl . . . this is the only place where her memory still is . . .*' Matina broke into sobs, then soothing sounds came from Spyros, causing the two women outside the door to listen intently, despite their growing guilt for overhearing.

But they cared about them, and it seemed like a wonderful breakthrough. At last, Spyros had aired his frustrations and helped Matina understand how he felt. This could only be good. Despite themselves, Katie and Eva approached the closed door. Now, they could hardly hear their employers' voices behind it. Whispering, Spyros was now speaking to Matina soothingly as she continued to cry.

Katie was about to pull Eva away, feeling awkward for witnessing this private scene, when a sweet *bouzouki* melody echoed from the courtyard. Katie and Eva looked at each other, gasping at the same time, then rushed outside. It was live music, no doubt about that.

###

When Katie and Eva emerged into the courtyard, they found three young men playing *bouzouki*, flanked by a half-dozen other musicians and singers, all standing by the BBQ. The guests had stopped eating and were watching the band play with rapt attention. Katie scanned the faces of the musicians, stopping to admire the young girl with the melodic voice who sang in the lead, then her eyes wandered to the rest of the people playing instruments. One played a *touberleki*, another held a *baglamas* at the ready, and last, a young man played the tambourine, shaking it high up, in front of his face.

Katie's twinkling eyes rested on him as she listened to the folk song playing, her wide grin faltering when she registered the familiar polo shirt he wore. That's when he lowered the tambourine in his hand and met her eyes. *Aggelos?*

Aggelos broke into a smile and raised the tambourine over his head, doing a little dance, then winked at her, causing her to burst out laughing. Katie shook her head, unbelieving. *He's full of surprises! And once more, he's saved the day. But how? Where did all these musicians come from?*

Katie heard footsteps from behind her. She turned to find Spyros and Matina stepping out of the kitchen door, his arm around her. Matina's eyes were a little puffy from crying earlier, but she seemed ecstatic to see the band.

Katie's employers came to stand between her and Eva. 'They play beautifully!' said Matina. 'But they're not the Stratos Band! Who are they, Katie? How come they're here? Do you know?'

Katie shook her head. They watched the band, their faces alight with mystification, and when the song ended, everyone erupted into applause. As soon as it died down, no one among the band members broke the line-up formation and went on to the next song. That's when Katie felt a tap on her shoulder. She turned and, to her surprise, saw Esmera standing there. The old woman's face was made up with discreet eye shadow, blush, and a glossy red lipstick that worked beautifully with her raven black hair. As always, it cascaded loosely over her shoulders but tonight it looked silky smooth. She wore a long patterned dress that reached down to her ankles, and an electric blue shawl. She looked amazing, and even taller, thanks to her high-heeled shoes.

'Wow, Esmera! You look lovely,' said Katie. She was so taken aback, it evaded her to wonder what she was doing there.

Esmera winked. 'I hope you don't mind. I've brought a few friends to liven up the party.' She gestured towards the band. Since Aggelos was among them, and Katie suspected Esmera was in the same covert profession as him, it made sense not to ask further questions. She imagined she wouldn't get any answers even if she did. So, instead, she turned to Matina, Spyros, and Eva, introducing Esmera as a friend from Athens. Seeing that everyone was happy to have the band for the evening that Esmera was thoughtful enough to bring along, no one else asked any questions either.

Yet, when Esmera followed Eva through the maze of tables to find a vacant seat, Spyros turned to Katie, his face bright. 'Katie, you're a treasure! How did you fix the problem so soon?' He nudged her elbow. 'What's your secret?'

Katie pressed her lips together, unable to find a suitable excuse. That's when she registered a wink Aggelos gave her across the courtyard as he played the tambourine. It occurred to Katie that the gesture served as a plea to keep a secret, not to allow any suspicions to be raised, for any of the strange interventions he had been making. And that was fine with her. It was futile, anyway, to try to explain Esmera's appearances out of nowhere, any more than it was to explain anything Aggelos did. After all, they both seemed to keep turning up in her life like guardian angels to save the day. And who would mind an angel coming into their lives to do that? Katie gave Spyros a wide grin. 'I seem to have some wonderful friends, Mr Spyros, and that's all there is to it.'

Chapter 35

The BBQ party was well underway. Everyone had finished their delicious meal. Eva and Julia, still wearing their widest smiles, were now bringing out to the tables plates of tiny *baklava* and *kataifi* treats, much to the guests' delight. Spyros and Matina seemed just as tireless, taking turns to dance with the guests and to sit at the tables, mingling with everyone.

The hotel guests danced to popular folk songs, laughed and kept refilling their glasses, their cheer rising into the night air that was rich with the aromas of jasmine and honeysuckle. Faint buzzing from a multitude of moths echoed from the lit lanterns, and in the lush greenery by the whitewashed walls, fireflies danced in the semidarkness, their radiant green flecks pulsating eerily.

High in the sky, the aura of the luminous moon reached out to caress the twinkling stars with shimmering tendrils. Underneath, the sea lapped gently on the shore, its alluring sigh only audible in the courtyard in between songs, a few quiet moments at a time.

After their meal, people kept getting up to dance to the lively folk music. Elise and Babis were among them; earlier, they'd sat together to eat. Seeing that his unfortunate shortcoming had vanished into thin air, Elise had no trouble sitting or dancing with him. Still, she never stopped observing Aggelos and Katie, never completely relaxing.

At some point, Elise and Babis got up to dance the *kalamatiano* and Aggelos went to join them.

Katie, on the other hand, remained seated beside Esmera, who had Chloe on her lap, a hand caressing the girl's hair. Chloe was gazing into Esmera's face, adoration alight in her eyes.

Katie watched them, her brow furrowed. The child had always been friendly, but she'd never seen her warm up to someone like that. If she didn't know better, she'd think she and Esmera were well acquainted. Chloe seemed to thrive in the old woman's affection, and her mere presence. She hadn't seen Esmera at the hotel before. *Then, how does Chloe know her? When did these two bond like this?*

'Hey! A penny for your thoughts!' piped up Aggelos taking a seat beside Katie, breaking her reverie. He slipped a hand under the table and squeezed hers that rested on her lap.

Katie sat up straight and smiled at him. 'Sorry, I was miles away. And it's way past my bedtime.' She put up her free hand to stifle a yawn as if to validate her response.

'Nonsense. The night is still young. Come! They're finally playing a slow song. Dance with me!' Aggelos pulled her gently to her feet and Katie didn't resist. As he led her to the dance floor holding her hand, she took in his strong shoulders and back, and the wispy little hairs that always teased her from the nape of his neck. She loved to brush them with her fingertips when she kissed him. Her heart gave a thump at the very thought.

They hadn't had a single moment alone tonight. *Shall I ask him to my room later? Would he mind if I took the first step, or would he prefer that I wait for him to do it?* Her mind drew a blank, but when he stopped by the other dancing couples to face her, she realized that was all by the by. What mattered was this given moment. It was enough to do what she was doing right now, just holding his gaze, feeling lost. Lost, and blissfully found. *One moment at a time, Katie. Happiness is now. Dance and let things unfold.*

Katie put her arms around his neck as he curled his around her waist. The feeling of closeness, as a slow, sweet melody played, was enough to make her feel lightheaded. He chuckled and she pulled away to look at him. 'What?' she whispered, so the magic of the moment wouldn't break.

Aggelos pointed with his head to his left. 'There! Look at Mrs Sparks dancing on her own.'

'Oh my goodness!' The two of them giggled, despite themselves, at the sight. As much as they loved the woman, she was such a mad hatter that it was impossible to watch her and not burst into laughter. Not only was she swaying to the slow song on her own, her arms raised to rest on an invisible man's shoulders, she was also chattering endlessly to herself. Her chin was raised, her heavily made-up eyes gazing into the neat lines of twinkling fairy lights hanging overhead.

'This woman is definitely a few French fries short of a happy meal,' said Aggelos. He'd heard the expression in a movie the night before as he watched TV sprawled out on a sofa in the hotel lounge. He broke into a wide grin, delighted he could use it.

It made Katie break into hysterics, then she slapped his arm playfully. 'Shame on you. Such a lovely lady and all!'

'Of course she's lovely. But she's also certified. Let's not confuse the two.'

'Katie tittered. 'I wonder who she thinks she's dancing with.'

'No one you know,' said Aggelos without thinking, then brought a hand to his mouth, alarm flashing in his eyes.

Katie arched her brows. 'What?'

He cleared his throat and looked away. 'Sorry, Katie. Don't pay attention to my nonsensical babble. I've drunk a lot . . .'

Katie smiled and looked around her as they continued to sway gently together. The band had moved on to slow songs, so she wasn't surprised she couldn't spot Elise and Babis dancing now. Elise's tolerance wouldn't reach that point. Katie's eyes scanned the sitting area and, sure enough, she found them sitting at their table, Babis puffing and fanning his face, while Elise was sitting up straight, her eyes pinned on the dance floor. *Is she looking at us?* Katie had long decided she liked Elise but found her over-protective attitude intense at times.

She looked away, and a satisfied smile spread across her lips when she spotted Matina and Spyros sitting together at a remote table with Eva and Julia. They all looked beat. Eva had removed her shoes under the table and was rubbing her feet together. Julia had her elbows on the table, one hand supporting her head. As for Matina, she'd leaned against Spyros, her head on his shoulder as he held her tenderly against himself. It was such a sweet sight.

'Aaah . . .'

'What is it?'

'My bosses. Look at them! They seem so happy together. You should have heard them earlier, though. They had the mother of all rows indoors. Eva and I didn't know what to do. Thank goodness, they seem to have made up now.'

'Yes, looks like it,' said Aggelos, a sweet smile playing on his lips.

Katie studied him, her expression bright. 'Look at you, huh? You came here and fixed everything.'

'Me?'

'Yes, you. For example, Mrs Matina used to be very stiff when I first got here. Now, she's all jokes and smiles.'

'Nothing to do with me, I assure you, Katie.'

'Perhaps. But you definitely had something to do with *that*!' She pointed with her head to their right, where Eddie was dancing with Sarah in his arms. He had a huge grin on his face and was holding her by the waist as if she were made of gold and porcelain, both precious and fragile. Their eyes radiated warmth and joy as they faced each other, lost to the world.

'Aww! I am glad I had something to do with that!'

Katie tilted her head. 'You're never going to tell me how you do it, are you?'

'How I do what?'

'You know, how you produced a Greek-English phrase book from your pocket when Eddie needed to talk to Sarah. How you happened to have cheese when Mrs Sparks' hamster escaped from its cage. How you seemed to know Chloe before even I and Eva set eyes on her. And she was so timid at first, Eva and I could hardly get a word out of her. Now, she's even warming up to strangers, like Esmera. And as for Mr Spyros, I'm still not convinced you didn't do something magical to save him from drowning at sea that day. Miracles never seem to cease around you, Aggelos . . .'

'Katie . . .' He leaned in, bringing his face so close to hers his breath tickled her lips. 'I'll let you in on a little secret. There's no such thing as magic or miracles. These things only happen when you have faith. Maybe Spyros believed he'd be saved that day. Or maybe someone else out there did.'

'Are you talking about God? Are you saying it had nothing to do with you at all?'

He winked. 'I didn't say that. I just don't want to take all the credit.' He gave a devilish smirk, then gave an easy laugh as he squeezed her against him.

'You're insufferable, you know that?' She caressed his cheek, her eyes widening. 'And yet, you've come here changing everything. I . . .' She bit her lip, her expression turning serious.

Sparks of mystification ignited in his eyes. 'Go on, what were you going to say?'

She chewed her lips, then gave a feeble smile. 'Well, if I didn't know better I'd think you're not even of this world.'

He held her closer, his hands gripping her waist. 'How do you mean?'

'I swear, Aggelos, your name means 'Angel' and that's exactly what you are to me. It's like this place is surrounded by a protective aura and, call me naïve but, I believe it's all because of you. There doesn't seem to be anyone and anything here you haven't taken under your wing. My bosses, Mrs Sparks, Chloe, Eddie . . . even that tourist lady you saved from drowning the other day.'

Aggelos stared at her aghast, not knowing how to respond to that. She took it as a sign of surprise and felt silly for having said these words. She swallowed hard and focused her eyes on the dancing couple beside them. 'I assure you, Aggelos, I don't often call people angels. I've known all sorts of people, but no one like you. You . . . you . . .' She met his eyes and lost her words again, this time for good.

'Oh Katie! If only . . . if only I could . . .'

'If only you could . . . what?'

Aggelos gave a soft sigh and squeezed her against him, then leaned in and kissed her tenderly. A few blissful moments later, when he pulled back and looked into her eyes, he found them huge, wistful, but pretended he didn't notice. He knew what the next logical step to take with her was, that is, what it would be, if only he were human like she was. He wanted nothing else more but didn't know how to go about it. Not really. How could he possibly do this?

'So . . .' she said, unaware of his inner anguish as she rested her hand on the nape of his neck, where those tiny hairs danced in the sea breeze, beckoning to her, wispy and glistening under the light like spider webs.

She exhaled slowly. 'It's getting late. I think I'll be leaving soon. How about you?' Her expression was hopeful and so transparent he'd have had to be blind not to see it. But he was afraid he'd let her down, or make a fool of himself. Sure, he had a vague idea of what intimacy with a woman behind a closed bedroom door involved. He'd watched enough late night movies to know that what stirred deep in his belly every time he kissed and held her to him, was real enough to help him along. Yet, the thought of actually doing this sort of thing panicked him beyond words.

'Aggelos?' she asked, her voice frail. He was chewing his lower lip, the look in his eyes distant.

'Katie, I—' He was shaking his head now, and she saw the rejection in his eyes. It caused her heart to sink. The song ended then, and the band announced they'd soon be leaving, and that they'd end their routine with a couple of *tsifteteli* songs. At the lively sound of *tsifteteli*, the couples retreated from the floor, while a host of women of all ages, from little girls to grandmothers, took to the stage to shake their bodies to belly dancing, Greek-style. It was the perfect timing for Aggelos to take Katie by the hand and return to their table.

Chapter 36

Back at the table, Chloe was sitting alone. Katie gave a beaming smile, doing her best to hide her disappointment from before. 'Chloe, how come you're sitting on your own? Has Esmera left?'

Chloe smiled widely, her eyes twinkling. 'Yes, you just missed her. She left in a hurry, without saying goodbye to anyone, but not before leaving this behind.' She pointed at a sealed bottle of wine on the table.

Katie hadn't noticed it till now. 'Wine? Esmera left this?' It was then that she caught a glimpse of Aggelos locking eyes with Chloe and giggling. He was sitting beside the little girl, his arm around her protectively. Katie grimaced. 'What? What's so funny?'

Aggelos waved his arms about. 'Nothing's funny. This is just Esmera all over, that's all. She has such a giving heart.'

'Giving? Towards whom? Who's the wine for?'

'It's a gift for Matina and Spyros,' replied Chloe. 'Esmera said to make sure to tell them to drink it on their own, and not to give a drop to anyone else.'

Katie curled her lip. 'That's weird.'

'Not if you know Esmera as well as we do,' said Aggelos. 'You forget she's a gypsy. And gypsies, well, they have their way to create magic for people who could use some help.'

'Magic? Are you serious?'

'Yes, Katie. Now, can you please do the honours and give it to your bosses for us?'

'But, is it safe?' She picked up the bottle, raising it against the electric light to peer at the liquid inside. 'What if she put something weird in there?'

Chloe chuckled. 'Like what? Bat wings and rat tails?'

Katie pursed her lips and put the bottle back down. She felt light-headed from all the drinking as it was. Having this surreal conversation certainly didn't help to keep her sane. Before she could find something to say, Aggelos put up a hand. 'No need to worry, Katie. Besides, remember what I said? There's no magic . . . only faith.'

'And love. Definitely love,' interrupted Chloe.

'Yes, love. Love more than anything else, actually,' said Aggelos tousling Chloe's hair. 'Esmera has been teaching you well, kiddo.'

Katie huffed and put up her hands. 'Hey, stop it. You guys are getting all weird on me.'

Aggelos winked. 'Just make sure to tell your bosses to drink the wine alone. And soon. Esmera's magic will do the rest.'

'It's her own wine, you know,' added Chloe, beaming. 'She has a vineyard near the hilltop.' The child pointed vaguely at the night scene in front of her. From the courtyard where they sat, guests could marvel at a panoramic vista of Asimi and the remote hills throughout the day.

Katie raised a single brow and took the non-descript, unlabelled bottle into her hands again. 'Her own wine, huh? A woman of many surprises.'

'That's for sure,' said Aggelos. 'It's very kind of her to do this for them.'

Katie cradled the bottle in her hands and gave a smile. 'Let's give it to Matina and Spyros then. Do you want to come with me, Chloe?'

Chloe's face hardened while Aggelos shook his head from side to side.

A deep frown etched Katie's forehead. 'What? Surely, you've met them both by now, Chloe?'

Chloe shook her head profusely, her eyes darting to Aggelos, who put up a hand. 'Katie, I think we've discussed this. You're not to ask questions about Chloe meeting or not meeting your bosses, remember?'

Katie opened her mouth to protest when she saw Chloe's eyes grow huge, her hands clutching the armrests of her chair. Katie turned around to see what she was looking at and saw Matina and Spyros approaching. They were smiling dreamily, their arms all over each other. *What's the matter with these two tonight? They're like a pair of love-sick puppies! Are they drunk?*

Katie waved them over, hoping to help Chloe get over her hang-up about meeting them once and for all. Yet, when she greeted Matina and Spyros and turned her head around again to make the introductions, she found she was the only one sitting at the table. *What the—?*

###

A few minutes later, having handed Esmera's gift of homemade wine to her bosses, Katie said goodbye and left the courtyard behind. By then, the band and most of the guests had already departed. Only a half-dozen guests had stayed behind, old friends of the owners, who were enjoying a couple of last quiet drinks before bedtime. Eva had retired earlier to bed and only Julia was still hosting with Matina and Spyros. Eddie was sitting alone with Sarah putting the odd cd in a portable stereo to entertain the last guests at low volume.

When she emerged via the gate into the front garden, Katie changed her mind about going to bed. Instead, she headed for the beach, drawn by the soft sound of the waves lapping on the shore in the semidarkness. She took her sandals off and gave a long sigh, the soles of her feet almost crying from relief when they touched the cool sand. They had been burning for hours from all the dancing. *This is bliss . . .*

As she began to amble towards the edge of the shore, she half-closed her eyes, relishing the cool breeze that tickled her face, neck and shoulders. She was so absorbed in the pleasure of it all, that she barely registered the sound of her name coming from behind her.

'Katie, wait.'

It was Aggelos walking over to her, his voice tender and soft, causing a shiver of longing to shoot down her spine. Somehow, instead of delighting her, the feeling caused her pain. She wasn't even sure she was pleased he had come looking for her. She was now standing at the edge of the shore. The sea foamed between her toes, tickling her, but she stood there expressionless, facing the water, waiting for him to near her, and still unsure she wanted him to.

As soon as he came to stand behind her, Aggelos took hold of her arm and gently swung her around. 'Katie? You okay?'

'Oh, what an honour! You decided to show up again, did you?' she spat out. Her anger had come out of nowhere and it caught her by surprise.

'Easy, tiger!' She was slurring. Badly. 'I think you've had a few drinks too many, missy. Care to sit down with me?'

'No! I won't do anything you ask me to.' She shook her head from side to side. 'Absolutely not. I don't trust you.'

'You don't trust me? Why do you say that?'

'What was that disappearing act back there for? You and Chloe. Why did you leave like that? Matina and Spyros don't bite, you know.'

Aggelos put out a hand to caress her hair but she pulled away. His touch hurt too much. So did all the mystery that surrounded him. She'd had big plans for tonight. Once more, he seemed too aloof to ever let things happen.

Aggelos tilted his head and let go of her. He watched her as she stumbled into the water a little further, kicking her heels up, splashing water all over her dress. Slowly, he walked up to her, not caring about his jeans and shoes getting soaked. He put his arms around her waist, pulling her to him.

Katie closed her eyes and, intoxicated as she was, tilted to the side, but Aggelos held her in time so she wouldn't fall. She gave a luxurious sigh, her head tipped back, her eyes half-closed.

His embrace felt warm. It shot arrows of bliss into her heart. Then, slowly, she opened her eyes and stared into the dark sea, the huge, flowing mass that sparkled like diamonds under the moonlight. The scene was so enchanting it caused her heart to swell and, just like that, tears began to flow down her face. *Oh no . . . So I love him enough to cry now? Well done, Katie. Welcome to the Land of Heartache. You bought the ticket. You boarded the flight. Enjoy.*

Unaware of her inner turmoil, Aggelos turned her around gently so she could face him. This time, when he placed a tender hand on her cheek to wipe her tears, she didn't pull away. Instead, she gave a faint smile and lowered her gaze, spent.

'Oh Katie . . . How I hate hurting you like this! If only I could tell you everything!'

She looked up, her eyes searching his. 'Yes! Yes! Tell me everything! I promise I will listen to the last word. And I'll try my best to understand. I think. But you may have to get me a strong coffee first.' She brought a hand to her forehead and winced.

'Katie, I am bound to secrecy. I cannot tell you. Not tonight anyway. But I promise, I will, before it's time to go. I'll tell you one thing tonight, though, and I don't care if you're too drunk to listen.' He gave a sweet smile that made the blue in his eyes seem deeper, like seas that invited her in. 'I love you, Katie. More than you can ever know.'

Katie's sleepy eyes snapped wide open, a huge smile lighting up her face. 'You love me?'

'Yes. Is my love enough, Katie? Will you settle for that?'

'Yes. Yes, of course! I love you too, Aggelos! I think I've loved you from the very first day I met you.'

He squeezed her against him and gave a wicked smirk. 'Really? Did I look that hot on the ferry with my t-shirt soiled in orange juice?'

Katie opened her mouth to tell him she probably loved him before even that, waiting for him all her life, when his lips came hot and urgent to seal hers, passion rising inside them like writhing flames, about to consume everything in sight. When they pulled apart, she took him by the hand and, without a word, led him to a further point along the beach, where the hotel's flood lights didn't reach.

There, under the shimmering moonlight, lying down with him on the cool sand, she gave him all the reasons he ever needed to stay, and he, in return, gave her all the love she needed to keep believing that, somehow, he'd never leave.

Chapter 37

When Katie walked into the kitchen early the next morning for breakfast, she found Eva and Julia giggling away. As soon as the women saw her, they waved frantically to her to approach.

Katie obliged them wide-eyed, a spring in her step.

'Katie! You won't believe what I saw this morning!' said Julia, Eva sniggering beside her.

Blank-faced, Katie waited. Julia leaned in and whispered, 'Spyros didn't sleep in his bed last night!'

Katie frowned. 'Didn't he?'

'He certainly didn't! And guess where I found him this morning!' Without waiting this time, Julia gave a loud guffaw, then winked. 'He didn't see me but I saw him coming out of Mrs Matina's bedroom with her! And get this: they were holding hands!'

Katie's eyes turned huge like dinner plates. 'Really?' They all knew the couple slept in separate bedrooms, and the discussions they occasionally had about this were harmless. If anything, they expressed the wish their bosses would find a way one day to come closer again as a couple.

According to Matina they no longer slept in the same bed because Spyros snored, and Spyros' reason was that Matina liked to read till late and her bedside light bothered him. Still, they all knew these were just excuses. The simple answer was they'd just drifted apart. But now, it looked like something wonderful had finally happened to bring them closer again. Literally.

'Do you suppose this was their first . . . you know . . . in a long time?' asked Eva.

Julia pressed her lips together and shook her head. 'Honestly, I don't know. Besides, it's none of our business. But I'll tell you this: those two left the party and went straight up to her bedroom last night!'

More chuckles and giggles ensued, and it all sounded wonderful. After the precious time Katie had spent with Aggelos on the beach the night before, she was already on a natural high. To hear this great piece of news about Matina and Spyros served to make Katie's morning seem just perfect. She had already put the kettle on for her tea and was about to help herself to some cereal when Spyros barged in through the double doors, a beaming smile on his face.

'Hello, ladies! And what a fine morning this is! I say, the party was an absolute hit! Never before have I seen so many guests stay behind that late!'

'Yes, indeed, Mr Spyros. And you look bright and breezy this morning! Did you have a good night's sleep?' said Julia. She picked up a piece of walnut cake from a tray and began to munch, turning away from him slightly so he couldn't see her wicked smirk.

'Yes, great, thank you. But, I must get on! Work can't wait, you know,' said Spyros rather nervously when he noticed the other two women shared a knowing look, then dropped their gaze to the fruit bowl before them at the same time. 'Erm, carry on with your work, ladies. Don't let me bother you.'

'Can I help prepare your breakfast, Mr Spyros?' asked Eva.

Spyros grimaced and flicked his wrist at her. 'No worries. I'll just get a cup of coffee, that's all, then I'll be off to do some planting.' He fussed about with the percolator, not sure if he remembered how to get it to work, while Eva brought him a large mug and a slice of walnut cake, then decided to sit at the table and let her prepare the coffee for him, after all.

Eva set the machine to make a few cups of coffee, just in case, while Julia began to comment about the previous evening.

'And I loved the band,' she carried on, 'where did you find them, Mr Spyros?'

'Don't look at me,' said Spyros. 'Our Katie was the one we owe this too,' then turning to Katie, 'I'd like to thank you once again for that. You saved our skin back there.'

Katie was standing near Eva nursing her mug of tea and gave a sweet smile in response. 'Oh, I don't deserve any credit for that. If we owe it to someone, that's my friend Esmera, who brought her musician friends to the party.'

Spyros tilted his head. 'Indeed. But how did she know, Katie? Did you ask her for help when it turned out I'd forgotten to call the band?'

Katie opened her mouth, then pressed her lips together again. How could she explain something that didn't make sense even to her? 'To tell you the truth, Mr Spyros, I have no idea how this happened. I never told her, but it's like she knew. I think she may be a little psychic . . . She has a tendency to come to the rescue. It's part of her charm.' She thought this could have been said about Aggelos too, but didn't voice it.

Instead, she turned to Eva, bright-faced. 'Say, did you see Aggelos play the tambourine last night? He seemed to have done this before. Such confidence!' Eva smiled and nodded to agree.

'Tambourine?' asked Julia. 'I don't remember seeing a tambourine player.'

'Neither do I,' said Spyros, huffing. 'Exactly how much did you ladies drink last night?'

'What are you talking about, Mr Spyros?' asked Eva.

'Mr Spyros, Aggelos is one of our guests,' piped up Katie. 'He's a tall guy. *Seriously* tall. How could you have missed him playing with the band?'

'A midget, more like!' said Julia, leaning against Mr Spyros, who let out a howl of laughter.

Eva put her hands on her hips. 'Don't mind them, Katie. They're having you on. Besides, Aggelos is too gorgeous to miss.'

Katie registered the shaking heads of Spyros and Julia and tried again. 'Granted, he played only during the first couple of songs and then sat for his dinner. Maybe that's why you missed him.'

'Maybe Julia missed him since she was serving at the time but I certainly couldn't have,' said Spyros. 'I was with you when the band played the first song, remember? But there was no tambourine player. I'd have remembered, Katie,' insisted Spyros.

For the first time, Katie was stunned to silence. When Eva protested again, Katie shook her head at her, signalling her with her eyes not to push the point further. Maybe Aggelos' weird stunts went further than she'd anticipated. One more mystery to pester him about, she imagined.

Now, her mind was whirling and she barely followed the conversation among the others that now moved on to other, light-hearted subjects. She took a few more gulps from her tea and tried to put her mind in order while the others chattered and drank from their cups.

Moments later, Spyros turned to Katie, his eyes sparkling with mirth. 'I say, Katie, your friend Esmera is something else! Not only did she save the party by bringing the band, but she brought an exquisite present as well. The wine she left Matina and me was pure nectar! Please thank her for us. Mind you, it went to my head, Matina's too. It . . .' He shook his head, then registered a giggle from Eva, who struggled to stifle it. She was doing dishes at the time, her back to the others.

Spyros stood to his feet and picked up his mug, then cleared his throat. 'Well, I'd better not waste another moment. Lots to be done in the garden. Where's Eddie, Julia? He wasn't at the front.'

'I hope you don't mind, Mr Spyros. I sent him to the pharmacy in Asimi to pick up something for me. He won't be long.'

'That's fine. Just send him round the back when he returns.' With these words, Spyros opened the back door and stepped outside into a glorious morning. The sun was rising on a clear blue sky where not a single cloud was to be seen. When the door closed, Julia gave a sigh. 'My Eddie sure enjoyed himself last night. I think he's in love!'

'You don't say!' said the other two in unison. They'd all been watching him dance with Sarah all night. More laughter ensued and then Julia relayed to Eva and Katie all about her love-struck son and how upset he was that Sarah was leaving soon. To hear all that, caused Katie's mind to wander.

As the others continued to chat, she pondered on how ephemeral and cruel summer love was, imagining that when it's all over, it must hurt like hell to lose the object of your desire overnight. But then, wouldn't it still be worth it? Wouldn't it be better to love and suffer the pain, rather than shy away from it all and miss so many precious, unforgettable moments?

Katie nodded, to no one in particular, deciding summer love was too sweet to ever turn it down. And even with the certainty of heartache at the end of it, there was still hope. Perhaps what she had with Aggelos was real. Perhaps it wouldn't be over the day he left.

She was engrossed in her thoughts so much she had long stopped contributing to the conversation. Eva noticed first. Katie was sitting at the table clutching her mug, her eyes staring, misty and glassy, into space. Eva opened her mouth to tease her when distressing shouting echoed from the corridor. The words were muffled, indecipherable, yet they all recognized the voice. Impossibly, it was Matina's. The three jolted upright and rushed out to find her.

Chapter 38

The three arrived at reception just in time to witness Matina swinging her door wide open, tears streaming down her face, her expression distraught.

Eva put her arms around her. 'Mrs Matina! What's the matter?'

Matina raked her hair that flowed freely over her shoulders, then planted a palm on her forehead with a groan.

'Come! Come sit here for a while!' offered Julia leading her to a chair.

Matina plopped herself down like a lump of lead, her hand still on her head, her eyes closed.

The others stood in front of her, shocked at the sight, not knowing what to think. Eva rushed to the kitchen to fetch her a glass of water and in the process called out to Mr Spyros to come over as well. They returned to reception, Spyros beside himself with worry. He knelt in front of Matina, his hands holding both of hers. 'What is it, my love? What on earth happened? Please tell us!'

Matina had a few sips of water, returned the glass to Eva with trembling hands, and drew an unsteady deep breath. 'I've just received a call from one of the village women. It's the community centre. Burglars broke into it last night.' She raised her eyes to meet her husband's, then began to cry. They gave her a hankie to wipe her tears and she continued, 'Many of the women are there now trying to help. The teacher, who has a spare key, let them in.'

'Is anything missing? What did they say?' asked Spyros.

Matina let out a laborious sigh. 'The burglars took the computers and the stereo.'

'How did they get in?' asked Eva.

'Through one of the front windows . . . The women found it open; the glass and the shutters were broken. Luckily the door was left intact. The teacher will call a repairer to install new glass panes and shutters on the window. No one has called the police yet. I said I'll do it. I just need a moment to calm down first.' Matina swallowed hard, a hand planted on her chest.

'Any damages inside?'

'Everything has been upturned, Spyros! It's a mess. Shredded paper and broken glass everywhere.' Matina grew increasingly upset, fresh tears brewing in her eyes.

'All right, Matina! Don't say any more. Calm down now,' soothed Spyros, putting his arms around her. She broke into tears again just as two guests approached from the entrance, so he took her to the office, away from prying eyes. He led her to sit in her chair, prompting Eva and Julia to leave them, but beckoned Katie to stay.

Katie closed the door and sat numbly on a chair. Spyros stood by his wife, a hand squeezing her shoulder. 'It's not so bad, Matina, if you think about it,' he soothed. 'Thankfully no one was harmed. That's what's important. And we are lucky to be part of such a caring, close-knit community. See how the village women rushed to the centre to help? I am sure they're doing a great job tidying up the place.'

Matina gave a faint smile. 'Yes, Spyros. You are right. And I should go as soon as possible to help as well.'

'Of course, you must, but our top priority is to call the police. Maybe they can retrieve the stolen goods, who knows? But even if they don't, material things can always be replaced. We are lucky it happened when no one was inside.'

Hearing these sensible, comforting words helped Matina to calm down at last. She couldn't help feeling admiration for her husband, who was so level-headed, so capable of saying the right things to soothe her angst. With a faint smile, she threw her sodden hankie in the bin and raised her red-rimmed eyes to smile at Spyros.

In return, he left a kiss on her cheek, then dialled the number for the local police station. Matina reported the burglary and, by the time she hung up, she looked a lot calmer.

Spyros seemed pleased. 'Katie, would you mind accompanying Matina to the community centre? I'm expecting a handyman to help with some maintenance work this morning and I can't leave, but I don't want her to go there on her own.'

Katie was happy to oblige. Matina expressed her gratitude for that on their way to the village as she drove them in her car. Once again, Katie was astonished by how casual, how easy, their conversations were these days, as if the scary woman she had met on that awkward first day at the hotel had never existed.

###

Matina parked the car outside the community centre to find its doors wide-open, locals of all ages coming and going. Everyone seemed to be there, children included, making a beeline to an empty barrel outside to throw into it torn up paper and odd scraps of broken plastic and wood. Some women had brought their brooms from home and were carrying dustpans full of debris to be disposed of outside. By the time Katie and Matina had left the car to stand by the gate and marvel at the busy sight, the locals had gathered before them, the children rushing to the front, grim colours of concern shadowing their little faces.

'Mrs Matina, you came,' said one of the little girls. It was Klara, the baker's daughter, a little angel of flowing blond hair and green eyes. She was only seven and had a pair of amazing dancing feet and the voice of a nightingale. But that wasn't the reason Matina loved Klara as one of her favourite pupils. It was because Klara had the knack of gazing at her deeply with her green mesmerizing eyes. Matina always cherished the sight. Once again, Klara gazed at Matina as she tilted her head and took her hand. 'Mrs Matina, I brought everyone here for you today. So you're not upset.'

'What? What do you mean you brought them?' asked Matina, kneeling in front of her.

'It's what the little girl asked me to do.'

'What little girl, my darling? I don't understand.'

Klara's mother approached them to put a firm hand on her daughter's shoulder. 'Don't mind her, Mrs Matina. She didn't make much sense when she told me either. I knew it was mindless children's talk so I nearly dismissed it. But she insisted so I came here to check, just to shut her up.' She chuckled loudly, her ruddy cheeks turning even more crimson. 'Turned out the centre was broken into, after all. That's when I decided to call you.'

Matina ignored the woman as she often did. She could never stand her. The reasons were many. For one, she was indifferent to so many precious things such as the words coming out of an innocent child's mouth. 'It was you who tipped off the village?' Matina asked Klara. 'But how did you know this? The robbers must have come in late at night. Weren't you in bed at that time, my darling?'

'Of course, Mrs Matina! I only found out this morning at the schoolyard where I'd gone to play.'

'Did someone tell you there? Who was it?' Matina saw Klara's mother roll her eyes but ignored that too. Once again, she was drawn by the girl's gaze that said so much. It had given her comfort many times. Today was no different.

'I don't know her name. I'd never seen her before today. She was around my age, and looked a little like me.'

'In what way?'

Klara shrugged a single shoulder. 'I don't know why I said that. I think maybe we have the same eyes. The same colour.'

Matina's heart gave a thump. She bit her lip and nodded, encouraging Klara to continue.

'But her hair was different. I am blond but she had long dark hair. It was frizzy too while mine is not. She was sitting by herself looking very sad. So I went and talked to her and she asked me to share a message with you all.' The girl took a deep breath before saying, 'She said this, word for word: "Tell everyone to go to the community centre and help my mummy. I don't want her to get upset".'

Matina gasped but then seemed to try to compose herself. She swallowed hard and mumbled, 'Who is her mummy? Did she say?'

'No, she didn't. But I think she meant *you* . . . Your eyes are the same,' she replied, raising her little hand to point a delicate finger at Matina. Beside her, her mother screwed up her face and looked skyward.

'Like I said, Mrs Matina, children's talk. And goodness knows my Klara loves to babble! Don't let her bother you any more. Come on, Klara, let's go inside and help put some more stuff into boxes.' Without waiting for a response, the baker's wife pulled Klara by the hand leading her up the steps and into the building.

As they walked away, the girl kept looking over her shoulder at Matina. The compassion in her eyes was palpable and with it, something else resonated in Matina's heart. It was something she'd been struggling for a long time to keep to herself and not express it. Once the girl and her mother had disappeared through the front door, Matina swallowed a painful lump in her throat and turned to Katie.

'Come on, Katie, we have a lot of work to do.' With that, Matina beckoned everyone to follow her inside, then marched up the steps. She delegated tasks and got everyone organised, her assertiveness surprising them all. And if they thought it was strange she seemed so unperturbed by this unprecedented upheaval in their quiet community, it was because only Matina knew the kind of comfort Klara's words had given her.

Chapter 39

In the early afternoon, Matina and Katie returned to the hotel. Spyros sat with them in Matina's office for a while but then had to go outside to finish the gardening. As soon as he left, Matina offered Katie to stay and have a cup of coffee and a snack with her.

Katie was happy to accept. A few minutes later they were sipping from their mugs and munching greedily some cheese-and-pepper pastries that Eva had brought in straight from the oven.

As they ate in silence, Katie thought about Matina's initial distress when she'd heard the bad news, and it was understandable. But something had changed about her since then. What was it? Could it be what little Klara had told her in the street?

Katie had watched their exchange and seen the look on Matina's face. What was that all about? She seemed to understand what the little girl had told her, yet her words had made no sense. How could Matina be that mysterious little girl's mother? Matina's only child had passed away.

When Matina spoke then, Katie snapped out of her state of deep contemplation, her shoulders jumping. She was still cradling her coffee mug on her lap as she glanced through the wide window pane at the distant view of Asimi.

'Sorry, I was miles away,' Katie replied with a distracted smile.

'That's all right, Katie. And I must apologize. I had you working very hard this morning, and I realize manual labour is not in your job description.'

Katie waved the words away. 'Please, don't mention it. I was glad to help. And it was wonderful that the village women all came to assist us. We tidied up in no time. Even the man who repaired the window came in a rush from Apollonia.'

'Yes, I am very grateful. Everyone was wonderful. It's just . . . It's just that . . .'

Katie leaned forward in her seat. 'Yes?'

Matina shook her head. 'Oh, never mind. But . . .' She raised her chin and looked at Katie straight in the eye. 'Katie, if I tell you a secret, will you promise to keep it to yourself?'

'Of course.'

'It's something I've been sensing very intensely for a while . . . at first, I thought I was going mad, but the feeling grew more and more real. And today, today when little Klara spoke to me, well, finally I knew I wasn't crazy.'

'I'm sorry, Mrs Matina, I don't understand.'

'I know, I apologize. Listen, it's about my little girl. I trust you may have heard from the staff I was the mother of a little girl once?'

Katie pressed her lips together, then nodded. Her voice came out frail when she said, 'Yes. Yes, I heard that she died.'

'I lost her from a terrible disease when she was only seven . . .' She wiped a single tear from her cheek. It had escaped from her eyes without her even knowing. Today, unlike any other day, it was hard to control the pain inside.

She took one look at Katie and knew it was all right. She saw the compassion in her eyes. Matina had confided in Eva in the past, Mrs Sparks even, but Katie felt different. She could tell Katie anything. Even that big secret she'd been hiding from her husband. Keeping it to herself had been driving her insane.

Matina took a steadying breath and leaned forward. 'Katie, do you believe in ghosts?'

'Ghosts?'

'Yes. Spirits of the dead. Because if you don't, you'll probably think I'm mad if I tell you what I think Klara said to me today.'

'Yes, I think I do believe. I've never had an encounter with a spirit, of course, but I believe in God . . . and in angels . . . I believe in life after death. So, why not? I haven't really thought about it much, to be honest, Mrs Matina. Just say what you have to say. I promise I won't tell, or judge, if that's what you want to hear.'

Matina smiled widely, a deep sigh escaping from her lips. 'Thank you. I guess that's what I'm after, yes.'

'Go ahead, I'm all ears.'

'Katie, I believe the spirit of my little girl is in this hotel. There! Now, I've said it.'

Katie gave a frown. 'You mean like, haunting it?'

'Yes. But not in the way you'd expect. Not like her spirit's trapped here. I feel it's more like she's here by choice. For me.'

'For you? Why do you believe that?'

Matina let out a long exhalation and gazed outside the window. Her gaze rested for a few moments on the sails of the distant windmill that turned slowly, effortlessly, in the quiet wind. The sight of the white, tireless sails that stood the test of time always gave her comfort. She turned to Katie again, her face bright this time. 'I think my little girl is here because she knows I haven't got over the pain yet. She's here to help me heal. But you know what's stranger than anything else, Katie? It's the fact that this is new. My daughter died ten years ago but it's only recently that I've started to, you know, feel her.'

'Recently? How recently?'

'I don't know . . . a month maybe, two, tops!'

'But, in what way do you feel her?'

'In subtle ways, small ways . . . like, often, when I work here on my computer, I may feel a tingle on my face or a caress on my shoulder, out of the blue. But instead of freaking me out, it feels comforting; full of love and compassion. And then, one morning, out of the blue, a note fell off my pinboard.'

She pointed to a cork-lined board on the wall beside her. 'You see that sticky note, Katie? It reads, "You're not a drop in the ocean; you're the entire ocean in a drop." It's my favourite quote by Rumi, and I put it on there to remind me that I am strong enough to endure hardship in my life. Then one day, like I said, it fell off the board on its own, pin and all. I never touched it, or had the door or the window open, so it couldn't have been moved by a gust of wind. And yet, there it was, flying off the board and landing on my desk right in front of me, the right way up and the right way around. As if placed there by an invisible hand for me to read.'

Katie felt a shiver coursing down her spine. 'Seriously?'

'Do you agree with me that this can have no logical explanation?'

'If it happened exactly as you relayed it, then, yes, I can only agree with you.'

'Yes, that's *exactly* how it happened. And do you know when that was?' Matina's eyes glinted and, without waiting for an answer, she added, 'The day Spyros nearly drowned at sea. The note fell an hour or so before the storm broke, when Spyros was out fishing.'

'What? Unbelievable!'

'Yes! And I believe it was my little girl who left me this message. Somehow she must have known this was going to happen, and she wanted to let me know in advance that Spyros was going to be all right. I think it was she who saved him that day. Of course, when panic struck I didn't think of it; it was only days later when I connected it to the note falling off the board. Then it all made perfect sense to me.'

Katie scratched her head as she contemplated this, her brow heavily creased. She'd thought Aggelos had intervened that day, having access to some top secret weather-controlling military device. But Aggelos had been vague about it. And now, as if that mystery weren't enough, her boss was saying it was a ghost that had saved Spyros that day, after all. *What is this? The Twilight Zone?* Still, Katie remained open to whatever Matina had to share. It was strange that note had fallen off the board of its own accord. What if she was right? *I work in a haunted hotel? Cool!*

'I can see how hard this must be for you to swallow,' continued Matina, 'But trust me, Katie, I'm not crazy. What Klara told me today made me sure of that, at last.'

'Klara?' *Yes, of course!* Katie's eyes lit up. 'Now, I understand! I heard what she told you but it didn't make sense back then. Are you saying Klara saw your daughter's spirit in the schoolyard?'

'Yes! She's such a gifted little girl . . . I wouldn't put it past her to be psychic on top of everything else. Shame for her mother, though. But we all have our crosses to bear. You know, I've always loved Klara; she has my daughter's eyes. And she's right. My little girl had my eyes too.'

Katie gave a faint smile. 'They were green, like yours?'

'Yes, except hers were bigger than mine. She was such a beautiful creature! Let me show you.' Matina reached over to the far side of the desk and took her wallet out of her bag. She handed the open wallet to Katie. 'And she had such adorable, curly hair! She never let us cut it or even pull it into a ponytail. She loved to wear it loose on her shoulders, my little darling . . .'

Katie dropped her gaze on a picture of a little girl in a short dress. She had radiant green eyes and floppy long hair. *What? She looks like*

. . . and that cute smile . . . 'What . . . what was her name?' she mumbled in a faint whisper.

'Chloe. Wasn't she a little angel?'

Chloe? But . . . how can it be? 'Oh my God!' blurted out Katie, before the world started to whirl.

Chapter 40

Katie remembered very little from the short exchange that ensued in Matina's office after she had received the shock of her life. From what she recalled, she had made an excuse about feeling unwell and needing to get some fresh air. But, instead of going out, Katie climbed two flights of stairs like her life depended on it and went banging on the door of Aggelos' room, too distressed and full of questions to care that she might disturb the other guests.

To her dismay, despite the incessant knocks on the door and even a few desperate cries, no one answered, so she took her angst back down the stairs with her and stormed out the front door. She roamed around the beach for a while, then headed to the fields, seeking solitude away from the crowds, alone to think and clear her head.

###

Back at the hotel, Elise had just found Chloe hanging out in the garden. Close by, Spyros held a large brush and was tending the trees with a hired worker, covering the bottom of the trunks with a coat of lime from a large bucket. Even though her semi-physical body had nothing to fear from exposure to sunlight, Chloe had picked up from the beach a forgotten hat with a wide brim and was wearing it as she sat under the vine trellis. She was playing *pentovola* with five pebbles by herself to the sounds of her father working and talking to the other man.

She wasn't worried either of them could see her. She'd been wandering around the hotel in the presence of many people these past few weeks and only a handful of them had been capable of seeing her. Her parents weren't among them.

Elise walked up to Chloe and, unlike what happened when she normally spoke to her, this time, her manner was urgent. Having no time to waste, she grabbed Chloe by the hand and pulled her upright.

'Elise! What's the matter?' responded Chloe with a groan, taken aback.

'You tell *me* what happened! I just heard your mother and Katie talking inside. What is this stunt you just pulled? Who gave you permission to talk to one of the villagers?'

A shadow set upon the girl's face and she visibly cringed.

'I see you had no permission. Just as I thought. What were you thinking? Esmera will be livid when she finds out you left the hotel! You were never supposed to leave the premises, remember? Let alone go to the school and tell that little girl who you are!'

'How did she know who I am? She wasn't even around when I still lived!'

'And yet she knew! And she told your mother so! But what I don't understand, Chloe, is why you would do this!'

When Chloe spoke next, her voice rang heavy with upset. 'I just wanted someone to know, to help Mummy! I knew these men planned to steal from her. They'd been watching her come and go from the hotel for days.'

'So, why didn't you tell us? Why did you keep it to yourself?'

'You were all excited about the party, so I didn't want to spoil your mood. And I thought it was the hotel they planned to break into! With it being so busy last night, I imagined they wouldn't try it. And I guarded the place for the rest of the night, like I always do, to make sure Mummy and Daddy, and everyone else, are safe.'

'And then, when you knew what happened, why did you decide to talk to that little girl?'

'I didn't! It was *she* who came and talked to me. Until she did, I didn't realize she could see me.'

'What were you doing in the schoolyard, anyway?'

'Early this morning, I . . . Well, I got a little upset. But I'm okay now.'

'Why? What happened?'

'At dawn, Esmera told me what was in the wine that she left with Mummy and Daddy. She told me what she was trying to do and I got very sad . . . So I ran away and Esmera didn't stop me. I wound up in the schoolyard . . . and on my way there I saw those bad men breaking the window at the centre.'

'Oh Chloe! You knew what Esmera had been trying to do for you all along. She did it to make your mummy and daddy happy again. Isn't this what you wanted?'

Chloe started to whine, trying to pull her arm from Elise's grasp and walk away, and Elise grew agitated. They were on stolen time. The only thing that saved them, that saved her, first of all, was to fess up to Esmera before she found out they had broken her rules.

First, Aggelos, with his wise ideas to make himself visible to his human, then falling hard for her, and now, the little girl, Esmera's protégé, was doing public relations in Asimi, starting with the local psychic, of all people, who could spill the beans to them all. Esmera would have a heart attack! But not before bagging them all into one cotton-white cloud and sending them back to heaven to repair harp strings for sweet eternity.

Chloe was whining still. It was getting too much for Elise to bear. 'Enough!' she shouted, grasping Chloe by the shoulders and shaking her, causing her to cry. Instantly, it made her sorry she had done it, for her heart went out to Chloe for her pain. She was an angel, after all. Of course, she cared for the little girl. But this was serious. Her dream job was on the line.

Elise stood up straight, letting go of Chloe's shoulders and just taking her hand gently in hers. She closed her eyes and, as the child's soft whimpers reached her ears, she formed in her mind the picture of Aggelos. Instantly, she heard his voice beside her.

'What is it? Why did you summon me so urgently? And why do you both look so glum?' Aggelos let out a light-hearted chuckle. The after effects of last night's love-making on the beach with Katie were still lasting even though he had no endorphins in his system to trip on. He'd spent most of the day sleeping and had woken up minutes ago. His semi-physical body only required a small amount of sleep, but the previous night's exertion had left him drained beyond measure.

Now he was up and somewhat refreshed, all he wanted to do was find Katie and lose himself in her arms and kisses again. He'd just gone to knock on her door but, to his surprise, she hadn't answered. And then, Elise had summoned him and he had no idea why she looked like the world was coming to an end. To him, a life that seemed like heaven on earth was just beginning.

Elise scowled. 'Aggelos! Wipe that silly grin of your face. We have a serious situation here.' Her eyes flicked to Chloe, who seemed ready to burst into tears, then back to Aggelos again.

Aggelos took in their expressions, this time fully, and alarm ignited in his eyes. He went rigid, his brows knitted tightly. 'What is it, guys? You're scaring me!'

Elise gave a loud groan. 'You're not scared *yet*, believe me. That's later, once we've told Esmera what Chloe has just done.'

Chapter 41

The first thing Katie did when she walked back into the hotel half an hour later was run up the stairs again. But if she thought the earlier shock had been bad enough, nothing could have prepared her for this one. In the place where the dazzling golden door of Aggelos' room had stood until today, now there was a brick wall that was heavily plastered in pure white. Katie stood in front of it gawping for a few moments, her feet heavy like lead, her eyes bulging, jaw dropped. Even her breath that rushed in and out of her chest burned. She felt her throat tightening. *'Is this a nightmare? God! If it is, I want to wake up. Please, Katie, WAKE UP!*

'Katie?' came Eddie's cheerful voice from behind her. He tapped her on the shoulder and when she spun around, her expression took him by surprise. Her eyes were swollen from crying, red-rimmed, and alight with panic. 'What is it, Katie?'

Before she could answer, Spyros, who had come upstairs with Eddie on a quick errand, walked up to them, his brow furrowed. 'What's the matter, Katie?'

Katie shook her head, her mind drawing blank. *What can I say? Where do I begin?*

'For God's sake, girl! Speak! Is everyone all right? Is it Matina? Is she okay?' Without meaning to, Spyros was squeezing her shoulder, causing her to hurt. But Katie welcomed the pain. It confirmed she wasn't dreaming, after all. Although this was bad news, she felt thankful to know. With a deep breath, she found new strength and her voice. 'No, Mr Spyros. Mrs Matina is fine, don't worry. But I'm not so sure about me.'

'Why?' asked Spyros, letting go of her and relaxing somewhat.

Katie squeezed her eyes shut and shook her head, realizing she had no time, or a way to begin to speak about what she knew and they didn't. Instead, an urgent question rose to her lips, seemingly of its own volition. 'Mr Spyros, has this hotel ever had a room number twenty-seven?'

'No. Never.' Beside Spyros, Eddie shook his head.

'That's what I thought. Thanks,' she mumbled, storming down the stairs without another word or explanation, Spyros and Eddie scratching their heads and shrugging their shoulders at each other.

###

When she reached the ground floor, Katie rushed out to the front garden and, even though the lawn and the beach were busy with guests, she didn't think twice before calling out to Aggelos, desperate to find him. Already, she knew it was futile. It was a logical assumption. Ever since she'd first met him, he seemed to keep showing up whenever she needed him, whenever anyone in the hotel, for that matter, needed assistance.

And yet, today of all days, even though Matina had been through all this upset, even though she'd just found out Chloe was a ghost, and even though she'd spent the past hour or so seeking him out, he was nowhere to be found.

That could only mean one thing, and her heart sank just thinking about it. She had no strength in her to admit it out loud but knew it deep down with certainty. He was gone. He was gone and he hadn't even bothered to say goodbye.

Spent, and having walked up and down the beach for a couple of minutes to no avail, she plopped down on a concrete step at the hotel entrance and sat with her face buried in her hands. Then, she heard a familiar voice call out to her. She whipped her head around and saw Mrs Sparks on the lawn. She was lying on her sun lounger in the usual place by the rhododendron bushes.

Katie walked up to her slowly, expecting the old lady to comment on her distraught expression and red-rimmed eyes, but she couldn't care less. When she came to loom over the frail, yet always upbeat Mrs Sparks, the old lady smiled bitterly and gestured to her to sit down.

Katie obliged her but couldn't manage a smile. She also wondered how come Mrs Sparks hadn't seemed surprised by the look on her face. But then, that was Mrs Sparks all over: loopy enough for you to never know what she'd do or say next.

'Hello, Mrs Sparks. Is there anything you need?' she said tiredly.

'I didn't call you here because of something I need, Katie. I called you here because it's *you* who needs something. Am I right?' She tilted her head, a movement that caused the sequins on her white turban—a new one Katie hadn't seen before—to catch the light and sparkle in a blinding way for a split second.

Katie looked away, squinting beside herself, then turned to the old lady again. 'You see a lot, Mrs Sparks. That's for sure.'

'I see a lot because I don't talk much, dear. I am not a talker. I am an observer of life. People give credit to the talkers, but it's the observers who catch the early bird, the observers who, at the end of the day, know it's the butler who did it.' She gave a wicked smirk that caused the heavy wrinkles at the corners of her mouth to pile up like a French accordion in the midst of a happy song.

'The butler? Are you talking about who-dunnits? The national pastime of the Brits?' Katie let out a light-hearted laugh that took her by surprise.

'There you go! I made you laugh. One of my missions for you today is accomplished.'

Katie furrowed her brow. 'Why? What other missions do you have planned for me, Mrs Sparks?'

Mrs Sparks gave a deep sigh but instead of talking she brought a hand to her neck, tapped on it with two manicured, bright turquoise fingertips, then pointed to Katie with her chin.

Instinctively, Katie brought her hand to her own neck and gasped. 'Oh my God!'

'You lost it, didn't you realize?'

'No! Just now I . . .' Her eyes widened. 'Wow! You noticed I lost it before I even did.'

Mrs Sparks winked. 'I told you, Katie, I'm an observer.'

Katie brought her hands to her head, trying to concentrate, then jumped to her feet. 'I had a walk in the fields earlier. I bet I lost it there. Better retrace my steps and find it before someone else does!' She made to go but Mrs Sparks put up a hand to stop her.

'No, my darling girl. Sit back down. You won't find it. It's gone. And it's not the only thing that's gone, is it, Katie?'

'What?' Katie sat down again, slowly starting to understand this time. The look in Mrs Sparks' eyes was unmistakable. She knew. She knew everything Katie needed to know. 'Please, tell me, Mrs Sparks! Where is Aggelos? Did you see him leave?'

Chapter 42

Mrs Sparks leaned forward in her sun lounger and placed a tender hand on Katie's cheek. 'Be strong now, my darling.'

'Mrs Sparks, please tell me! Where is he? Isn't he coming back?'

The old woman swung her spindly legs around, her turquoise toenails glinting in the sunlight as she put her feet on the soft grass. She gave a long sigh. 'I wish I had better news for you, Katie, I wish I did. You're such a darling. I could tell you and Aggelos were in love.'

Katie swallowed the lump in her throat and fought back her tears by blinking fervently as she took a deep breath. 'Please. Just tell me what you know.'

Mrs Sparks rested her kindly eyes on Katie. 'Your amulet is gone. And this is why Aggelos has gone too.'

Katie knitted her brows. 'Huh?'

'Haven't you worked it out yet? Aggelos was here *because* of the amulet! It's that gypsy woman who—'

'Esmera?'

'That's right. She brought Aggelos here on the island to take care of you, to protect you. Esmera brought a whole party of them for some kind of training over here, including the busty blond and that . . . that stinky guy.'

'Elise and Babis?'

'Yes. Them. Surely you worked out all of them knew each other.'

'I knew that, yes.'

'What did you think they were doing here?'

'Honestly? I knew nothing. They wouldn't say.'

Mrs Sparks rolled her eyes. 'I'm not surprised.'

'Are you saying they're all gone now? For good? But why? What's changed?'

'*Everything's* changed overnight, Katie. For one, Chloe blew her cover. Her mother now knows her dead daughter is haunting the hotel, and that she never found peace. How is Matina ever going to let go now and move on with her life? And don't get me started with you and Aggelos!' She tutted and shook her head. 'You two were never supposed to fall in love!'

'But why?'

'He's not human, Katie. He's an angel! They *all* are!'

'Angels?' mumbled Katie, her eyes flicking left and right as she recounted memories.

'Duh! 'Aggelos' means 'Angel'. Hello?'

Katie shook her head and twisted her lips, then looked up. 'Are you sure? How is this possible?'

Mrs Sparks sighed. 'Katie, just face it: you've been working in a hotel frequented by a bunch of angels and a ghost. I wouldn't advise you to put that on your résumé, though!' She let out an easy laugh, a low gurgle rising from her throat. 'I'm sorry. I've had the gift all my life. I couldn't have handled it without learning to exercise my humour muscle.'

Katie flicked her wrist to dismiss the apology. 'So Chloe is a ghost?' She'd already worked that one out but needed to hear it. It still felt impossible to believe.

'Yes. That's right.'

'But how? *How*? And where did she come from? Did Esmera bring her too?'

'No. Chloe has been here all along. I've been detecting her presence for years in this hotel, but I never actually saw her until this year. And what a delightful little creature she is . . .'

'So, all this time, every time she hid when Mrs Matina or Mr Spyros turned up, she was just pretending? For us? So we don't suspect? When all along, they couldn't have possibly seen her anyway?'

'That's right.'

'But how . . . how did she suddenly turn up like this when all these years, not even *you* could see her?'

'Esmera gave her a different form this year to help her comfort herself and her mother a little better. Chloe could never leave her mother behind while she was so upset over her loss. So Esmera granted Chloe some kind of semi-physical body this year, the same she gave the angels. Among us humans, only those with a gift to see the unseen can see them all. They can appear human because you can touch them, talk to them; they can eat, drink, and . . . well, in

Aggelos' case do a little more than that,' Mrs Sparks added with a wink.

Katie lowered her head, then shook it, unwilling to give shelter to all the craziness entering her head. 'This is insane . . . too much. Too damn much to swallow,' she said, her voice wavering.

Mrs Sparks reached out to her and held her, soothing her against her bosom. 'Hush, hush now,' said the old woman, 'For I believe there is still hope.'

Katie wiped her tears with the back of her hand. 'Hope?'

'Yes. Only a tiny one, mind you, but you never know. Go and talk to Chloe. I think perhaps she could help you find Aggelos again, if only for a chance to say goodbye.'

Katie looked around. 'Where is she? Is she still here?'

'Not for much longer. She's sitting on the jetty over there. See the large straw hat? That's her. Please tell me you can see her.'

Katie jumped to her feet. 'Yes! Yes, I can see her! Thank you!' She kissed Mrs Sparks on the cheek and made to go but stopped short and spun around again, tilting her head. 'Wait a minute! You said only those with a gift to see the unseen can see the angels and Chloe. I know you have this gift, but I don't. How come I could see them, talk to them, all this time?'

Mrs Sparks shrugged. 'I am not sure, but I think it's because you had the amulet. It gave you powers.'

'And how can I see Chloe now?' She pointed to the jetty. 'I no longer wear it.'

'That's a mystery. But maybe it was meant to be. Or maybe Esmera's magic allows this. That's hopeful in itself.'

'Mrs Sparks, thank you! It's all starting to finally make some sense. I can see now why Matina and Spyros never met Chloe at the hotel, even though she seemed to practically live in it. And I can understand why Aggelos remained unseen by everyone other than you and me. Although . . . Wait a minute! How could Eva see him? And, she spoke to Chloe every day! We chatted, we joked . . . she spoon-fed her a few times, for God's sake!'

Mrs Sparks gave a loud guffaw, then fixed Katie with a cheerful stare, her eyes twinkling. 'I'm glad you asked. I know all about Eva. She looks at me and thinks I'm some batty old lady. But I know better.' She placed a finger on her temple and winked. 'Eva has the gift. She just doesn't know it.'

Chapter 43

'Why didn't you tell me?' asked Katie as soon as she came to sit on a bench beside Chloe at the edge of the jetty.

The little girl turned around slowly. She tilted her head and looked up, revealing sorrowful eyes from under the wide brim of her sun hat.

Katie's heart constricted with feeling at the sight. She took Chloe in her arms and held her, rocking her back and forth. Chloe was quiet. She didn't cry or speak. After a while, Katie let her go and sat up again, just holding Chloe's hand now, her fingers entwined with hers. 'How are you feeling?'

'Sad . . . worried . . . but most of all, sorry. So very sorry. Because of me, Aggelos went away earlier than planned. I didn't mean to cause this, Katie. I'm so sorry! I just didn't know that little girl could see me. And when she did, I guess I was too sad, thinking how Mummy would be upset about the robbers. It came out, before I could stop myself.'

'Please don't apologize. I know you didn't mean it. But it's okay. I know you think your mummy must be upset to find out you've been around, but believe me, this was a comfort to her. She is happier today than she's been in years. She's been feeling your love, Chloe. This can only be good for her.'

Chloe looked pensive, her eyes focusing far as she chewed her lower lip. She turned to face Katie, her expression urgent. 'But . . . but Aggelos is gone because of me! Esmera has just called up all the angels in her legion, ending their training immediately. She's dispatching them all to their newly appointed posts today.'

'But, why?'

'One thing she cannot risk is the humans knowing about the angels being here. Angels like to keep things quiet, you know.'

'What exactly is Esmera? She's not just a gypsy with magical powers, is she?'

'No, of course not. She's an archangel and the commander of the Cyclades Angelic Division. C.A.D. for short.'

'Commander of *what*?'

Chloe rolled her eyes. 'Basically, Esmera's job is to train new angels that are posted in this world. She also uses magical gifts to help humans at will, then assigns angels in her legion to help them along the way. The way she did with you.'

'By giving me the amulet.'

'That's right. Aggelos was the angel assigned to help you. Except . . .'

'Except we fell in love. And I'm guessing Esmera didn't like it.'

'Not one bit. Elise insisted we fess up to Esmera today before she found out. So that's what she, Aggelos, and I did. But Esmera was so mad . . . I can't imagine how she would have been had she found out herself.' Chloe shook her head forlornly. 'At some point, I thought she was going to send us all to heaven mid-sentence. Especially me! But then, Aggelos spoke to her in private, and she calmed down. I don't know what he told her, but she announced I could stay at the hotel a little longer, after all. As for the angels, she forbade them to come back to this hotel ever again.'

Katie's heart sank, her voice a mere whisper. 'Ever?'

'Uh-uh. To make sure of that, she came down here herself and snapped the amulet from your neck. She found you sitting under a tree in a field crying. I know. I saw.'

Katie knew exactly where and when. She'd stayed a while crying her eyes out in that place. Yet, she hadn't seen or sensed Esmera. 'Why did she take it?'

'To make sure Aggelos doesn't disobey her. Without the amulet, he can't come near you, and even if he did, you wouldn't be able to see or hear him.'

'If that's the case, then how can I see *you*?'

Chloe gave a faint smile. 'Esmera may be a large and often scary woman, but she doesn't command me. She has no power over me, the way she does with the angels. It is my will that you can still see me. I love you, Katie. I'm going to miss you.'

'Oh Chloe! I love you too, and I'll miss you so much. So will your mummy.'

Chloe set her jaw. 'It's okay. I know she will be all right from now on. I am ready to leave her behind.'

'Really?'

'Yes. And I've made up my mind about the when and the how. But first, I need to ask you a question, Katie.'

'Sure, go ahead.'

'If you had to choose between your happiness and Aggelos', what would you choose?'

'I'd choose for Aggelos to be happy. Any day of the week.'

Chloe gave a wide grin and nodded. 'I knew it! That's why Esmera gave you the amulet in the first place. She's a great judge of character. She could tell you have a pure heart.'

'I don't understand, sorry.'

'It's simple, Katie. Your pure heart means hope's not lost. You'd be happy to sacrifice your happiness for him, and he did the same for you. He allowed Elise to tell Esmera what had happened, knowing she'd remove him from your life at once because he didn't want to risk hurting you more in the long run. And I don't think he had the heart to say goodbye, knowing he'd have to disappear forever after that. You guys had no future, don't you see?'

'I'm sorry, Chloe. I still don't understand. You spoke of hope. I still don't see it.'

'Katie, it's because of your pure hearts that I can help you.' She puffed up her chest and sat up straight. 'I'm going to ask Esmera to take his place in her legion so he can be free to return to you.'

'What? How is that even possible? You're not an angel.'

'Technically not. Or rather, not yet. But I have a plan!'

Katie leaned forward, her eyes turning huge. 'Is there anything I can do?'

'Yes. But first, I want to say goodbye to my parents. I mean, properly. Will you help me?'

'What can I do?'

'I need you to tell them a few words for me, seeing I can't speak to them myself. And then, you'll need to ask them to drive us to the windmill on the hill.'

'The windmill? What on earth for?'

'That's where Esmera is dispatching them all from tonight.'

'The top of the hill? Really?'

'Yes. They gather up there often in the evenings to command the winds. That's what they do. They use the wind and their pure heavenly energy to distribute goodness, kindness, and joy throughout every part of Greece. What do you think keeps the Greeks strong and positive, despite the many hardships?'

'Really? That's what it is?'

'What did you think it is? *Chalva, baklava,* and *ouzo* that keep us perky?' She pulled a cute face. 'Well, maybe, in a small degree, but certainly not all the way!'

'And that happens all over Greece? And they use the winds, you said?'

'Yes. But this angelic activity is at its strongest on the islands in the Aegean, such as this part: the Cyclades. That's why Elise, Aggelos, and Babis have been hoping to be posted here after the end of the training period. It's a greatly sought after post for earth-dwelling angels, you know.'

'Wow!' said Katie as she followed Chloe down the jetty.

Chloe chortled as she hopped along up ahead. She turned to look at Katie over her shoulder and winked. 'You look so surprised! Why do you think it's so windy in this part of the world?'

Chapter 44

Spyros drove his car blurry-eyed, Matina sitting next to him wiping tears from her eyes as numbly as he did, as the car trudged along uphill, sending puffs of fine dust twirling and rising high in its wake. In the back seat, Katie sat with Mrs Sparks and Eva, or rather, that's what Matina and Spyros could perceive. The three had told them their little daughter, Chloe, had come along and was also sitting in the back, but they had no physical evidence to back that up. All they had was blind trust towards the people they knew, who swore they were serious and telling the truth.

Half an hour earlier, when Katie had knocked on the door of Matina's office, the latter had answered it, letting in more people than she bargained for. And if it would have been easy to dismiss loopy Mrs Sparks for announcing her deceased daughter was in the room and wanted to talk to her, it was impossible not to listen when Katie and Eva said the same. For some reason, it was Eva that managed to convince both Matina and Spyros in the end. Without Eva's testimony, it would have been impossible to believe the crazy things they said could possibly hold a modicum of truth.

Eva had described Chloe in every detail. Not just her cute mannerisms, the funny quips she'd often come up with, but even her affinity for pets, hats, and the fact that *moussaka* was her favourite meal in the whole wide world. How could Eva know all that when she hadn't even been around when Chloe was still alive?

And then, Katie began to speak for Chloe, asking Matina to fetch the little girl's diary 'from the bottom left drawer in the wardrobe' where Chloe knew her mother kept it. After the initial shock, Matina rushed to her private room to get it. The rest was a blur. Half-convinced and half-feeling as if they were slowly going insane, Spyros and Matina agreed to drive everyone uphill where Chloe needed 'to have her last wish come true by the angels before her spirit could be free.' It made no sense. But, they felt compelled to help make it happen all the same.

As soon as they reached the plateau on the hilltop where the windmill stood, the car pulled to a stop and everyone got out. They weren't alone, although not all of them could see everybody.

Chloe, Eva, and Mrs Sparks saw Esmera standing in front of a dozen angels, recognizing Aggelos, Elise, and Babis as well as some of the angels that had come to the BBQ party with Esmera.

As for Katie, Spyros, and Matina, their faces grew animated with mystification to find Esmera standing alone before the windmill. Spyros and Matina couldn't fathom what the gypsy lady from the BBQ party could be doing there. Was this a pre-arranged meeting? Had she been waiting for them and why?

Matina spoke first, turning to Katie and Eva. 'Is it Esmera we're meeting here? What's going on?'

Mrs Sparks leaned over to Katie and whispered to let her know all the angels were present, including Aggelos. Katie's heart bloomed at the very thought that he was near. Her eyes darted frantically here and there across the distance, yet she couldn't see anyone else but Esmera standing before the windmill.

At the same time, across the few feet that separated them, Aggelos ached to run to Katie. He could tell she couldn't see him and his heart was breaking. He imagined Esmera had done that. Now, he was torn. Was it worth it to run to her to hold her and give her the shock of her life since she couldn't see him? Could he risk hurting her more? This was goodbye, after all.

Elise, who stood beside him, decided for him when she grabbed his arm, digging her nails into his flesh. She was dressed in a smart evening dress, the only one among all the angels who wasn't dressed casually. Elise kept chewing her lips in agony, all the while clutching Aggelos' arm, her eyes darting to Katie, Esmera, and Aggelos on a loop.

As for Esmera, she looked livid. She could tell the humans weren't there for a good reason and wasn't looking forward to an awkward scene in front of her legion. She balled her hands into fists, took a deep breath, then signalled to Aggelos and everyone else to stay put. Then, she turned to the humans again and arranged her features into an expression of mild annoyance as she waited for them to make the first move.

Chloe rushed up to Esmera, a cute smile on her face. 'Esmera, please listen before you say anything.'

Esmera took the girl's hand and turned around, leading her to the edge of the precipice, as far from the humans as possible.

The view before them was breathtaking; the sun was still high in the sky, casting golden sun rays onto the world from behind fluffy white clouds. The bright cobalt blue of the sea had the power to steal the air from your lungs.

'What have you gone and done now? What are your parents doing here?' growled Esmera in a hushed tone. She turned and darted her eyes behind them and was pleased to see that at least Aggelos had obeyed her for once. He was standing away from Katie and the other people. Elise stood beside him, her jaw set, her fingers squeezing his arm hard.

Across the distance, Katie's expression was intense as she looked blankly into space, her eyes feverish. It broke Esmera's heart, but she knew she had no choice. The angel was needed in the legion. There was no time to train someone else. Heaven couldn't wait because one of them fell in love, as sweet as it sounded. Heaven had better things to do than grant angels pleasures meant only for humans. Chloe's sweet voice brought her back to the moment.

'Esmera, I'm sorry for interrupting you. But I have a good reason. Read this first, and I'll explain.' She offered Esmera the diary she had been holding. The gypsy gave a soft sigh and opened it to a page where a ribbon had been placed to mark it. There, she saw the last diary entry, written in Chloe's hand. Well-rounded letters in pink perfumed ink. A faint smell of strawberry rose from the page. Esmera took a pair of reading glasses from her flowery skirt's deep pocket and began to read:

Today, Mummy said that when the angels come to take me to heaven I will become an angel too. She said Granny and Granddad are angels as well, and that they're waiting for me up there. Mummy says heaven is very beautiful but I don't want to go yet. She is so sad! She cries all the time, making Daddy and everyone else sad too. So how can I go? I want Mummy to smile all the time. I want her to laugh. No, not just Mummy. I want EVERYONE in the hotel to be happy. Only then I will be ready to fly away with the angels.

Esmera pressed her lips together, looked up and peered at the girl from over her glasses. 'I don't understand, Chloe. Why are you showing me this?'

'It's my last wish, Esmera. I want you to make it come true.'

Esmera shook her head. 'My darling, you died ten years ago.'

'Yes, but when the angel came to get me that day, I refused. I wasn't ready to go. But I'm ready now.'

Esmera returned her glasses to her pocket, then knelt in front of Chloe. 'So, you're ready to go? Just like that? I thought you needed a little more time. Isn't that what you told me? That while your mummy's sad you cannot go?'

'It's all right. I know and you know that she will be happy again soon.'

'Well, if she's going to be happy soon, your wish is already granted. No one can stop you from going. I'll get a guide to fly down and pick you up. But can it wait an hour? Sorry, darling. I'm busy now as you can see.'

Chloe tapped the open diary that Esmera still held. 'Don't pretend you can't see. It's right there, Esmera. It says that *everyone* should be happy.'

Esmera gave a titter. 'You're a clever little thing; I'll give you that. But sorry, no can do.'

'But why not?'

'I can't help you, Chloe. There is no way Katie and Aggelos can have their happily ever after. Aggelos isn't human. You know that. He's had his training and now he has to be posted like everyone else to do his job. Period.'

'No! He doesn't have to work for you. Not if someone else can take his place.'

'Chloe, we've spent a long time getting to know each other. I've told you how things are. I work on tight schedules and can't get back to my superiors admitting to last-minute disasters. They are within the Seraphim and Cherubim ranks. You don't mess with those guys. They have daily meetings with The One. You know? The One and Only? The Almighty One? I don't want any mess-ups of mine being discussed among the highest ranks of angelic hierarchy.'

Chloe winked. 'No one will know. You and I will fix it right here right now.'

'And where do you suppose we find a replacement angel, all ready and trained, just like that?'

'You're looking at the angel you're after.'

'Huh?'

'Come on, Esmera! I've been present in so many training sessions with your legions! Over the years I've met them all! You might as well have trained me dozens of times too. I know the job and I could start tonight.'

'What exactly are you suggesting here? You can't possibly—'

'I suggest you let Aggelos stay with Katie, and you place me wherever you intended to place Aggelos. I'll do the job just fine.'

'And you don't mind not going to heaven?'

'Pah! Heaven! It's overrated! If heaven is so cool, then why does The One recycle the souls, sending them back down to earth over and over again for more training? Don't you see Esmera? Here, it's much better, and way more interesting. I doubt heaven has this kind of beauty!' She pointed to the stunning landscape unfolding before them and continued, 'Besides, I hardly think they serve *moussaka* up there!'

Esmera pursed her lips. 'What if I said no? Would you take the humans and go without making any fuss?'

Chloe crossed her arms before her chest and stamped her foot on the ground. 'No! You can't say no to me! It's my last wish. And according to Chapter 10 paragraph 2 in the Manual for Spiritual Guides and Guardian Angels, a child's last wish is non-negotiable, especially—'

'Especially when in writing,' interrupted Esmera to finish Chloe's sentence.

'That's right, Esmera. And now, seeing that I never got my wish when the angel came to get me, now that I ask, now that I'm ready to leave Mummy behind, you have no choice but to accept it. As I wrote in my diary, *everyone* must be happy before I can go. You'll just have to do exactly that for me.'

Esmera thought for a while, then shook her head. 'I'm afraid I can't help you. I have to do things by the book, you see. Katie and

Aggelos are not members of your family. You know the rules. They can't benefit from your wish.'

Chloe didn't even flinch. You could tell she expected that argument because she didn't waste any time with her response. 'Yes, you're correct! Except, Aggelos and Katie are both pure of heart! And according to the final chapter in the Basic Guide to Angelic Procedures & Human Encounters, you should never refuse to assist the pure of heart because—'

Once again, Esmera finished the sentence. 'Because it is only love that drives them.'

Chloe gave a triumphant smile. 'You can turn this round and round in your head, Esmera, but you won't find anything else. I've taken a long time to think this through.'

Esmera pressed her lips together and bowed her head in deep contemplation for a few moments before speaking. 'Okay, so Aggelos is pure of heart, I'll give you that, but how do we really know Katie is too?'

Chloe half-closed her eyes and tutted. 'Oh please. If she's not, you'd never have given her the amulet in the first place. You told me yourself you pick only the purest of hearts.'

Esmera heaved a long sigh, then turned to face angels and humans alike, who all waited in silence. Some of them looked mildly amused, others indifferent, and a few seemed to be in torment. Esmera scratched her head and turned to Chloe, her eyes dancing with mirth. 'You cunning little thing! You read those manuals I lent you cover to cover, didn't you?'

Chapter 45

Esmera took her time walking up to Aggelos and Elise, Chloe trailing behind her in the same leisurely pace. All this time none of the others had heard a peep from the conversation but could tell from the body language that their argument was intense.

When Esmera stopped in front of the two angels everyone held their breaths, including Matina and Spyros. Eva had assured them that a group of angels was standing close by, and they had been shocked to silence, their eyes bulging out as they clung to each other, seeking desperately visual evidence, but to no avail.

'Aggelos . . . Elise,' said Esmera, a deep frown etching her brow. 'I had such big plans for you! You are truly the best in the team. When Chloe and her friends arrived, I was about to announce that I was posting you right here, on this hilltop, angel guardians of Asimi, but now . . .'

'Now, what? What do you mean, Esmera?' asked Elise, gesticulating wildly with both hands. Even though she'd let go of Aggelos' arm, the finger marks from her fierce grasp were still visible on his skin. Beside her, Aggelos seemed patient with her as always, realizing the very idea of her being stationed on the same post with Babis was the worst thing she could ever imagine happening to her. He knew why, and that's what made him so patient with her.

'Elise, I'm sorry. You'll be a guardian of Asimi with someone else. I'm transferring Aggelos to another post.'

'Noooo!' yelled Elise. 'Please! You can't do this to me! I'll do anything, I'll go anywhere! Just don't place me with *him*!'

'Who? What on earth are you blathering about, girl?'

'I know Babis is third in line and Asimi is the most sought-after station in the Cyclades! You can't place me with Babis! He stinks, you understand? And I don't just mean smell-wise. The man is *foul*!' shrieked Elise, her eyes wide with distress. 'He never changes his socks unless they become crusty and mouldy like old cheese! He sleeps on the ground, often in fields, and never washes his clothes! When he eats, he holds a fork in one hand and a cigarette in the other! And he sucks pasta noisily, faster than a vacuum cleaner! You can't place me with this Neanderthal! I'll go to the far corners of the world, just keep him away from me. *Please*, Esmera!'

Babis stepped closer. 'Hey! I thought you liked these things about me! You said they were the trademarks of my charm!'

Elise rolled her eyes. 'You're kidding, right?' then turning to Esmera, '*Please*. Save. Me. I beg you!'

'Relax. I'm not placing you with Babis. Babis is going to Mykonos. He—'

'Whoa-hey! Mykonos, baby! Here I come!' interrupted Babis who started to dance to an inaudible beat, kicking his legs up in what looked like a cross between the *Lambada* and a crazy chicken dance. As he strutted, legs and arms akimbo, towards the humans, Mrs Sparks took a perfume spray bottle out of her bag and strode up to him, leaned over and began to sniff him like a hound dog. Babis did a double take and sobered up, looking at her stunned.

Mrs Sparks huffed and sprayed his torso, then handed him the can. 'Here! That's the last one I give you. Don't forget to buy your own on Mykonos!'

Babis smiled in response. Being taller than her, he had to double over to leave a peck on her cheek. Mrs Sparks gave him a cuddle, then retreated back to the others holding her nose surreptitiously. 'Yikes,' she said, 'That boy still needs a bit of work.'

In the meantime, Aggelos had stepped in to speak in Elise's favour. He explained to Esmera that Babis reminded her of her older brother, who had tormented her throughout her childhood. Being brought up on a farm, born into a poor family, her brother had never smelled nice. He loved to work with the cows, the sheep and the pigs, and knowing how much his little sister loved the finer things in life, he never missed to touch her on purpose, soiling her clothes with dirt, mud, and other things he found in the animal pens that weren't even mentionable. Her disgust for uncleanliness had survived in her psyche even after she'd gained her angel wings.

Upon hearing this explanation, Esmera turned around and brought Chloe in front of her, her hands on the girl's shoulders. 'Elise, you don't need to worry any more. Not only am I not placing you with Babis who reminds you of things that bothered you once, but I'm not even placing you with a guy. With your new partner, you can talk girly things and fineries to your heart's content!'

'You? But how?' asked Elise as she gawped at Chloe. Beside her, Aggelos had completely lost his voice. He ventured another glance towards Katie and the others. For the first time, the yearning to be near her was overwhelming. Without realizing, his feet unglued themselves from the spot he'd been standing on and began to rush towards her. As he ran with open wide arms, his body suddenly flung backwards just as he was about to reach her. It was like he had bounced off an invisible wall, and he fell flat on his back on the dirt. *What on earth?*

He jumped back on his feet and dusted himself off. That's when he noticed Katie was no longer wearing the amulet. She was gazing into his face from just a couple steps away, her eyes wild, searching, yet she didn't seem to know she was looking straight at him.

Aggelos whirled around and strode to Esmera. 'Can you please let me say goodbye to her at least? Before you . . . *Please*, Esmera! I *need* this!'

Esmera let out a deep sigh and put her arm around his shoulder. She wasn't as tall as him but was tall enough to be able to do this without looking silly. As she led him towards the humans, the grace and magnificence of her stature were in full bloom. When they reached the point where Aggelos had bounced off earlier, she put up a hand and exposed her open palm, the amulet materializing on it. Then, she simply walked through the invisible wall, taking Aggelos through with her.

When she reached Katie and the others, she took Aggelos' hand and placed it in Katie's, then put the amulet on top of their hands. In a flash of bright white light, Aggelos' form came into view and Katie gasped. He remained transparent for a few split seconds, sparkling and shining, then his form turned solid, perfectly human.

Katie and Aggelos felt it at once. A rush of heat coursed through their bodies and they fell into each other's arms as they realized they'd been given the greatest gift of all: the freedom to live the rest of their lives with the one they'd chosen. Smiling brightly they turned to face Esmera.

The old gypsy rolled her eyes and flicked a hand at Aggelos. 'What are you waiting for? Kiss her already!' she said with a chuckle and he was happy to oblige her to the sound of cheer from everyone else.

When the couple pulled apart they turned to Esmera, their faces beaming. 'Thank you, thank you Esmera! Thank you so much!' they kept repeating.

Esmera patted Aggelos on the shoulder. 'When you and the others told me earlier what had transpired overnight, and this morning in the schoolyard, I was mad. I'll admit it. I wanted to remove you and Chloe from the island immediately. But when you begged me to remove the memory of you from Katie's mind so she doesn't hurt any more, you broke my heart. I knew then you two should be together since you'd prefer she doesn't remember you rather than feel the emotional pain of your loss. But I guess I was stubborn and sticking to the plan with a heavy heart. Until Chloe came, of course, bringing her diplomatic skills to the table.' She gave a joyful little laugh. 'Still, if I were you, I wouldn't hurry to be so thankful for turning human.' She gave Aggelos a wink. 'Let's hope you don't change your mind when you catch a cold or stub your toe or something.'

As the sweethearts giggled happily to that, Esmera put out a hand and caressed Katie's cheek. 'I don't know if you've worked it out yet, so I'll explain now why I came to you in the first place. When I met you, you were angry at your boss back in Athens; you seemed to have sussed her out completely. But you know, Katie, you need to give other people the benefit of the doubt. No one knows what lies in other people's hearts. Not fully. I'll let you in on another little secret: the most difficult people are the ones who suffer the most. So don't be quick to judge them. You simply don't know what they're going through inside.'

Katie's eyes widened. She darted her eyes to Matina, darling Matina, whom she'd also judged in the same way at first. The thought caused her to hang her head in a mixture of shame and quiet contemplation. Esmera smiled sweetly and patted Katie on the head, then her eyes lit up when she remembered she was still holding the amulet.

'Here!' she said, handing it to Aggelos. 'A little head start in your life together.' Without waiting for a response, she turned to Chloe. The girl had been waiting patiently for her turn to have her miracle.

'I'm sorry to have kept you waiting, my darling,' Esmera told her. 'But I had to make your last wish come true first, as you asked me. And now, it's time for the final goodbye. Come!' She took Chloe by the hand and led her to the other humans, who were waiting a few feet away, shocked to silence.

Esmera stopped before Matina and Spyros and placed her hands on their shoulders. They still couldn't see or hear their daughter but, by now, were convinced she was there. Matina was so overwhelmed that the tears were flowing freely from her eyes. As for Spyros, he had an arm around his wife, forever her protector, but in a way, he needed to hold her to draw strength from her too.

As soon as Esmera touched them, a sweet numbness overtook them. It felt warm, comforting, like a thick blanket at the end of a tiring day in the cold.

'Matina and Spyros, Spyros and Matina. Truly, you're both amazing and admirable. Life was cruel with you once, but you never let the pain or the sorrow beat you. When fate deals people a bad hand, as nasty as the one you were dealt, they have two choices: the first, the easy one, is to close their hearts and live the rest of their days shutting out the world, feeling miserable and bitter. But when you take that road, other people's happiness becomes your own brand of hell. You get to begrudge the smile and the joy of others. The only thing that gives you comfort is to know others are suffering as much as you do, so you only keep around you those who feel the same as you. But this is no way to live. You two, you went the other way – the right way: you opened your hearts to the world, giving selflessly happiness and joy to others even though you had little inside for yourselves. And, of course, that's the very thing that saw you through. You're still doing wonders for the people of Asimi. And, in your hotel, you give joy to people daily with your big smiles, warmth, and wonderful hospitality. I've seen inside your hearts and I know joy is hard to find. And yet, you've been sharing it as if you had lots to give. And that makes you winners of life. It makes you worthy of *this*!'

As soon as she finished her little speech, Esmera removed her hands from their shoulders and placed them in front of her in mid-air. At once, a mass of light appeared before her, and it was so dazzling that, at first, Matina and Spyros squeezed their eyes shut and winced. And then, as the shimmer before them diminished gradually, they realized their child, their sweet Chloe, was standing before them just as they'd hoped. She still had the same semi-physical form, except now Esmera had allowed them to see her for the first time.

Matina flung her arms open and held Chloe, and they cried tears of joy. Then it was Spyros' turn to hold her, kiss her, and caress her cheeks. Eva and Mrs Sparks took over to cuddle her and say goodbye, and that's when Matina noticed the legion of angels standing in a perfect line-up across the distance. When she heard her utter a cry of surprise, Spyros looked up from Chloe and confirmed he could see them too. Under their stunned gaze, huge, spotless wings slowly unfurled on the angels' backs. Today's agenda included commanding the winds again. It was time and they were getting ready.

Esmera turned around to check on her angels, then faced the humans again. 'I'm sorry. We have to let you go soon. Chloe, are you ready?'

The little girl nodded, still holding her mother's hand. Esmera placed her palm flat on the girl's head and Chloe began to radiate, her body shimmering and sparkling like diamonds. Magnificent, cotton-white wings sprouted from her back, reaching up to twice her height. The humans gave a gasp and Chloe smiled.

'Goodbye. I love you. All of you!' she said with a huge grin. 'But even if this is goodbye, always remember I'm never far.' She gave a little jump and flapped her wings at the same time, flying over their heads, then landing between Elise and Babis on the angel line-up. Elise took her hand and cheered, and Chloe smiled at everyone across the distance as the wind picked up and the sails of the windmill slowly began to turn.

Esmera looked at her watch and gasped, then held Matina and Spyros by their arms. 'I'm sorry, but you have to go now and let us do our holy work. Remember: Chloe is an angel of Asimi now. Be proud and comforted! Rejoice and get on with your lives. I know there are happy times ahead from now on.' She winked at Matina. 'You'll know soon. My magical gifts never fail!'

Chapter 46

As it turned out, the value of the amulet was higher than Katie and Aggelos had thought. Having had it estimated in Athens during a short break, they sold it on the same day and returned to Sifnos to live the rest of their lives there in the corner of paradise they'd chosen. A fortnight later, they bought a tiny house on the beach, halfway between Asimi and Pefki.

They afforded it easily, seeing that the pendant on the amulet wasn't silver, as Katie had thought, but 18K white gold. As for the gems, they weren't zirconia, but a set of diamonds of perfect clarity. As well as the house, Katie and Aggelos also bought an old derelict beach bar, a stone's throw away from the hotel and got to work, painting and cleaning, sweeping and refurnishing, and when it opened, the people of Asimi and other parts of the island began visiting in droves.

Soon, it became the favourite hangout of Matina and Spyros too, who often came to relax there at the end of a tiring day.

It was early October, the summer season winding down effortlessly to an end. Days were getting shorter, the scorching heat giving its place to a cooling breeze, the odd drizzle, and cloudy spells on most days. That late afternoon was no different. Aggelos was behind the bar as usual, while Katie sat at a remote table on the sand with Matina and Spyros.

Matina was pregnant, her big bump evident under her paisley-patterned summer dress. She held a glass of orange juice, her face tanned, her hair dyed in copper-red highlights. It was flowing around her shoulders, wispy strands dancing in the breeze. Spyros sat beside her, enjoying a bright red cocktail and smiling brightly as he listened to her speak.

Katie watched them and allowed her mind to wander for a while. She still couldn't believe what had transpired in the last few months. Since that magical afternoon on the hilltop, the miracles had never ceased. Esmera had been right. Happy days had followed. For all of them. Even Julia had changed her mind and told Eddie he could go to England to visit his father.

For years, she'd felt embittered towards her ex-husband, who had fallen in love with a British tourist girl and followed her to England, divorcing Julia and leaving behind two small children as well. He'd been sending monthly payments and Julia had allowed him to send letters and to phone the children but, out of spite, she had refused to let them visit him in England. It was the only thing she could do to mar her ex-husband's annoying, blissful marriage that he dared run away to, without giving her and the children a second thought.

Over time, Eddie had stopped asking his mother if he could go to England, even though he missed his father, to avoid upsetting her. But at the BBQ, Julia had seen the joy on her son's face as he danced with Sarah, and then, his upset the following day when he expressed his sorrow about her leaving soon. It all brought it back – the feeling of loss she experienced when her ex departed for England. And so, she told Eddie there and then that whenever he wanted, he could go and visit his father, and this way he could also meet Sarah again.

Little did either of them know that this development was the result of Elise's excellent work. She'd been working hard in her unseen, transparent form to cause Eddie and Sarah to meet by chance around the hotel grounds, over and over again, making sure his mother witnessed the shy words and tender glances they exchanged. It had also been Elise who'd put that phrase book in Aggelos' pocket, asking him to deliver it to Eddie.

These days, Eddie was doing well with his English lessons in Apollonia and couldn't wait to visit his father and Sarah this coming Christmas. But, among all the incredible developments in people's lives at Hotel Asimi, the greatest miracle was still at play and was growing in Matina's belly. Katie had put two and two together and realized the bottle of wine Esmera had left that night at the BBQ had caused the miracle in question.

'Hey, Katie,' said Aggelos placing a hand on her shoulder as he took a seat beside her.

Katie came to with a start as she turned to him. 'I'm sorry, I was miles away,' she said, then noticed all three were looking at her as if waiting for her to say or do something. 'Sorry, what did I miss?'

'I was only asking,' said Spyros, 'What do you think about one last BBQ this weekend before the season's end? Will this mild weather last? And could we ask for your help maybe? Because Matina is expecting, I'd rather she didn't have to stand for hours like she did last time.' He put out a hand to rub his wife's belly.

Matina gave a huge grin, relishing his attentions, and left a kiss on his cheek.

'Of course, we'll both help!' said Katie, and Aggelos nodded profusely.

'See? Don't be such a stress ball, Spyros,' said Matina, pinching his cheek. 'And as for the weather, I'm sure it'll be fine on the day.' She cast a tender glance towards the hills, the windmill that stood on the highest peak in particular. 'I expect not a leaf will be stirring in the trees. Our two precious angels up there will see to that.'

Katie opened her mouth to agree but then her mobile began to ring. The caller took her by surprise, being someone she hadn't heard from in ages. It was Vasso, one of her old colleagues from her office job in Athens.

Katie answered the call and was surprised to find that the girl was in Sifnos for a short break. 'Of course, Vasso! I'd love to meet you!' she said, eager to see her again. Then, the girl started to tell her news from work that Katie found hard to believe.

The others watched, puzzled, as Katie let out one exclamation of surprise after another. When she hung up with the promise to talk again soon and arrange to meet, Katie shook her head, stunned by what she'd heard.

'What is it? What could be so earth-shuttering?' asked Aggelos.

'You wouldn't believe what happened.' Katie then began to explain that the news was about Roula, her evil ex-boss. It turned out she had met somebody and fallen head over heels in love. What's more, she had left the country, following her man to New York as he was Greek-American. On her last day at work, she had taken all the office girls on her floor out for dinner, then for drinks at two different bars. In the wee hours of the morning, when she said goodbye to them all, she'd kissed and hugged them but not before confessing to them that she'd been miserable all her life.

But this guy, she said, he'd come to change everything, showing her that happiness was possible for her too, something that until then, she'd never believed. Even work, for her, had been a drag. She'd studied Business Administration to please her parents when all she'd ever wanted to do was become a dancer. But her guy, who'd come like a prince in shining armour to sweep her off her feet in a fairy-tale manner, was a professional dancer who owned a dance studio in New York.

Roula had kept in touch with a few of the girls so they knew she was now learning Jazz and Ball Room Dancing. She'd sent pictures of her in leotards at the studio, looking skinny and sporting a wide grin in all of them, her guy, tall and handsome, holding her as if she were the most precious thing in the world.

An hour later, Matina and Spyros returned to the hotel, but Katie remained at the table with Aggelos. The breeze had died down, and the sun was beginning to set. Sitting side by side, they faced the water's edge as the sun began to say its goodbyes while leaving the world its generous gifts of gold and wonder.

Soon, the sun disappeared under the horizon followed by an orgy of pinks and purples. With the murmuring sea lapping at their feet, Katie sighed deeply and leaned on Aggelos, putting her head on his shoulder.

He put an arm around her, squeezing her tight, then kissed the top of her head. 'What is it, my darling? You seem so deep in thought tonight. Is there something wrong?'

Katie looked up, her eyes dancing with joy. 'Wrong? Why, you must be joking. I am the happiest girl in the world.'

Aggelos gave a bright smile. 'Good. So you're not sorry we had to sell the amulet.'

'Who needs an amulet, or all the gems in the world for that matter, when I get to keep my own guardian angel?'

'Huh! But you forget, I am not an angel any more. Just your everyday, hard-working husband.'

Katie raised her chin and sought his lips. His eyes seemed to melt as he leaned in to kiss her sweetly, slowly, as the sea that foamed softly on the sand released the sweet murmur that pleased their ears.

Then, she pulled back, held his gaze and said, 'To me, you'll always be my very own guardian angel.'

THE END

Thank you for reading The Amulet! Keep turning the pages to check out a FREE book by Effrosyni, an important note from the author, and more!

Did you know? Every time one of my readers forgets to write a review, a Greek gets so upset that they forget to pick the olives from their trees. It just breaks my heart! Tell me what you thought of my book and help the Greeks continue to pour olive oil in their salads!

Please leave a short review on Amazon. It will be greatly appreciated!

Visit Amazon

US:
https://www.amazon.com/dp/B01MCZ2UOU
UK:
https://www.amazon.co.uk/dp/B01MCZ2UOU

A note from Effrosyni

Although I've written this book in British English, I tried my best to pick words that will make sense to every English-speaking reader, no matter their nationality. I hope I've succeeded in doing that.

As I often do in my books, I've peppered The Amulet with mentions of delicious Greek dishes. To taste them first hand, visit my blog to grab my family recipes for moussaka, cheese and pepper pastries, biftekia, tzatziki, and lots more. You'll find them all here: https://effrosinimoss.wordpress.com/category/greek-recipes-2/

To receive my news, best offers and an exclusive free book, join my mailing list. Very sparse emails and your privacy is guaranteed! http://effrosyniwrites.com/newsletter/

I'm always delighted to hear from my readers, and highly value any comments. I'd love to hear from you!

**Email me at contact@effrosyniwrites.com or ladyofthepier@gmail.com

**Visit my website to download FREE excerpts and to watch book trailers: http://www.effrosyniwrites.com

**Like me on Facebook:
https://www.facebook.com/authoreffrosyni

**Friend me on Facebook – I love to connect with readers there!
https://www.facebook.com/efrosini.moschoudi

**Follow me on Twitter: https://twitter.com/frostiemoss

**Find me on Goodreads:
https://www.goodreads.com/author/show/7362780.Effrosyni_Moschoudi

**Follow my blogs. The first one below is perfect for bookworms (many author interviews and reviews). On the second blog you'll find all my yummy Greek recipes!

http://www.effrosyniwrites.com

http://www.effrosinimoss.wordpress.com

Acknowledgements

First off, huge thanks to my wonderful beta readers who have helped make this book as perfect as can be. I owe the same eternal thanks to them all so this is in no particular order – heaps of gratitude to: Jean Symonds, Colleen Cheesbro, Cheryl Michaelides, Ann Marie Hanson, Nicholas Rossis, David Wind, and Kerry Hall.

As always, I am thankful beyond words to my husband and best friend, Andy. Because he believes in me, my dream continues to unfold and to bring me joy. The least I could do was dedicate this book, a book about guardian angels, to him.

I'd also like to offer my heartfelt thanks to the wonderful romance author and friend, MM Jaye. If it's possible to have an online sister, then that's what I've found in her. Her generosity of spirit is limitless, her tireless provision of valuable information and moral support priceless, and I'm incredibly lucky to have her.

Last but not least, many thanks to all of you who read my books, and/or share my posts on Twitter and Facebook. With your kind comments and feedback you continue to give me wings. You're all superstars; the best supporters an author could ever have.

About the author

Effrosyni Moschoudi was born and raised in Athens, Greece. As a child, she often sat alone in her garden scribbling rhymes about flowers, butterflies and ants. Today she writes books for people who love all things Greek. Her novels are Amazon bestsellers, having hit #1 several times. She lives in a quaint seaside town near Athens with her husband Andy and a ridiculous amount of books and DVDs.

Her debut novel, The Necklace of Goddess Athena, is a Readers' Favorite silver medalist. Her historical romance, The Ebb, is an ABNA Q-finalist and is inspired from the author's blissful summers in 1980s Corfu as a youngster.

Effrosyni loves Corfu with passion! Her FREE online guide to the island is unmissable if you plan to visit Greece! Check it out here: http://effrosyniwrites.com/your-guide-to-moraitika-corfu

Effrosyni's books are available on Amazon in kindle and paperback. The paperbacks can also be ordered at any bookstore or library.

More from this author

Get "FACETS of LOVE" for FREE!

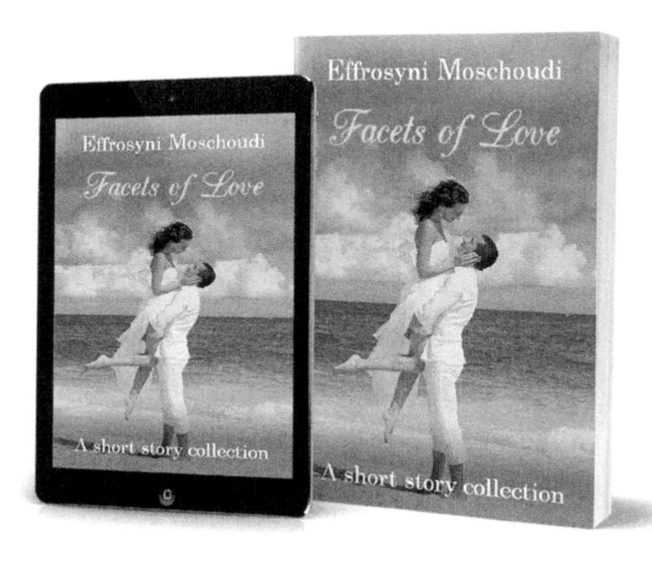

Treat yourself today to this wonderful collection of short stories that highlight various kinds of love. Not just the romantic kind, but also love for family, pets, and country. Facets of Love will introduce you to stunning locations around Greece. The fantasy elements contained in some of the stories are bound to enchant you!

Visit:

http://effrosyniwrites.com/yours-for-free/

Running Haunted is a paranormal romantic comedy set in the alluring town of Nafplio. Kelly ran a marathon and wound up running a house. With a ghost in it!

Visit Amazon
US: https://www.amazon.com/dp/B0853CMP1V
UK: https://www.amazon.co.uk/dp/B0853CMP1V

The Lady of the Pier – The Ebb is an award-winning historical romance set in Corfu, Greece and Brighton, England. If you're a romantic at heart or if you enjoy Greek island romances, this #1 Amazon bestseller is the perfect choice for you.

US: **http://www.amazon.com/dp/B00LGNYEPC**
UK: **https://www.amazon.co.uk/dp/B00LGNYEPC**

Order Effrosyni's paperbacks on Amazon, at your nearest bookstore, or ask at the library.

Fabulous reads by other authors

DERRICK ~ Book 1 of The Single Daddy Club

Ex-military man Derrick is solitary and satisfied—until Timmy's dropped into his lap and Derrick must become a daddy. Fate has denied Anna a family of her own, but she has plenty of love to give, if only someone would notice.

"…delightfully entertaining!"

"…heartwarming, you feel the characters' pains, agonies and joy. Love happy endings. Highly recommended."

Available for Kindle for just 99¢

USA Today Bestseller Donna Fasano is the author of over 35 award-winning romance and women's fiction books.

Can two wrongs win Mr. Right?
An aspiring thriller writer, Trish Swan would rather write violence, not witness it. Yet, on her first day in Athens, Greece, she turns in a cop, presenting footage, evidence of police brutality. Her civic duty done, she goes to a small Greek island to pursue her dream. Markos Venetis wants nothing more than to get his hands on the meddling tourist that ruined him professionally. Against all odds, he does. And she screams. Not out of fear. But when she tarnishes his family's name, this Greek heir's blood boils. And someone is bound to burn.

"An intense romance in a stunning setting."
"Markos will get your attention!"

Visit Amazon:
https://www.amazon.com/gp/product/B01EXLXYWM

Printed in Great Britain
by Amazon